"He's very sweet..."

Mike smiled hesitantly. "I don't know how to take care of him, and that scares me a whole lot. I'm better with perps and bad guys than I am with babies."

"I can see that," Paige said wryly.

"I can pay you for your time," Mike added. "Basically, I'll need to get some sort of childcare arranged, but in the meantime, I'm looking for someone to take care of Benjie while I'm at work, and to teach me everything I need to know."

It should be simple—a few baby-care lessons and a little baby minding for a couple of weeks. Maybe it would help her get out of her head so she could decide on what to do with the rest of her life. Was she sticking with social services, or was she quitting for good?

"I'm not a long-term solution," Paige said.

Mike met her gaze, those gray eyes locking on to hers so powerfully that her breath caught. "I'm not looking for long-term. I'm just looking for some help right now while I _____ _____ance. What do you say?"

Dear Reader,

When I write, I often think about my reader—
what she might look like curled up in a comfy
chair, sitting on a bus, standing in a long lineup
somewhere—and what she might get out of the
story I'm writing. If there is one thing I hope you
feel at the end of this story, it's brave! I hope
you'll feel courageous enough to take a risk
when it really matters. Love is complicated and
oftentimes messy. But it's always worth it.

I write for Heartwarming and Love Inspired here
at Harlequin, and I hope you'll check out my
other books. You're guaranteed to get sweet
romance with a lot of heart!

You can find me on my blog at
patriciajohnsromance.com, on Facebook and on
Twitter. I'd love to hear from you.

Patricia Johns

HEARTWARMING

The Lawman's Baby

—

Patricia Johns

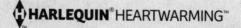

Recycling programs
for this product may
not exist in your area.

ISBN-13: 978-1-335-51074-7

The Lawman's Baby

Copyright © 2019 by Patricia Johns

Printed in U.S.A.

Patricia Johns writes from Alberta, Canada. She has her Hon. BA in English literature and currently writes for Harlequin's Love Inspired and Heartwarming lines. You can find her at patriciajohnsromance.com.

Books by Patricia Johns

Harlequin Heartwarming

Home to Eagle's Rest

Her Lawman Protector
Falling for the Cowboy Dad

A Baxter's Redemption
The Runaway Bride
A Boy's Christmas Wish

Love Inspired

Montana Twins

Her Cowboy's Twin Blessings
Her Twins' Cowboy Dad

Comfort Creek Lawmen

Deputy Daddy
The Lawman's Runaway Bride
The Deputy's Unexpected Family

His Unexpected Family
The Rancher's City Girl
A Firefighter's Promise
The Lawman's Surprise Family

Visit the Author Profile page
at Harlequin.com for more titles.

To my husband, my very own happily-ever-after.
I love you!

CHAPTER ONE

PAIGE STEDLER WALKED up the front stairs to the Eagle's Rest Police Department and tugged her coat a little closer. It was a chilly fall morning, and an eddy of wind whipped a pile of leaves against the police station front doors. The police chief had called her in as a special request. Everyone knew that Paige was on stress leave, but this wasn't exactly related to her job as a Social Services agent. Or so the chief had assured her.

She did feel a lot better than she had three weeks ago when she'd had her fifth panic attack while at work. But Paige wasn't sure what the chief even wanted from her. Here was hoping it was just a form to sign or something like that. She pulled open the front door and headed into the station's warmth. The receptionist, Ellen, shot her a smile.

"Paige!" the chief's voice boomed across the office.

Paige returned Ellen's smile on her way past and headed toward Chief Simpson's office in the back. The chief was an older man with a potbelly and a demanding stare that softened when he waved to her. He strode across the bull pen and met her halfway.

"Thanks for coming in, Paige," he said, lowering his voice.

"No problem." It was only half a lie. "What can I do for you?"

"We have a situation, and I think you're the person we need. One of our new officers just became guardian of his sister's newborn, and he's overwhelmed, to put it mildly. He needs a hand getting used to child care. For a bit. Just while he sorts things out. And since you were on leave..."

As if stress leave were paid vacation!

"Why do you think I'm the only one who can handle it, Chief?" she asked.

"You're the best," the chief replied.

"I'm on stress leave," she countered.

"You're still the best." He met her gaze. "And your brother's worried."

Paige's brother, Nathan, was a cop, too, but he was stationed in a small town a couple of hours away. Serving the public was in the Stedler blood…except Paige didn't seem to have what it took anymore.

"You could ask pretty much anyone to help out with a baby," Paige said.

"This particular baby is pretty small, and he was born with cocaine in his system. He doesn't seem to be going through any withdrawal, miraculously enough, but it's still a touchy case," he said. "And no one else is available. I did ask around, for the record. If not you, we're moving on to some local grandmothers who might lend a hand, and I'd rather recommend someone who's trained in social services. You have…more of the experience that we need, considering this infant's shaky start."

"Oh." Yes, that did make sense. Still…

"Nathan's not the only one who's been worried about you," the chief added with an apologetic shrug. "I know you pretty well, Paige, and I want to help you get back in the saddle. I'm guessing you want that, too, or you wouldn't be here."

"Did you run this past Dana?" Paige asked with a teasing smile. Dana was Chief Simpson's wife—twenty years his junior, short, slim, and with a mop of curly hair that set off a pair of sparkling eyes. She and Paige had always gotten along.

"No," he said, but he returned the wry smile. "She would have told me to mind my own business and let you deal with things your own way."

"So this baby care thing—this is for me," she said.

"Come see the situation," Chief Simpson suggested quietly. "Meet the officer, the baby... And if you don't want to help out, then no hard feelings and I'll start talking to local grandmothers."

"And you can tell Nathan that you did your best," she said.

"Something like that. Unless you want me to tell him I tried but you're not interested. I'm not going to push you into something you're not ready for."

From across the bull pen, the soft cry of a baby filtered toward them, and Paige's heart softened. A new dad and a new baby...complications aside, she was curious.

"Let's go," she said, and the chief shot her a grin.

"Thanks for this, Paige."

Paige followed the chief through the bull

pen. A couple of officers who stood by the coffeemaker nodded at her. Three others were working at their desks. She knew most of these cops from various cases she'd been called in to. The chief led her to his office, and gestured her in first, then followed, shutting the door behind him.

A large, muscular man sat inside, a baby car seat cradled in his lap. He looked to be around thirty, with short-cropped brown hair. His attention was fixed on the car seat he was holding in his lap. He was rocking it—the entire car seat—and the baby seemed to be settled again. He looked up, his steely gray gaze drilling into her. Paige glanced between the men.

"Hi," she said feebly.

"This is Officer Mike McMann," Chief Simpson said. "He's just transferred over from Denver."

"Pleasure." Mike reached out to shake her hand, and she was struck by the sheer size of him. His arms were thick with muscle, but as his broad palm engulfed hers, that iron gaze of his melted, and she caught a flicker of emotion under his professional reserve. And he looked—scared?

From the car seat, another little mewling cry arose, and she bent down to get a closer look. Inside was a tiny newborn baby who couldn't have been much over five pounds. He was swimming in a blue newborn sleeper that had been rolled up at the sleeves, but the legs just flopped empty underneath him.

"This is my, uh, nephew," Mike said hesitantly. "His name is Benjie. Well, Benjamin Alexander McMann. It's kind of long for a guy this small, though."

"Benjie…" Paige bent over the car seat, and the baby squirmed again and wrinkled up his tiny face in a cry. "Have you held him yet, Mike?"

"Um. Once. I put him right back, though."

"Once!"

"I didn't want to hurt him," Mike said, eyeing her.

"You won't. He's not that fragile. Babies are meant to be held—it's good for them. They need the contact. Do you mind if I pick him up?"

"No, that'd be fine."

Paige unbuckled the straps and lifted the tiny infant from the restraints. "You're supposed to hold him as much as possible," she said. As she pulled the baby up to her shoulder, Benjie instinctively nuzzled into her neck, tucking up those little legs underneath him. There was just something about that milk-sweet scent and the tiny rump in her palm that slowed her heartbeat down. She leaned her cheek against his downy head.

She needed the contact right now, it seemed, and when she looked down at the baby, he opened his mouth in a tiny yawn. She smoothed a hand over that little back. He was thin—which was natural when a baby was born a few weeks early. He didn't have any of that healthy newborn chub.

"I kind of knew that, but he's pretty little, and I'm kind of—" He looked down at his hands. "I'm in over my head."

"He's your nephew, you said?"

"Yeah. I only found out about him at one this morning. That's when the hospital tracked me down. He was born four days ago. It took them that long to find me and to be certain that he wasn't born addicted. He, um, had cocaine in his system."

"Yes, the chief filled me about that," she confirmed quietly.

"My sister left him after he was born,"

Mike went on. "I'm her only living relative, so he's in my hands now. I'm obviously working full-time, and add to that, I have no idea how to take care of babies."

"So you need to learn how to care for a newborn," she clarified.

"That among other things, I guess. I just need…" He shrugged weakly. "Help."

Paige could see that much. Mike looked down at the car seat in his lap, and then placed it on the floor. His movements were carefully controlled—she could see the police training in him as he kept himself contained in the chair that was too small for his muscular frame. He rose to his feet and rolled his shoulders, then let his gray gaze move over Paige, finally settling on the baby in her arms.

"Did Chief Simpson tell you that I'm on stress leave?" she asked.

"He mentioned that you had some time off," Mike replied, glancing toward the chief. Yeah, she was sure the chief had explained more than that.

"I've been working in Social Services for seven years now," she said, "and I'm burned out. You should you know that up front. I need a break—desperately."

"And helping me out…isn't exactly the break you're looking for."

"Not exactly," she agreed. The baby nestled closer against her neck, and she patted his back gently. He was so tiny and so desperately in need of love, and she looked over at the infant, her heart melting in spite of her. "He's very sweet, though."

It was this sort of scenario that had drawn her to Social Services—parents in need of support, children in need of love. But there was always deeper heartbreak underneath, and that was what made this career so draining. She couldn't fix it all. She couldn't fix much actually. Everything she did for the good ended up hurting whoever was on the other side. There was never an easy right or wrong decision.

Mike smiled hesitantly. "I don't know how to take care of him, and that scares me a whole lot. I'm better with perps and bad guys than I am with babies."

"I can see that," she said wryly.

"I can pay you for your time," Mike added. "Basically, I'll need to get some sort of child care arranged, but in the meantime, I'm looking for someone to take care of Benjie while I'm at work, and to teach me everything I need to know."

It should be simple—a few baby care lessons and a little baby minding for a couple of weeks. Maybe it would help her get out of her head so she could decide about what to do with the rest of her life. Was she sticking with Social Services, or was she quitting for good?

"I'm not a long-term solution," Paige cautioned.

Mike met her gaze, those gray eyes locking on to hers so powerfully that her breath caught. "I'm not looking for long term. I'm just looking for some help right now while I get my balance. What do you say?"

CHIEF SIMPSON HAD recommended Paige Stedler because he claimed she was the best. And looking at her with the baby nestled next to her chin, her undecided blue eyes meeting his, Mike had to wonder if this was a good idea.

When the chief mentioned a Social Services agent on leave, Mike had figured she'd be older, and maybe a little less attractive. Instead, he was faced with a petite blonde, her hair loose and wavy around her face. Her blue eyes were expressive, and he could read all the concerns flitting through the clear gaze that regarded him.

Paige broke eye contact and looked down at the baby again, adjusting him so that he lay in the crook of her arm. He looked snug and cozy in her arms—and she seemed so confident holding him. Mike had been scared that he'd drop the baby, or hurt him somehow. Benjie was just so small, with thin little arms and legs he was afraid he'd snap if he held him wrong.

"Here's what I can do," she said finally. "You have me for three weeks, so make sure you line up some alternative child care for after that. In that time, I'll teach you everything you need to know about baby care and help you get comfortable. While you're at work, I'll take over, but when you're home I expect you to be hands-on."

"Okay," he agreed.

"My stress leave is up in three weeks, so I'll either be going back to work or tendering my resignation there," she added.

"You're thinking of quitting?" Mike asked in surprise, then he softened his tone. "Sorry, I just thought—"

"I have decisions of my own to make, is my point," she said. "But maybe helping you with Benjie will get my feet wet again so that I can be sure of my choice."

Mike saw Paige's gaze flicker toward the chief, whose eyebrows were raised. Color rose in her cheeks. Obviously, this was news all around. But it shouldn't matter to Mike. She was offering him three weeks of help, and he was grateful.

"Thanks," he said. "I appreciate you being willing to give me a hand. All things considered."

"You're welcome." Paige looked back in control again, her confidence in place. She was so petite, but she intimidated him a little. Maybe it was that he needed her help so much. He was more comfortable in the role of rescuer than…this.

"Take the day off," the chief said, turning to Mike. "You can start fresh after you're settled in."

"Thanks, sir," Mike replied. He looked down at Paige, feeling better already. Until he figured this out, he'd have some support from someone who knew what she was doing when it came to infants.

"If you're willing to start now, we can head back to my place," he said.

"Sounds good." For the first time, she smiled, and he was struck by how it transformed her face. She went from pretty to stunning, and he turned his attention to the car seat instead. He was glad she was willing to give him a hand, but he'd have to stop noticing just how attractive she was if they were going to make this work.

He wasn't sticking around Eagle's Rest for long, anyway. This was a demotion, and everyone knew it. If he'd had a better relationship with the chief in Denver, Mike might have been able to pursue getting on to the SWAT team there, but things had gotten complicated between him and Chief Vernon. To say the least. If Mike stuck around Denver any longer, Chief Vernon would find some reason to write him up again, and his career as a cop might be over completely. Accepting this position in Eagle's Rest was the smartest move under the circumstances.

SWAT *was* where Mike belonged, and he

knew it. Not only was he built for the job—two hundred and fifty pounds of solid muscle—but he was also in peak physical shape and an excellent shot. But he was hungry for this position on more than a testosterone level. This was personal for him…atonement for past mistakes. He hadn't always been this capable.

"Let's get him back into the car seat," Paige said, and for the next couple of minutes they got Benjie settled into the seat and buckled in. Paige tucked the blanket around him, and then stood back for Mike to pick it up.

"Thanks for the introduction, Chief," Mike said, shaking the older man's hand. "I'll be back bright and early tomorrow morning."

"Good luck." Chief Simpson reached out and shook Paige's hand. "To both of you."

Mike and Paige headed out the door of his office and out into the bull pen. Paige glanced up at Mike, and he gave her a small smile. She was pretty, and she had a confidence about her that set his own frayed nerves at ease. They didn't say anything else as they wound their way around desks and headed out of the station and into the chilly, autumn air.

"Let's get him buckled into your car," Paige said. "I'll follow you back to your place."

"Right. Sure."

He'd gotten the car seat into his vehicle before, and it didn't take him too long to get the car seat clicked into place now.

"I do appreciate this," Mike said as he closed the door gently.

The wind ruffled Paige's hair and she hunched her shoulders. "It's no problem."

"All the same…"

She smiled again. "Don't thank me too soon. I'm a toughie. I'm going to make you do all this yourself, you know."

"Probably for the best," he said with a rueful smile. "So… My place is in the west end of town. You said you'll follow me there?"

"I'll be right behind you. I'm parked just over there." She hooked a thumb toward a little blue hatchback, then raised her hand in a farewell and started off in that direction. He watched her for a moment, then heaved a sigh. He'd figure this out.

When Mike got into his cruiser, he glanced into the backseat. He couldn't see into the car seat from that position, so he turned front again and sucked in a deep breath. He hadn't slept since that phone call telling him about his nephew, and he hadn't had a chance to process it all, either.

He started the car. Feeling any of this was just going to have to wait.

On the drive, Mike kept an eye on his rearview mirror, and Paige's little blue car stayed steadily in the center of it. Eagle's Rest was a small town in Colorado's Rocky Mountains, and it didn't take him long to get to his place and park out front. Paige parked beside him. Having her here to help him out did make him feel a bit better.

It was midmorning and the sun was shining despite the chilly wind. Mike got the car seat out of his car on his own. Benjie was covered up in that blanket that Paige had tucked around him, but even so, Mike hurried to unlock the front door, balancing the car seat in one hand as he fiddled with his key ring in the other.

The door swung open, and Mike gestured Paige in ahead of him.

"Here we are," he said, casting a quick glance around the place. It looked like the bachelor pad it was. He had a couch—relatively new—a TV, a kitchen table that sat between the tiny kitchen and the living room. The master bedroom was down the hall, along with a second bedroom that was full of packed boxes. Where was the baby supposed to sleep? The thought only occurred to him now. He looked over at Paige in mild panic.

"What?" she asked.

"I only have one bedroom that isn't full of boxes right now," he said.

"I'm not staying the night," she said wryly. "You're doing night duty on your own."

"No, I meant—" He smiled at her dry humor. "The baby. Where is he going to sleep?"

"He's a newborn. He'll be in your bedroom," she replied.

"Yeah?" It wasn't very big in there, either.

"I'll suss up a bassinet for you and a couple other necessities. But he'll sleep in your room so that when he cries, you can feed him more easily. It's good for bonding, too."

"Bonding."

"He needs to know that there's someone who will respond when he's lonely, or when he's hungry, or when he's scared."

"A mother," he murmured.

"A parental figure," she corrected him. "That's you."

"Yeah, right." He was still getting used to that concept. He was going to be like a dad to this kid. For a while at least. It felt wrong, though. He was Benjie's uncle. This was Jana's child. Not his.

"Your sister…" Paige began, then winced. "Can I ask about her?"

Jana was out there somewhere—alone, for all he knew. She'd be recovering from childbirth, and he had no way to find her. At least not immediately.

"Why not?" Mike sighed. "The administrator at the hospital told me that she gave my name and said I was a local cop. She didn't know I'd moved out to Eagle's Rest—I had no contact information to even let her know. Anyway, the Denver department passed along the message."

"But what's her situation?" Paige asked.

"Jana's an addict." He swallowed hard. "I haven't seen her in a long time. She ran away as a teenager a couple of times. The second time, she didn't come back. This was the first contact I've had with her in about three years. And I'm not sure it really counts as contact, if I never saw or spoke to her, does it?"

"I guess not," Paige said softly. "I'm sorry."

"Yeah, well…" He wasn't sure what to say. He didn't talk about his sister—she wasn't an easy topic. There weren't any answers.

"What caused her to run away?" Paige asked.

"We were raised by our grandmother when our mom took off. Grandma wasn't really equipped to raise two kids. Her health was failing, and frankly, she was just tired. But it was better than nothing. Anyway, Jana and I handled our upbringing a little differently, I guess. I toughened up, and she… didn't. She was sensitive, and we went to a rough school. I didn't notice that she was struggling until it was too late."

"Was there abuse in your home? Addiction?" Paige asked. Yeah, that was the social services shining through. She would probably have seen a lot of this sort of thing in her career.

"Mostly it was neglect," he replied. "We raised ourselves, and I was pretty busy with my own friends, drowning my own sorrows. I thought she was doing the same thing—just riding it out. Grandma hated Jana's boyfriend. He got arrested a couple of times, and Grandma had enough, told Jana to stop seeing him. So she ran away with him. She came back when they broke up after a couple of months. I thought it was over, but she never did settle back in, and the next time she took off, she never came back. And we didn't find her."

"How old was the boyfriend?" Paige asked.

"Three years older than her. She was fourteen. He was seventeen. Looking back on it now, they were both pretty young."

"You didn't find her until now?" Paige asked.

"No, I tracked her down a couple of times. Once she found me and asked for money. Another time I found her when her name came through the system—arrested for petty theft. I don't know where she is right now, though. They can't tell me anything under the Safe Haven law that gives a mother the right to relinquish her infant within three days of birth, no questions asked. I guess she did the same thing Mom did with us—

dropped her kid off with someone she knew would care, and left."

"The police are still looking for her, though, right?" Paige asked.

"I'm *personally* looking for her," Mike retorted. "I'm not going to let her down again."

The baby started to whimper from the car seat, and he looked over at Paige expectantly.

"I told you that you'd be the one doing the baby care," Paige said with a small smile. "No time like the present to get started."

He stared down at the little guy, trepidation rising up inside of him. He reached down and undid the buckle.

"I'm not sure how…" he admitted.

"One hand under the bum, one hand under the neck and head," she said, standing back, her arms crossed over her chest.

"Right." He did as she instructed and lifted the infant out of the car seat. The little arms and legs flailed as Benjie opened his mouth in a plaintive wail. Mike pulled the baby into his chest, and Paige draped a blanket over him as Mike got adjusted. Benjie felt so small in his hands, and as the baby wriggled, squirming toward his neck, he was surprised as the little guy's strength.

Mike boosted him higher on his chest, and Benjie let out a soft sigh as his head made contact with Mike's neck just under his chin. He couldn't see the baby anymore now—just feel him as he settled over Mike's heartbeat.

"Okay…" Mike breathed. "Got it. He's really small, isn't he?"

"They start out that way," Paige said. "Especially if they're born a little early. I'll cut you some slack and get the bottle ready. At his size, he's going to be eating every hour or two. He's got some catching up to do."

"As in twenty-four feedings a day?" Mike asked incredulously.

"Give or take." She bent down, picked up a box of supplies that had come from Social Services in Denver and headed toward his kitchen. Her cheerful voice filtered back to him as he heard the tap turn on. "You're about to find out what tired really feels like!"

And then she laughed, this buoyant, cheerful tinkle of laughter that made him feel a little better, in spite of it all.

CHAPTER TWO

PAIGE STOOD BY the kitchen sink shaking up a bottle of formula. Mike's kitchen was neat—a pot in the farmhouse-style sink waiting to be washed, but other than that, the counters were wiped and everything looked in order. Paige could appreciate a neat kitchen. It was soothing.

The milk frothed in the bottle, and she paused, let it settle, then shook it again. The view from the kitchen window opened up into a backyard with a lawn that seemed to fade into some brush and forest. Trees flamed red and gold; the wind rippling through autumn leaves clung resolutely to the branches. Beyond the trees, the mountains loomed. A cape of evergreens mingled with a few deciduous trees that were in full fall display climbing up the mountainside toward the bare, rocky peaks that were obscured by cloud.

"It's quite the view," Mike said behind

her, and she turned. The baby was still snuggled up under his chin.

"It really is," she agreed, and she turned on the hot water tap to warm the milk in the bottle. "I've lived here my whole life, except for my college years, and I never get tired of that view."

"Really?" Mike raised his eyebrows. "All your life?"

"It's as good a place as any to grow up," she said, turning off the tap and shaking up the bottle again. "I love this town. We have more than our fair share of eagles, which draws in a lot of tourists. Have you ever seen one up close?"

Mike shook his head. "Not yet."

"It's only a matter of time around here," she said. "Most people want to come out this way for the wildlife."

"Not me." His voice was a low rumble.

"So why did you?" she asked.

"I didn't have a whole lot of choice," he replied. "My boss strongly suggested I transfer out, and Eagle's Rest was the only place hiring."

"What happened?" She eyed him for a moment, standing there with the baby in his arms and an irritable look on his face. "Never mind. I think I can guess."

"Yeah?" He shot her an amused look. "Go ahead. Give it your best shot."

"My brother's a cop, and I've worked with police officers for a long time. The one thing you all seemed to share in common is a tendency to balk at authority—ironically enough. It takes a certain personality type to want to chase down bad guys...and that personality doesn't like authority, either."

He laughed softly. "You're insightful."

"I am." She shot him a smile back. "So, I'm right?"

"Sort of," he said. "I want to join the SWAT team, but that involves both a passing mark on the qualifying exams and a recommendation from my boss to even get into the Denver SWAT training. Chief Vernon wasn't going to give me the recommendation. He said if I wanted to start fresh somewhere else, I was welcome to. There was an opening here, and I figured I'd take his advice and see if I couldn't get a new chief to help me get there."

"SWAT." She eyed him for a moment. "That's elite. Have you done the exams?"

"Yep. Just waiting on the results."

"If the chief didn't think you had what it took, why let you sit for the exams to begin with?"

"I think he was hoping I wouldn't pass and he could shut me down for a while. I'm more stubborn than that."

She could see it now—the cocky cop, the determination, the attitude... Now this officer was here in quiet little Eagle's Rest with a newborn. He was going to hate this.

"You don't plan to stay, do you?" she asked.

"Only as long as I have to, honestly," he replied. "I know what I want. I know where I can contribute the most. And it isn't here."

Paige handed him the bottle. "Benjie's going to be hungry pretty soon."

The baby wriggled and opened his mouth like a little bird as if on cue. Mike's confidence seemed to evaporate and he looked from the bottle to the baby and over to her with an expression of misgiving.

"How do I do this?" he asked.

"Here—" She took the bottle back. "Just tip him onto his back in the crook of your arm."

Mike took a moment to get the baby into the right position, then she handed him the bottle again.

"Test it against your wrist," she said. "There are a lot of nerve endings there. The milk should feel warm but not hot."

Mike tapped the nipple against his wrist, nodded, then held it over the baby's face. A drip of milk splattered across the infant's forehead, and Benjie let out a squawk of annoyance. Paige chuckled, then stepped closer, put her hand over Mike's broad one and guided the bottle to Benjie's searching mouth. The baby latched on and started to suck.

"There you go," she murmured.

Paige was standing close, and when she looked up at him, she found his steely gaze locked on her. He smelled good—the wrong thing to be noticing right now.

"Thanks," Mike said.

"Sure." She shot him a brief smile, and his gaze moved back to the baby. He probably had no idea what that stare of his did to a woman. He was just so…male. It had been a while since she'd noticed a man in this way.

The bottle was dwarfed in Mike's big hand as the baby drank, the milk in the bottle steadily disappearing.

"So, you've figured me out," Mike said quietly. "What about you? How come you want to quit? You have that trouble with authority, too?"

"No, not me. I just…lost my faith in being able to make a difference."

His eyes flickered up toward her again. "One case in particular?"

"It was a dad with two young children," she said after a beat of silence. "He struggled with alcoholism and was doing well for a while, but then slid back down into it. I came by to check on the family and found the kids alone in the trailer. It was a mess. No food in the fridge, just a TV blaring to keep them company. I had to call in Children's Services, and they were taken away."

"Sounds like it was the only call you could make," he replied.

"It was."

"So what was the problem?"

"The dad came by my office a week later, sober again. He sat down and sobbed. His heart was just breaking. He said he loved his kids. This was the kick in the pants that he needed. He'd never drink a drop again."

Mike was silent, watching her, and the memory came back with the force of a load of bricks. That heartbreaking sob torn from the chest of a broken man. The way he'd pleaded with her, begged for another chance. She couldn't give it. She knew she'd made the right call…but somehow, that man's desperation had sunk past all her defenses.

"I had his kids taken away," she said, bracing herself against the memory. "And while I know I had to, I broke three hearts that day."

"It was the right call," he said.

"I felt it too deeply, though," she said. "I didn't have that professional glass between me and that man's pain. I used to have it…"

"You don't think you'll get it back?" he asked.

"I don't think I *want* it back," she replied. "That's my problem! When I think about getting professional reserve back, being able to protect my heart from other people's pain… It's kind of depressing. Maybe I don't want to be tough again. Maybe I just want to be normal."

"What's normal?" he said with a short laugh.

He meant it as a rhetorical question, but Paige had a very good idea of what normal looked like.

"I want a regular life," she said. "I want a job that doesn't break my heart. I want a white picket fence and a view of the mountains. And that's it. I want hobbies, and friends and work stories about Karen from Accounting."

"You want to be a civilian again," he said quietly.

"I really do."

"No one likes Karen from Accounting," he added, his expression deadpan, but she could hear the humor in his voice. "She's awful. You might want to consider that."

Paige chuckled. "I want regular, civilian annoyances. Including Karen. At least she doesn't break my heart."

"I suppose."

"Don't you see the appeal of that?" she asked, meeting his gaze. "I mean, after all you've seen...don't you ever look at a regular Joe and think how lucky he is?"

"Nah," Mike replied as the baby drained the last drop from the bottle. He pulled the nipple out of Benjie's mouth with a pop. "I'd rather know the worst."

"Really?" She eyed him for a moment.

"I missed out on what was really going on with my sister," he said. "I just wanted to focus on my own stuff back then. I was only seventeen, after all. Same as her boyfriend. I liked cars and girls. But if I'd opened my eyes and actually recognized what was happening with my little sister, I might have been able to help her. So, no. I don't want to shut my eyes to it again. I want to chase it down and toss it behind bars. I want to find out who's to blame and make them pay. That's how I feel better."

She nodded. Sure. Faced with the tough stuff, he wanted to beat it up. But when she faced the same tough realities, she was left a heartbroken mess. He belonged out there in the middle of it all. She just didn't think that she did.

The baby started to squirm, and Paige grabbed a dish towel and tossed it over Mike's shoulder. "Time to burp."

He took a moment to awkwardly reposition the baby up on his shoulder.

"Just rub some gentle circles on his back," Paige instructed, and Mike did as she told him with the tips of two fingers. Benjie squirmed and lifted his head, then dropped it back onto Mike's shoulder.

"Is he okay?" Mike asked, turning his head to look at the baby.

"He's working up a burp," she said.

"He doesn't like this towel," Mike said, and he pulled it out from under the baby. "Do you, buddy?"

"You might not want to—" Paige began, when Benjie came up with a resounding, wet burp. The dribble of milk ran down Mike's uniform, and the baby stopped squirming, settling down into comfort. Mike looked from the towel to the baby, then over at Paige.

"That's why we use a cloth," she said with a small smile. "Live and learn."

She picked up the towel again and came over to wipe up what she could. Mike's breath brushed the top of her head as she wiped, the heat from his chest emanating against her. He felt comforting, and she knew that had very little to do with who he was and very much to do with her current state of mind. She was feeling vulnerable, and a big, strong guy was comforting on a DNA level. Who didn't want to be protected by a man like this? Except the reality was, this bulky cop was filled with attitude and misgivings and was hip-deep in the life she was running away from.

"You're going to need a bassinet for him

to sleep in," Paige said, stepping back and tossing the towel onto the counter. "And a few other things I can pick up for you. If I keep the receipts, you can reimburse me. I won't be long."

"Wait...what?"

And the tough cop seemed to evaporate, leaving behind a slightly panicked man with a stain on the front of his uniform. His hand on Benjie's rump covered the baby almost up to his little shoulders, and those gray eyes softened to charcoal as he met her gaze in dismay.

"You'll be fine," she replied, forcing herself to smile. "I'll make up another couple of bottles for you before I leave, but this will be good for you. I promise."

And Paige would be even better once she got out of here for an hour or two and could think straight. Maybe what she really needed wasn't a muscular cop or a job that could let her get her feet wet again... but a nunnery. She needed some solitude and then some bracing older women to tell her what to do.

But that wasn't likely, and she'd already taken the job.

PAIGE WAS GONE longer than Mike had anticipated. He didn't have anywhere to put the baby down besides the car seat. Funny, he hadn't thought of that before—where to put the baby. The car seat was by the door, and he moved it over to the couch and tried to get Benjie settled inside it again, only to have Benjie's little mouth turn down. Then his eyes welled up and that plaintive cry erupted from deep inside his tiny chest. So Mike picked the baby back up and paced through the living room to the front window, then across again to the kitchen, all the while wondering what he was supposed to do with himself. If nothing else, he was getting his steps in on his fitness tracker.

Mike glanced toward the TV as he headed back into the living room, and that seemed like a good idea, so he sank into the couch, the baby on his chest, and flicked through some channels, keeping the volume low. Benjie wriggled a little bit, but when Mike put a hand over his back, he settled down and fell asleep. Twice, Mike tried to sit up to get Benjie into that car seat, but Benjie woke up each time, and that cry would start up again, so he'd lean back again and flick through a few more channels.

An hour passed, and Benjie woke up, his little mouth searching against Mike's shirt, so he got another of the bottles Paige had prepared from the fridge and warmed it under the tap like she'd shown him. Feeding the baby was a little easier this time because Mike didn't have an audience, and he sat down on the couch, a talk show keeping him company, the baby propped in his lap. Benjie's eyes were wide open as he slurped back on that bottle, and Mike couldn't help but smile.

"You're cute," he murmured as milk dribbled down Benjie's chin. He was so tiny yet so solemn as he went to town on that bottle. And in the baby's face, Mike thought he could see a little bit of his sister.

Jana had always been overly solemn, too. He would tease her when she was little. And when she'd get upset about something at school—some mean girls making fun of her clothes, a teacher telling her off for not trying hard enough—he'd counsel her to just ignore it. It was what he did, after all. He always blocked out the stuff he didn't want to see. He'd been just as abandoned as she was, after all, and he didn't let it get him down.

Looking back on it, he wished he could change some of those reactions. He hadn't been helpful. But then, he'd been a kid, too, and it wasn't fair to expect him to know how to fix problems that adults struggled with. Jana hadn't needed him to tell her that the things that made her sad shouldn't. She'd needed…what? Maybe just to be understood. And he hadn't even managed that much for her. She'd run away from home…and from him.

"I'm going to do better by you, buddy," Mike murmured, and he felt his throat tighten with emotion. Somehow, even with all his failure when it came to his sister, she'd still chosen him to take care of her little boy.

Did she think he'd do better now that he was grown, or was she simply desperate?

And where was she now? If he knew, he'd find her, bring her here. He'd keep her safe at long last. But his only connection to his sister was her tiny baby.

Benjie finished off his bottle, and Mike dropped it onto the couch next to him. He looked around for a cloth, found one and put it up on his shoulder. He wouldn't make that mistake twice.

Mike's cell phone rang, and he glanced down to see the station's number. Work—that was actually a good thing right now. He flicked off the TV and hit the speaker button, then lifted Benjie up to his shoulder for that burp.

"Officer McMann," he said.

"Hi, Mike, it's Ellen." The receptionist at the station. "How are you?"

"Not bad. You?"

"I'm fine." He could hear the smile in her voice. "The chief wants to know if you're free Sunday afternoon."

"I don't think I'm scheduled to work," he said. Benjie squirmed and let out a little whimper, and Mike kept doing those circles on the little guy's back with his fingertips.

"Good, because we want to throw you a baby shower," she announced.

"What? No."

"Yes." She sounded so matter-of-fact.

"Ellen, I appreciate the thought, but I'm not really a party kind of guy. Besides, I'm not…a mother…"

"We're having a baby shower," Ellen said.

"If you don't come, it's going to be a really awkward party."

Mike sighed, and shut his eyes. Benjie let out a loud burp, and Mike looked down at the little guy, who looked rather pleased with himself.

"Sunday," Ellen said when he hadn't replied. "This is coming from the chief."

Great. It was an order from the one man he needed to impress. If he'd come to Eagle's Rest without family complications, he would be spending his time at the firing range and doing physical training. How was he supposed to prove to the chief he was SWAT material when he was being mollycoddled at the precinct?

"Thanks, Ellen," he said.

"No problem," she replied cheerily, and hung up.

The very last thing he needed right now was some stupid baby shower. This wasn't funny—some joke played on the muscle-bound cop who now had a baby to take care of by himself. Hilarious. He hardly knew these people.

It was then that he felt a rumble in Benjie's diaper. It started out small, and then started to grow. Mike looked down at the baby in surprise and saw that Benjie's face was scrunched up in a look of intense concentration. The smell came next, and Mike held Benjie out in front of him like an unwanted Christmas fruitcake.

"Better out than in," Mike said. He felt the obligation to say something encouraging, and he waited until the rumbling stopped. "Done?"

Benjie blinked a couple of times, and then there was another rumble.

"Wow. Kiddo. This is really something," Mike said, looking around the room. Some leaks were starting to seep into the sleeper, and Mike quickly realized he was in a bind. This baby needed a new diaper—heck, maybe two, at this rate—and he had a very faint idea of how to make this happen.

"Benjie, you and I have a problem," Mike said, pulling the baby back against his body again. There was going to be a smell, and probably some leaking, but he couldn't just walk around for the next ten minutes, holding a five-pound newborn like an offering to the gods. He'd have to survive a little baby poop.

The diapers were in the box in the kitchen. So he headed in that direction. There would be wipes, too. He knew that much. He rummaged around, past bottles, soothers, some plastic doodads he didn't recognize…and emerged with a small package of diapers. He tossed them overhand toward the couch, then snatched up the tub of wipes.

He was feeling better already. This wasn't so bad. He'd been a little freaked out when Paige took off to run those errands, but maybe she was right—he was doing okay.

There was a sweatshirt hanging over the arm of the couch, and he tossed it onto the floor to give a bit of padding. Then he sank to the floor next to it, lowered Benjie onto the sweatshirt and started undoing snaps on that little sleeper. Getting him out of the soiled sleeper was easy enough, but the diaper was a whole new challenge. He couldn't figure out how to get it off Benjie, and it was more than full—it was overflowing. Mike eyed it for a moment, considering his options. He briefly considered just using some scissors and cutting the kid out of the diaper, but pointy scissors and a tiny, squirmy baby were a bad combination.

But then it occurred to him that he could just slide the baby out of his diaper like a pair of shorts. The whole diaper, now that it was overflowing, was hanging rather loose and low, anyway, so he gave it a little shimmy, and his plan worked...for the most part.

He now had a dirty diaper, and a baby dirty from the waist down, since he'd pulled Benjie through the diaper to get him out of it. He left the diaper where it was on top of the sweater and carried Benjie out in front of him, thumbs under his arms and fingers supporting his tiny head from behind, and headed for the kitchen.

He needed the sprayer nozzle on the tap, but before he could do anything with the sprayer, he needed a hand free. That meant the dirty baby went back up on his shoulder, and one hand went over the dirty bottom. He grimaced. There was an easier way for all of this, he was sure.

Once he got some warm water, Mike rinsed off his hand under the tap, then lowered the baby into the empty sink and sprayed him off, too. He was being gentle, but Benjie scrunched up his face and started to cry.

"Hey, buddy…it's not so bad. You've got to be clean. I'm sorry, okay? I'm sorry…"

Behind him, Mike heard the front door open.

"I'm back!" Paige's voice filtered over to the kitchen. There was a pause. "Oh, my God! What happened in here?"

"I'm in the kitchen," he called, and he turned off the water, then scanned the room for something to wrap the baby in. Benjie's plaintive wail made him feel bad—no one liked being hosed off, even if the hose was warm and gentle.

Paige appeared in the doorway, her eyes wide as she took him in.

"There is baby poop literally everywhere," she said.

"Except on the baby," he said, lifting up Benjie as proof. He was feeling rather proud of that achievement. He snatched a dish towel off the handle of the stove and wrapped it around Benjie, who stopped crying the minute he was wrapped up again. "Would you mind holding him?"

Paige stepped forward and took the baby without complaint, staring at Mike with a look of bewildered shock.

"I'll just…change," he said, looking down at his now smeared uniform. "This comes out in the wash, right?"

Paige didn't answer, and he headed for the bedroom to find something else to wear. The smell of the diaper followed him, and he wrinkled his nose.

"So what did you pick up?" Mike called as he grabbed a pair of jeans and a T-shirt from his dresser.

"A bassinet, some burp cloths, a few preemie sleepers, since he's pretty tiny still," Paige called back. "Mike, what did you do to that diaper?"

"Nothing." Mike emerged from the bedroom fully dressed. He went over to the sweatshirt protecting the carpet, picked it all up with one swoop and headed for the garbage. Whatever—he wasn't attached to that sweatshirt, anyway.

"I think we need some diaper lessons," she said. "Grab me a diaper, and I'm going to run through the basics."

Mike passed a diaper over, and she held it up in front of her one-handed, the baby in the other arm. "This is the front. This is the back. These little tabs work like stickers."

And for the next five minutes, Paige gave him a brief overview of diapering and dressing a baby—Benjie getting buttoned into a sleeper in the process. So, yeah, there had been an easier way, but in his defense, he'd panicked. Looking over at Paige's sparkling blue eyes as she gave her super-detailed explanation of diaper duty, he realized that he was more than glad she was here to help him out—he was deeply grateful.

"They're throwing me a baby shower at the precinct," he said when she stopped talking.

"Good."

"I don't think so."

"You need baby things," she said, rising to her feet and cuddling Benjie close in her arms.

"What about that box in the kitchen? And you just *bought* baby things, I thought."

"I got a few necessities," she said with a small smile. "Trust me, Mike, you need a whole lot more baby stuff than you already have, and baby showers are a great way to get it."

"I don't like this," he said.

Paige shrugged. "You'll survive. You also

might end up with something really useful, like a stroller, so…"

He found her lack of pity annoying, but he shot her a grin, anyway. "I take it the baby stuff is in the car still?"

She rummaged in her pocket for her keys and tossed them over to him. He caught them and headed for the front door. "I'll write you a check."

He was a lot more comfortable carrying boxes out of the car than he was dealing with his infant nephew, but when he glanced back at Benjie snuggled up in the crook of Paige's arm, already fast asleep, he felt a wave of tenderness. Funny how an explosive diaper could be so bonding.

He and Benjie would be okay. Eventually.

CHAPTER THREE

PAIGE AWOKE FIVE minutes before her alarm went off the next morning, and she rolled over to grab her cell phone from the bedside table. When she pushed a button to light up the screen, she saw she had no missed calls. She yawned and put it down, then rubbed her hands over her face. She'd left her number with Mike before she left last night, just in case he found himself in over his head and in need of help. So she had slept lightly, expecting the phone to ring.

But it hadn't, and she wasn't sure what that meant. She'd agreed to be at his home by seven in the morning. So she flung back the covers and shivered in the chilly pre-dawn. She grabbed a bathrobe and pulled it on before she flicked on her light and opened her closet.

Paige got dressed in some warm layers, ending in a soft, mauve sweater and a pair of jeans. It felt good to be dressing down for a change—she had to admit that. But waking up this early and plunging out into the morning cold still felt like it was a workday.

She'd had a few appointments with a counselor about her panic attacks and decisions for her future, and one of the things the counselor had pointed out was that Paige had never taken a proper break. What would life look like if Paige didn't have this job? Stress leave was about more than giving her frayed nerves a rest—it was an experiment in what life would be like without her duties as a social worker.

So far, that had meant ordinary days—grocery shopping, watching Netflix, looking through the want ads at the jobs that came up in Eagle's Rest. She hadn't found an encouraging number of jobs she was qualified for, or interested in.

She'd considered getting another appointment with the counselor, but she needed to make her own decision. No one else could do this for her. If she left her career, she'd be the one to reap the rewards or live to regret it. And this assignment with Mike and Benjie was a bit of a relief. It was less time in her own head. Less agonizing about her decisions.

Paige's house was a two-bedroom bungalow with an unfinished basement and ancient plumbing, but it suited Paige just fine. She stopped in her little kitchen for a cup of hot tea and toast with extra butter. Then she cleaned up, put on a bit of makeup and let herself out into the chilly predawn darkness.

The sky was clear of clouds, and she paused in the driveway in front of her house to look up. It was a habit from childhood—looking for the constellations she knew. But she could see only the brightest of the stars still visible. The mountains loomed like a black wall to the west, and she shivered as a gust of icy wind wormed its way against her neck.

Paige unlocked her car and got in. She turned the key and rubbed her hands together, then pressed them between her legs while the engine warmed up and the frost melted off her windows. Winter was coming—and soon enough the mountain snow would work its way down to them.

This really did feel like going to work, except for the casual dress, and she had to remind herself that this wasn't. Not really.

Mike had agreed to pay her a fair wage for the three weeks, but this wasn't the job that had her heart in knots. This was a strange break—a newborn, a clueless guardian and a couple of weeks where she could put off making the biggest decision of her career. She sucked in a few deep breaths, counting four seconds in, holding it for four seconds and then releasing for four seconds. It helped to center herself in the moment.

"I'm fine," she murmured to herself. "It's early, and I'm tired, but I'm fine."

Her phone dinged, and she looked down at an incoming text. It was from her friend Liv Hylton. She'd just gotten married and was both pregnant with her first child and running a successful bookstore in downtown Eagle's Rest, but she'd made time to chat with Paige last night. For that Paige was grateful.

Speaking of new career ideas, ever think of running a day care? Eagle's Rest could use one.

What were friends for, if not to help a girl brainstorm a whole new career? She was too young to call this a midlife crisis, but it *was* a crisis. She flicked on the heater in the car before she started texting back.

Not a bad idea actually. I'm looking forward to being a nanny for a few weeks. This baby is so adorable… 5 lbs of cute!

She was making light of things, as if a cute baby and three weeks with a ruggedly good-looking cop could solve her problems. They couldn't, obviously, but neither could Liv, so Paige wouldn't unload on her pregnant friend this morning. Paige might feel overwhelmed, but that was no reason to be a burden on her friends. She wasn't even willing to call her brother this morning, and she and Nathan had always been close.

She tossed her phone onto the passenger side seat and put her car in Reverse. She didn't want to be late.

Her phone pinged again, and Paige glanced at the incoming text from Liv.

The 250 lbs of cute can't hurt, either.

"Har, har," Paige said aloud, then chuckled as she backed out of her driveway. But

Mike wasn't quite the diversion from reality that Liv seemed to think.

The drive across town only took ten minutes, and most of that was stopping at empty intersections. This time of year, there were fewer tourists to clog the roads, but they still had the traffic lights that were so necessary in the busy season, and Paige seemed to hit every single red light. She stopped at the elementary school, the window already aglow this early, and then she stopped again at the corner with the laundromat and the diner. The next red light was by the bus station, and she watched a teenager sitting with a backpack inside the well-lit waiting area.

Going somewhere…alone. It sparked Paige's instincts because she had dealt with a few runaways in her career. But then an older woman appeared at the girl's side, handing her a can of pop and sitting down next to her. The light turned green, and Paige pressed on the gas again. Eagle's Rest was her town, and she felt like one of the guardians here—keeping it safe and secure for everyone else.

When Paige pulled into Mike's driveway,

the sun had started to peer over the horizon, flooding the sky with pink, setting the snowcapped mountain peaks into a golden glow.

Lights shone from the windows of Mike's little bungalow, and when she knocked on the side door, it opened almost instantly.

Mike stood in the doorway barefoot, Benjie wrapped in an afghan, his little eyes open wide and his downy hair standing up straight. Mike's uniform shirt was unbuttoned and hung open, revealing a white undershirt beneath, and he looked like he'd had a rough night.

"Morning," he said, stepping back. "Am I glad to see you."

"How'd it go?" she asked. She closed the door behind her, then bent down to touch Benjie's soft little cheek with the back of her finger.

"Long. He kept waking up hungry. Like, every hour."

"I warned you," she said. "That's actually a good sign."

"Yeah, yeah." Mike yawned. "You want to hold him?"

"Sure."

Mike eased the baby into Paige's arms, and she looked down at Benjie with a smile. She smoothed a hand over his ruffled hair and sighed. This was soothing… She glanced up, expecting Mike to head back the bedroom to get ready for work, but instead he yawned again and opened the fridge.

"Have you eaten yet?" he asked over his shoulder.

"Not much," she admitted.

"I fix a mean omelet," he said. "Interested?"

"Will I make you late?" she asked.

"Nope, I'm cooking, anyway," he said, pulling some ingredients from the fridge.

Paige peeked into the living room and spotted a few cloths strewn across the couch, three empty baby bottles sitting on a side table.

"How do you feel about me taking Benjie out today?" Paige asked. "I might want to go out for lunch or something. Are you comfortable with that?"

"Sure." He glanced over his shoulder. "That's not daunting for you?"

"Not really," she said.

He turned back to the stove. "You weren't the one up all night."

"You could have called," she said. "I actually expected you to."

"Nah." He stifled a yawn. "I've got to soldier through, right?"

Paige headed for the coffeemaker. "How do you take your coffee?"

"Black. Why?"

She poured a mug and slid it across the counter toward him. "Drink up."

Mike accepted it without another word and gingerly took a sip.

"Here," she said. "Take the baby. Drink your coffee. I'll make breakfast."

"It's my home, I feel like I should do the cooking," he said.

"This is also your baby, and I think he needs a change," she retorted with a grin.

Mike chuckled. "Just you wait until I'm all the way awake."

But he did as she asked, and took the baby from her arms. He blew on the coffee, took another sip, then headed into the living room. Paige started sautéing some mushrooms and onions for the omelets, and for a few minutes there was nothing but the hiss of frying food.

"There you go, buddy…" she could hear Mike say from the other room. "You're awake now, aren't you? Well, I'm not. No one lets me nap like they do for you. You could get away with murder because you're smaller than a loaf of bread. I'm bigger than a loaf of bread, so there's more judgment there."

She couldn't help but smile as she listened to Mike talk to the baby. He didn't seem to have the regular baby talk that most people used on infants. His was earnest and logical…and he sounded exhausted.

By the time Paige poured the egg mixture into the pan, Mike emerged into the kitchen, the baby in one arm and wheeling the bassinet ahead of him.

"Almost done," she said.

Mike laid Benjie in the bassinet, then straightened, stretching his shoulders and back.

"I'm not normally this helpless," he said, coming up beside her and opening an upper cupboard. He pulled down two plates and put them on the counter next to her. "I feel like I need to say that."

"I believe you," she replied, then used the spatula to cut the omelet in half and serve it up. "Maybe it's lucky you're here in Eagle's Rest right now. At least your shift should be an easy one."

"Yeah, that's part of the problem," he replied, and she could hear a note of bitterness in his tone. "I'm the kind of guy who doesn't relax too easily. I need a challenge. A bad guy. A crime ring. Something."

"A baby?" she said, raising an eyebrow.

Mike passed her a fork. "That came out of left field."

"This boring tourist trap is actually a great place to raise kids," she said. "I grew up here. It's calm. Safe."

"How calm is it if you're burning out in Social Services?" he countered.

"To be fair, I service the surrounding towns, as well," she replied.

But he had a point. That was the problem with this job. She could live in a gorgeous little tourist destination, and still be faced with the most heartrending cases. No community was immune, because it was *life*. She believed in the job, in the importance of what social workers did for the community.

She just wasn't sure she could do it anymore. There were tougher people who could pick up where she left off.

Paige followed Mike to the table and sat down. He pulled the bassinet a little closer and looked inside. Benjie had fallen back to sleep, and for a couple of minutes they both ate in silence.

"You know what it's like," she said. "There's always someone getting hurt, needing help. And for the longest time, I thought that if I could just offer that help, I'd be doing something for those vulnerable people."

"But it's always more complicated than that," he concluded.

She nodded, then leaned back against her chair. "Aren't you ever tired of being seen as the bad guy? I mean, you're the one who has to arrest the abusive dad in front of the kids. You're the big, bad authority figure. For a lot of people, you're the enemy."

"It's all perspective," Mike replied. "I'll be the bad guy to someone. Especially, if I'm locking him up. But I'm the good guy to someone else who's being protected."

"Even if you're doing the right thing in arresting the abusive dad, the kids don't think you're the good guy," she countered.

"Sure. I guess."

"The very people you're protecting are going to hate you," she said. "At least, that's the way it seems to turn out all too often."

"I figure anything worthwhile is going to tick off somebody."

Paige wanted to make a difference, too, but how much of her own emotional health was she willing to sacrifice in order to do that?

Mike finished the last of his omelet and stood up.

"Thanks for cooking breakfast. Leave the mess in the living room. I'll take care of it tonight."

"I can tidy up," she said.

"I'm not the kind of guy who expects a woman to cook and clean. You're here for the baby, not for me. I should be able to take care of myself at this point."

"You're part of the job, Mike," she said.

"Not really."

"Oh, completely." She smiled ruefully. "I'm teaching you baby care, aren't I? And Benjie won't thrive unless you're okay, too."

"I'm okay," he said.

"If you need anything, you have to tell me," she said. "You've got me for three weeks, so make the most of this."

"Yeah." He met her gaze with a small smile. "I will."

He started doing up his shirt buttons, then slowly turned and headed out of the kitchen, still buttoning. She watched him go. Mike was very much part of her job. Unfortunately, her emotions were at risk of getting entangled wherever she put her energy— into caring for a baby, or into the floundering dad.

"OFFICER McMANN," THE chief said as Mike came into the station that morning. Mike had a travel mug in one hand, and he took a sip of coffee as he turned toward the chief.

"Good morning," Mike said.

"You look like a train wreck," the chief said with a short laugh. "How's the baby?"

"Eating often," Mike replied. "But otherwise good."

"Glad to hear it. Is Paige working out?"

Working out. She wasn't a housekeeper or something… She was turning out to be a lifesaver, and an image of her concerned gaze and her hair tucked behind her ears as she shook bottles full of formula crowded his overtired mind.

"Yeah, she's…great. She knows what she's doing, and that's what I need, right?"

She was also comforting, and a little distracting. Not that he'd tell the boss that.

"If you need another few days off—" the chief began.

"No, no," Mike said with a shake of his head. "I'd rather get back to work."

"You sure?"

"Positive." Work had always been his solace, and right now, he didn't need to be leaning on the too-pretty nanny. She said he was part of the job, but he didn't intend to be. He'd take care of himself.

Mike headed toward his desk in the back corner of the bull pen, rubbing a hand through his hair. It was going to be a long day, but he had good reason to want to be here, and it had nothing to do with impressing his boss. It wasn't only the baby that had kept him up last night. He was worried about Jana. His sister had just abandoned her newborn, and while Safe Haven laws meant that

Jana was perfectly within her rights to hand her newborn to a hospital employee with no questions asked, Mike was her brother—and he was damn well asking a few questions. He just wasn't sure how he was going to get those answers.

He logged into his computer and pulled up the phone numbers for the hospital where Benjie had been left. His sister had given the nurse a lot more information than most mothers did who were taking advantage of the Safe Haven laws. She could have simply handed the baby over and walked out, but she'd obviously wanted her son to go to family.

Was Jana going to change her mind? Would she want the baby back?

He had too many questions, but the main one was what had happened to Jana to make her give up her newborn baby? She had been together enough to know about the laws, to remember to give his contact information… Was she still with the father? Was she on her own and desperate? Or was there some loser involved who she couldn't get away from? She was obviously doing some drugs, and that was never a good sign. But if he was going to help her, he needed detailed answers.

Mike called a few different numbers, and was transferred three times before he was put in touch with the hospital social services worker who had done the paperwork for Benjie.

"Officer McMann," she said with a smile in her voice. "How's the little guy doing?"

"Good. Really good," Mike said.

"I'm glad to hear it. What can I do for you?"

"I was hoping to get a little more information about my sister."

"You know I can't do that." Her voice softened. "She was within her rights to relinquish the baby, and if we don't respect those privacy rights, the whole system fails."

Yeah, he did. The Safe Haven laws were in place so that babies need not be abandoned in unsafe environments. If a mother didn't want her baby, she could simply hand it over to a hospital employee or a firefighter within three days of the birth. If they started chasing down parents who abandoned those babies, people would be afraid to do the right thing and those babies might be left in much worse environments.

"I'm worried about her," Mike said. "She's my sister. She's recently given birth. She might be in medical distress—it's a possibility! I just want to find her and make sure she's okay."

"I can't do that, Officer McMann," she repeated. "I would if I could. I do sympathize with your worries, but—"

"Was there any hint of where she might be living?"

"None."

"Was anyone with her when she left the hospital?"

"I can't reveal that information unless you're investigating a crime. Are you?"

"No." He sighed. "I'm not."

"May I give you some advice, Officer?" the woman asked gently.

"Might as well."

"The baby is safe. Your sister knew where to find you—even if you didn't know where to find her. Wait a few days or weeks. Maybe she'll come see you herself."

"Did she seem…okay?" he asked. She was silent, and he sighed. "Just wait. Right."

"It's all I can say."

"Thanks," he said. "I guess I don't have much choice."

Mike hung up and rubbed his hands over his face. Those blasted laws... Yeah, he understood how they worked, but what about the times that the mothers might need medical intervention? She wasn't okay—if she were, she wouldn't have left her baby, he knew that. She'd been abandoned when she was tiny, too. She grew up wondering why her mom had just dumped her with Grandma and disappeared. So she wouldn't do that to her own child—not if she could help it.

"Mike?" He looked up to see Jack Talbott coming across the bull pen. He and Jack had worked together in Denver before Jack transferred out here to Eagle's Rest in order to get married.

"Hey," Mike said. "If you mention how tired I look, I'm going to deck you."

Jack laughed. "That's going to be me soon enough."

"When is Liv due?" Mike asked.

"Six weeks."

"Yeah... This *will* be you soon enough," he agreed.

"Are you okay, though?" Jack asked, pulling up a chair opposite Mike's desk. "Have you heard from your sister?"

"No," Mike said. "I left instructions for the Denver precinct to give her my contact information if she tries to find me. The Social Services agent who dealt with her when she relinquished the baby won't give me any other information."

Jack nodded slowly. "Have you checked for any arrests or detained individuals in the last few days? I mean, not saying she'd have been in trouble, but…"

"It's something to check," Mike agreed, and he turned to his computer. He'd found her once before the exact same way. "I called the Denver precinct last night and asked around if anyone knew anything, or had any idea of where she might have gone. It was a long shot, but they don't have anything, either."

"You might just have to be patient," his friend replied.

"What would you do, if you were me?" Mike asked.

"If I contacted her, I'd be worried that she'd want her baby back," Jack said.

"That crossed my mind," Mike agreed. If he found his sister, would she even want his help? Or would she want Benjie back? A mother didn't give birth and then just cut all her emotions off—he knew that much.

"But I'm worried about her, too. She needs help."

"Yeah, I get it."

Mike shrugged. "If you hear anything, let me know."

Jack tapped Mike's desk in a farewell. "You bet. Take care, buddy. See you out there."

Mike nodded a goodbye, but remained at his desk. He was just going to have to wait for his sister to contact him. Because as much as he wanted to treat his sister's situation like he treated every other challenge in his life—go conquer it with testosterone pounding through his system—he couldn't. SWAT tactics weren't the answer here. Jana might have given him her child, but so far, she didn't want to be found.

He pushed back his chair and rose. Patrol of this sleepy little tourist spot wasn't exactly exciting, but it did give him time to think. His sister needed his help—he was sure of it—but this was going to take a softer touch than he was accustomed to using.

He'd come to Eagle's Rest to prove himself tough enough to be part of the most elite squad in the force. So far, he was being forced to soften up in ways he'd never anticipated—a newborn baby's care, and possibly his sister's life, depended on it.

CHAPTER FOUR

THE NEXT MORNING, Paige stood by Mike's kitchen window, looking out over the frost-tipped grass of his backyard and the dead flowers that hunched over in brown flower beds along the edge of the lawn. The frost was melting away in the pools of golden, late-morning sunlight.

"So what should I expect at this baby shower today?" Mike asked, passing a mug of tea to her. "With milk and sugar. As requested."

"Thanks." She picked up the tea bag string and bobbed it up and down in the mug. "It's nothing to worry about. There will be a few games, probably. People will want to see the baby, maybe hold him."

"Games?"

"And gifts," she added, taking a sip of sweet, milky tea. "You need those, Mike. So don't put your nose up about this. The people who come to this baby shower will know more about what you need than you do. Trust them."

"But games?" He grimaced.

Paige chuckled. "Yes, games. That's what usually happens. It makes it fun for everyone."

"I'm allowed to hate this."

"But you aren't allowed to show it," she retorted. "This is for you. So be a bit appreciative."

"No, I get it…" He heaved a sigh. "Everyone means well."

"Including me," she said.

"Wait—are you part of this?" he asked.

"Well, in so much that I've been tasked with getting you there and not letting you off the hook," she replied with a small smile. "And with getting some information for the shower. This is a small town, Mike. Everyone knows everyone, and things like this are a team effort."

"Everyone?" He smiled faintly.

"Just about," she replied. "We're a tight-knit community."

"And what information are you supposed to get from me?" he asked, and his gaze turned wary. She couldn't help but smile at the fact that this beefy cop was unnerved right now.

"Hang on." Paige went over to her purse and rummaged through, then pulled out her phone. "Ellen emailed me earlier. She figured I might have better luck than she would." Paige opened the email. "Okay, so question number one. How much can you bench-press?"

"What does this have to do with a baby shower?" he asked, barking out a laugh.

"It's a game—everyone will write down their guesses, and the person who gets the most answers right wins a door prize. Most of the guests are going to be cops, so this is the sort of thing that seems appropriate. Sometimes they guess at the exact due date, or the baby's weight at birth…it's supposed to be fun. But since you're a cop, and the dad, they wanted to make it more guy friendly."

"I'm not the dad, though," he countered. "I'm Benjie's uncle. That's an important distinction here."

"It's not one that Benjie's making right now," she said, then sighed. "I get that this is complicated. I do. Just for argument's sake, you're doing the job of a dad. All of it. So we're trying to take care of you. That's all."

Mike chewed the side of his cheek and looked at her for a moment. "Okay. Fine."

"Yeah?" She hesitated.

"Yeah."

"Okay." Paige looked back down at the email. "So how much can you bench-press?"

"Three-seventy."

"Wow." She eyed him again, impressed. "Three hundred and seventy pounds?"

"Yeah. I've been training for a while. It comes in handy when dealing with perps."

Paige typed in the answer. "Okay, and how fast can you run a mile?"

"Carrying gear or without?" he asked.

Paige blinked, then shrugged. "Um, she didn't specify. Let's say without."

"Seven minutes. Or around there."

Paige typed in that answer, too. Then she looked up at him. "Mike, how do you separate your emotions from the job?"

"That's not a question on there, is it?" he asked with a small smile.

"No, that's *my* question. I'm just…" Paige sighed. "You're tough. Physically, you could just about bench-press three of me. But a job in public service requires a different kind of toughness. How do you do it? How do you chase down bad guys, see all the ugliness that goes down and then still face another day of it?"

Mike was silent for a moment, then he shrugged. "I guess there's a certain satisfaction in catching them."

"But you don't catch them all," she pressed. "And the victims left behind in some of these cases... I mean, I know what you see out there. Social Services comes in later to help clean up the emotional messes. And there is just so much collateral damage. So much pain. So many hurt people."

"We're part of the solution," Mike said. "Not the whole solution, but part of it. I'm a cop, so I catch them. You're a social worker, so you come in and help give kids a new start, or get some much needed counseling for victims. It's better than not doing anything."

"I always thought so," she agreed. "That was why I got into this field to begin with. But lately, I find that just before bed is the hardest time of day. After I've eaten. Maybe even after I've watched a bit of TV. When I'm done doing stuff and being busy and my mind starts to slow down..."

"What happens?" Mike fixed his gray gaze on her.

"That's when I remember the people I couldn't help, and I just can't sweep them aside. I know all the logical arguments— I've done my best, I can't do everything..." Paige ran a hand through her hair. "Never mind. Sorry. This isn't your problem."

"I'm listening," Mike said. "Keep going."

Paige eyed him for a moment and saw his expression was serious and focused. Great— he had that cop mask up, the one professionals used to distance themselves from the hard stuff. So did that mean *she* was the hard stuff right now?

"No, it's fine," she said, forcing a smile. She headed for the counter and took a towel off some sanitized baby bottles. She was here to help with Benjie, not dump her issues onto him. She'd gone over this with a counselor repeatedly, and Mike was dealing with enough upheaval.

Mike came up next to her, opened the cupboard and pulled down the tin of baby formula. He opened it, fished out the plastic scoop and wordlessly handed it to her.

"I go to the gym," Mike said, his voice low.

"Hmm?" She looked up at him.

"When I remember the faces of the people I couldn't help. That's when I hit the gym. And I imagine pummeling the bad guys into a pulp. I take all the frustration and helpless feelings, and I turn them into adrenaline while I pump iron. That's what I do. That's how I deal with it."

She met his gaze for a moment. "Oh."

And by the looks of his muscular physique, he'd had a whole lot of conflicted feelings to pour into his workouts.

"Are you really thinking of quitting?" Mike asked.

"Yes." Paige poured a scoopful of powder into the first bottle and topped it up with water. Then she put the lid on and started to shake it.

"Ever consider hitting the gym instead?" he said with a small smile.

"Not like you do," she said with a short laugh. "I don't know, Mike. I've never been the gym-going kind of girl. I like bookstores and tea, rainy days and long walks. Besides, after the gym, I'd still be left with that dreaded time just before bed, wouldn't I?"

"Yeah, I guess so."

"It's my personality, I think," she said. "I don't have a thick enough skin."

"Sorry. I wish I had some great fix."

"I don't think there is a great fix for this one." She reached for the next empty baby bottle. Her empathy was her strength— but it was also her greatest weakness. She cared so much that it broke her heart, and she couldn't take it anymore. "I was hoping you might have some insight that I hadn't come across yet."

"Still hoping to save this career path, deep down, aren't you?" he asked.

"Maybe."

Paige had gone to school for social services. She'd worked hard. She'd been passionate about her job, and she'd poured herself into it. It had been an integral part of her identity. The answer to "What do you do?" said a lot about a person. She'd chosen a profession, one where she could make a difference for the most vulnerable people in the community. This wasn't just a job for her.

Paige shook up the next bottle. "So, back to this baby shower."

"You sure you can't just go for me?" he asked ruefully.

"Not a chance. The chief would never forgive me."

"How well do you know him?" Mike asked.

"He's my high school best friend's dad," she said. "So he's known me since I was a dorky freshman."

"Yeah?" Mike chuckled. "I can't imagine you dorky."

"Add braces to this look, and an earnest belief in rules," she said. "And that was me in high school."

Mike eyed her for a moment, then grinned. "You might be a little dorky now..."

She laughed and smacked his arm, and his gaze softened.

"I take that back," he said. "Sorry, I shouldn't tease. You're not dorky in the least. You're downright intimidating."

"To a big guy like you?" she said.

"Yeah. A woman like you is everything

I'm not, and that covers a whole lot of territory."

She put the freshly shaken bottle aside and wiped her hands on a towel. Was he flirting with her? It was hard to tell. But she had to tread carefully here, so she pulled out her cell phone again. "There was one more question."

"Yeah?"

"What's your favorite kids' song? Whoever guesses all of the answers will get two tickets to the movie theater."

"Good prize," he said.

"Well?"

"'Wheels on the Bus,'" he said. "I used that with a lost five-year-old to keep him busy until we could locate his parents."

"That's sweet." She typed in his answer. "I'm pressing Send now. You okay with that?"

"Sure."

"I'm willing to bet you're a good cop, Mike."

"I try. I'm good at standing between victims and perps. I'm good at chasing down the bad guys. It's the stuff that you find easy that's tough for me—the relationships, the soft skills."

"It's not easy," she countered. "It puts your heart in a vice."

"I believe that." He met her gaze, and for a moment she thought he'd say something else, but then a whimper came from the other room. Paige angled her head toward the living room where Benjie's bassinet was.

"You're up," she said.

"No sympathy from you?" he asked, the seriousness evaporating as a grin tugged at his lips. He picked up one of the newly prepared bottles from the counter.

"Not a drop. Get in there."

Mike ran the bottle under hot water for a few seconds, then headed out of the kitchen, and Paige stood listening to the sound of Mike's low voice. The whimpering stopped. He was better at baby minding than he seemed to think. It was just a matter of bottles and diapers…and some heart. A baby needed love—the unconditional, openhearted, overflowing kind. The kind that could hurt.

She shook up another bottle. This little guy was going to go through a lot of formula, so they'd need to bring a few bottles with them.

Mike came back into the kitchen, Benjie in his arms fervently drinking a bottle.

"I haven't had a shower yet this morning, and I need one," Mike said.

"Okay."

"It just occurred to me… How do you do that? I mean, while watching a baby. Is it safe? Can you just…go close yourself in the bathroom and… Like, a simple shower is seeming complicated now."

Paige chuckled. "This time around, I'll hold the baby. But when you're on your own, you use a bouncy chair. It's a little seat that you can strap a baby into, and you take your shower and leave the curtain open a bit so you can look out a him. Just think—you might get one as a gift at the party."

Mike shot her a rueful look. "You're enjoying this."

"A little bit," she admitted. If she had to honest, she was enjoying *him*. "Here—hand Benjie over. I think I'd prefer you showered, too."

MIKE WASN'T WORKING TODAY, so he put on jeans and a long-sleeved shirt. He felt better having Paige out there watching Benjie, and he had to admit that he was nervous about being left alone in this. It was daunting.

When he came out of his bedroom, he found Benjie asleep in his bassinet. The house was quiet. Paige stood looking out a window, her back to him. She was slim, but her shape was womanly, and he found himself admiring her. There was something about the way she stood—her arms crossed in front of her, her feet close together—that looked rather vulnerable. What was she thinking about, staring out the window like that?

He ambled up behind her, trying to get a glimpse at what had her attention.

"Penny for your thoughts," he murmured.

Paige jumped, landing solidly against his chest, and he shot out a hand to catch her, holding her. She laughed softly, then lifted her gaze. He loosened his grip on her, but didn't drop his hand, either. She felt good right there in his arms—warm, fragrant, her blue eyes sparkling with laughter. She was gorgeous, he realized, looking down at her. Not pretty. Not girl-next-door comforting. This woman was gorgeous, and holding her like this was waking him up in ways that were definitely not professional.

His gaze dropped down to her lips, and he had to push back thoughts of bending down and covering them with his own...

What was he thinking? That had escalated quickly, and he cleared his throat.

"Sorry," he murmured. He should definitely step back here...but she hadn't moved yet.

Paige sucked in a breath, and for a moment, they just looked at each other. He could see the way her pulse beat at the base of her throat, and she hesitated there against him, then stepped back and let go of his hand.

Good. That was for the best. He felt some heat creeping up his neck. Would she think he was some sort of jerk now? Or had he managed to hide what he'd been thinking?

"What were you looking at?" he murmured.

"There was an eagle circling," she said. "Those big circles—it was hunting something."

Mike leaned over, taking in the strip of sky above them.

"I don't see it," he said.

Paige leaned to look again, too, and he could feel the warmth of her emanating against him. He shut his eyes for a moment—he'd have to be careful with her. Not that she was overstepping, but he was a red-blooded male, after all.

He normally went for the tough, wise-cracking female cops he worked with. The relationships were passionate, quick and generally ended before he'd met any family members or got too deeply involved. The gentle, sweet women he came across— friends of friends, blind date setups—always felt a little too pure for him. He didn't know how to be normal and functional, and he tended to pull back.

Paige wasn't his usual type, but pulling away from her wasn't going to be as easy. She was in his house every day. He'd have to get used to being around someone "normal and functional," for a little while at least.

Paige shrugged. "It's gone."

She shot him a quick smile and stepped away from the window. But this time as she strolled toward the kitchen, he was seeing something he hadn't quite seen before—the simmering beauty of a vulnerable woman.

Funny—in the past he'd always been afraid of breaking the sweet, vulnerable types—and maybe it was his time with Benjie that was changing his perspective a bit, but right now, he was feeling more protective. He didn't want to banter with her or go shooting with her—one of his go-to dates with the women cops. Instead, he wanted to keep her safe and maintain this strange, warm feeling inside of his home.

And he couldn't even say that was for the baby's benefit, either, although Benjie wouldn't suffer from it. It was for him.

Except he knew himself. He was better with a woman who had thicker skin, who could deal with his shortcomings and put him in his place if she needed to. He wasn't always terribly sensitive, and he didn't always know how to be the kind of man a woman needed. That would explain why he was still single.

So maybe he was kind of scared of hurting her. He sucked in a deep breath, trying to regain his mental balance.

She was helping him with the baby, and

then she'd be gone. He'd best keep whatever he was feeling tamped down.

MIKE DROVE TO the station in his SUV, Paige beside him and Benjie in the back. She smelled nice—soft, floral. And he was trying really hard not to notice that. Now that he'd seen her in this strange new light, he was trying not to go there.

The rest of the morning had been casual. They'd watched some TV together, and Mike had made sure to sit on the easy chair, leaving the couch for her. But listening to her laugh along with the jokes in *The Big Bang Theory* reruns had been oddly comforting. Benjie had slept through most of it.

Now, driving together, he realized that he liked the silence they shared as he navigated the tree-lined streets. Maybe it was just that she was here to make the upheaval of a newborn easier, but she did improve things just by being around. It was a taste of a life he'd always known wasn't meant for the likes of him. And maybe that was dangerous. It was like giving a poor kid a taste for caviar. It wasn't helpful.

The baby shower was being held in one

of the precinct's meeting rooms, and Mike found a visitor's spot and parked. He glanced over at Paige as she undid her seat belt.

"I have to say, this isn't what I expected when I came out here," Mike said.

"Babies tend to turn everything upside down," she said.

"I'm not sure I'm going to be able to convince the chief that I'm SWAT material this way," he said.

"SWAT officers don't have families?" she said, shooting him a quizzical look. "You can have a life and a career, you know."

"I've always been the kind of guy whose career and personal life blended together," he said. Guns, target practice, bulletproof vests and the women he took out… "I'm all or nothing. Call it a personality defect."

"We have that in common," she said.

Maybe not quite so much as she thought, though. She gathered up the baby bag, then turned her glittering gaze on him again.

"I've been told that there are people who actually balance home life and career," she said with a teasing smile.

Mike chuckled at her dry humor. "I've

heard of those people. In fairy tales. Like unicorns. They exist?"

She pushed open her door. "Oh, they exist, and one day I hope to be one of them."

Yeah—that was right. He had personal goals to get into SWAT, but hers were different. She wanted balance and—how did she put it?—a white picket fence. And he was the proverbial bull in a china shop. She'd asked him before if he ever envied regular civilians, and up until now he hadn't. He never had fit in with regular people. He'd always been the odd one out, the broken one, the guy who'd been through too much for others to identify with him. But when he got into law enforcement, he realized that it wasn't just his personal issues that made him different—it was something deeper, a part of him that found satisfaction in righting wrongs. And the other cops were a lot like him.

But today, looking at Paige, with her sparkling blue eyes and her hopes to one day have that calm, ordinary life, he found himself envying the guy who would get to live that life with her. They'd enjoy ordinary things like brunch and baby showers. That guy would get Paige's smile in the morning and her joking banter after work... He'd get to pull her into his arms and kiss those lips. But envy was where it stopped, because he couldn't fit into that life. He had a sister to find, and bad guys to make pay for all the times he hadn't been able to protect her.

Mike carried the car seat and Paige took the baby bag as they headed into the precinct. Meeting room B was normally rather sparsely furnished with some chairs, a display screen for information and a coffee-maker. But when Mike walked into the room, Benjie's car seat held in one hand and Paige close behind him, he stopped short. The chairs were moved into a large circle, and to the side there was a table piled with pastel gift bags. Light blue helium balloons bobbed, held secure by their strings, from various surfaces like tabletops or tied to chair backs. Some twisted streamers looped across the ceiling, and he ducked to miss one as he stepped inside.

"Hey, Mike's here!"

Most of the precinct had squeezed into the room—cops and their spouses, too—and Mike's mouth went dry. This wasn't his domain—this was where the ordinary people did their thing. He'd never fit in well with that.

"Does everyone have one of these?" Ellen called from the back of the room. She fluttered a pale blue piece of paper in the air. "Fill it out with your best guesses to the questions. There are going to be prizes! So do take part!"

Mike looked back at Paige and she shot him a grin. "Relax."

"Easier said than done," he muttered.

"You'll be fine." Paige pointed to the only swivel chair in the room, festooned with balloons. "That's your seat."

"Is this the little guy?" one of the women asked. She was in full uniform—probably on a break from her shift.

"Hey, Donna," he said.

"Hi." She smiled. "Can I hold him?"

"Um—" Mike glanced back at Paige again. He wasn't sure why. He didn't need her permission, but he felt completely out of his depth. "Yeah, sure. Let me get him out of the car seat, though."

He put the car seat down on the chair and undid the buckles. Benjie was fast asleep, his little tongue stuck out as he made sucking movements with his lips.

"So tiny…" Donna breathed as Mike lifted Benjie out. He was still getting used to how small this infant was, too, but he didn't feel like he was going to break him anymore. That was something. When Donna had him snuggled in her arms, everyone came over to have a look at him, and Mike scrubbed a hand through his hair.

"You okay?" Paige's voice came at his shoulder, and he glanced down at her.

"I—um—" He wasn't sure how he felt, but he kept his gaze locked on Donna's back as she moved across the room.

"You're feeling protective of him," Paige said.

"Yeah—so? Is that weird?" Quite honestly, he had no idea if any of his instincts were "right" or not.

"No, it's healthy," she replied with a low laugh. "But relax. Everyone here is a cop, and no one is leaving the room. Benjie couldn't be safer."

"I know. It's not logical." He looked at the ridiculous swivel chair. "Do I have to sit there?"

"Yep." She shrugged. "Sorry, there are social rules here."

"This is all so…girlie."

"Excuse me?" She pulled a balloon forward—this one with a picture of handcuffs on it. "There was a lot of effort put into masculinizing this party, I'll have you know."

He could see the humor in her eyes, and he was suddenly deeply grateful that she was here with him.

"Very masculine," he said with a chuckle.

"Those were from a retirement party, I think," Paige said. "But really, any party at the police station could use a few handcuff balloons."

"A solid point." He met her gaze and they both smiled.

"Mike! How're you doing, buddy?"

It was Jack Talbott, and Mike shook his hand with a rueful smile.

"I'm doing fine. Have you met Paige Stedler?"

"Yeah, of course. She's friends with Liv," Jack said, shaking her hand. "So you're taking Mike here under your wing, are you?"

"I'm helping out," she said with a smile. "He needs me less than he thinks."

"Mike will have to show me the ropes soon enough," Jack said.

Mike could feel Paige's hand touch his arm lightly. "I'm just going to say hi to Liv." She shot Jack an easy smile, then slid away, leaving Mike on his own. He stood there for a moment, watching as she walked across the crowded room, and he wished she would stay. Whatever. It was probably better that she didn't. His attraction to her was probably linked to how out of his depth he felt with Benjie right now. That was all.

"You'll have Liv, Jack," Mike said, picking up the conversation. "You won't be quite so desperate as I am."

"True, and she also has a huge extended family, so I don't think we'll ever be short of babysitters or unwanted advice."

Mike barked out a laugh. "You should be more grateful for that!"

"Who says I'm not?"

Family. A beautiful wife. A baby on the way. Jack was getting there in the right order, and Mike could feel just how much more difficult it was going to be for him. Instead, he had a baby to care for and a beautiful woman in his home he had to try not to feel anything for. It was a weird balance.

"What are you going to do for child care?" Mike asked.

"For a while, Liv will just have the baby down in the store with her, but when the baby gets older—I don't know. We'll figure it out, I guess."

Unlike Jack and Liv's baby, little Benjie didn't have a mom in the picture. Mike had called a couple of day cares that morning, but both were booked up with waiting lists. He wasn't going to have much time to settle into his role, was he?

Jack looked across the room, then he nudged Mike's arm. "They're talking about us."

"What?" Mike looked over to where Paige and Liv stood together, and he caught both women looking at him. He met Paige's gaze curiously, and she laughed, shook her head and looked away.

Had she noticed anything this morning? He'd tried to hide it, but he felt a wriggle of misgiving in his gut.

"That's what it looks like when the women discuss you," Jack said. "For the record."

"There's nothing to discuss," Mike replied. "I'm a helpless cop with a newborn. She's helping me out for a few weeks. It's pretty straightforward."

"Yeah, of course."

Jack had agreed to that too quickly, and Mike glanced across the room again. Liv was watching him this time, her eyes narrowed and her head cocked to one side. They were two beautiful women—why did they scare him just a bit?

"All right, everyone!" Ellen called. "It's time to get started! Please choose a seat around the outside of the room, and we have a few games to play!"

"I'd better go get a seat next to my wife," Jack said. "Have fun."

Mike was suddenly feeling very exposed, and he looked at the balloon-festooned chair behind him. Great. Now he was going to feel like an idiot for the next hour or so because it was socially expected of him—and he was doing this on next to no sleep.

The baby started to cry, and Mike saw another woman pass him over to Paige. He felt better knowing that Paige had him. But Benjie's cries didn't stop like he expected, and Paige wove through the room toward him.

"Is he hungry again?" Mike asked when she made it to his side.

"I'll get a bottle," Paige said. "Here—"

And she passed Benjie into his arms, but as soon as the baby settled against his chest, the cries stopped and Benjie heaved a shaky little sigh. Mike looked down at the infant in surprise.

"I guess he just wanted you," Paige said.

"You think so?"

"Looks that way to me."

Mike patted Benjie's diaper gently, a small smile on his face. Funny how satisfying it was to be the little guy's preference.

"Have a seat, everyone!" Ellen called, and this time Mike did what he was supposed to do, and sat down in the middle of those bobbing balloons.

"I hate this," he whispered to Paige.

"Think of it as work-life balance," she whispered back, and he rolled his eyes.

"Now, everyone, pull out those papers I gave you, and we're going to go over the answers," Ellen said. "The first question was, how long has Mike been a cop. If you said ten years, then you're right!"

The chatting and murmur of voices started to slow down as people turned their attention toward the front.

"The second question was, how much can Mike bench-press," Ellen said. "And if you said three-seventy, then you're right!"

"Seriously?" one of the cops barked. "Remind me not to arm wrestle him!"

There was some laughter, and the baby squirmed a little, turning his face toward Mike's shirt. Hungry. He knew that move by now. He turned to Paige and whispered, "You have that bottle?"

Paige pulled one out of the diaper bag, and Mike tipped Benjie back into his arms and popped the bottle into his mouth. The baby care was starting to get easier already, he realized. Benjie sucked away at the bottle, his tiny hands opening and closing in his eagerness to get milk inside of him, and when Mike glanced over at Paige, she pulled a cloth out of the bag and passed it over. Yeah, he'd need that in a minute, wouldn't he?

He liked this—the teamwork. It was okay with Paige by his side…but it wasn't just the baby care, either. She was gorgeous, and he found himself feeling a level of attraction that he wasn't comfortable with. She seemed to wake up his nerve endings, and he could sense just how close she sat to him.

The last thing he needed was to be seen mooning after some women in front of all his colleagues. He wasn't planning on sticking around long, anyway. His strength had always been in his ability to stay focused and hit his next target. As soon as he could turn that focus back to SWAT preparation, he would. This was just a minor hitch in his plan until he could get a day care lined up.

"A seven-minute mile?" one of the cops moaned. "You're killing me, man! I haven't gotten anything right!"

Mike realized he'd tuned out.

"And the last question was, what is Mike's favorite kids' song," Ellen said. "And the correct answer is 'The Wheels on the Bus.' So, who got one out of four correct?"

A few hands went up.

"Two out of four? Three out of four?"

Mike looked across the room, and he saw Jack with a self-congratulatory grin on his face, his hand raised.

"And no one got all of them right?" Ellen said. "Okay, we have our winner with three out of four. Jack Talbott, come get your prize!"

Jack headed over to get his envelope, and Mike glanced around this room filled with colleagues. He'd come to Eagle's Rest with a definitive plan, but so far, it had been derailed. Standing here with a tiny baby in his arms, he felt as far as possible from the life he'd envisioned for himself. All of that preparation was useless when it came to taking care of his sister's baby... And yet, he knew that he had to make things right for Jana, and for all the other people victimized by criminals. His plans hadn't changed. One day, when Benjie was older, he'd teach him about stubborn persistence. That was what had gotten Mike this far—stubborn persistence in life, and in the gym, and in surviving when things had been toughest growing up.

A guy did best if he stuck to his strengths. A healthy work-life balance probably wasn't in the cards.

CHAPTER FIVE

THE GIFT OPENING came next, and Ellen sat on the other side of Mike, a pad of paper in her lap as she recorded the gift and giver in a neat list for his benefit. Somehow, Paige didn't see Mike as the thank-you-card kind of guy—especially after work and sleepless nights with his new charge. But that wasn't Paige's place to say. These were his colleagues, and this party was for him and Benjie. Paige was sure he could deal with his own social obligations.

At least that was what she kept reminding herself about. Things with Mike had been too cozy this morning. There had been something smoldering in his eyes when he looked down at her, and she hadn't been able to tear herself away. Not at first.

It was stupid of her. They were supposed to be cordial and friendly, but she was feeling herself slipping into a relationship that was just a smidge past professional. Babies could have that effect. They insisted upon love and open hearts. They didn't allow for professional reserves, and she needed some careful distance when it came to Mike. She couldn't keep colliding with that broad chest and looking up into eyes that revealed just a little too much. Benjie and Mike required different things from her at the same time, and it was getting harder to balance. And that was a whole lot like her difficulty in balancing her social work job. She seemed to have a life theme—her heart knocking everything off-kilter.

When the party broke up for refreshments, Mike was chatting with a few officers, and one of their wives was holding Benjie. He had it under control, and she felt a wave of satisfaction. This was her job, to show him how to be a dad, and then step back and let him do it.

A uniformed officer came up beside Paige, a plastic cup of pop in her hand. "You're back, Paige!" Officer Layla Sanders was in her midforties and was out of uniform today, which meant she'd come in on her day off. She shot Paige a smile. "How are you doing?"

"I'm good." Paige smiled back. It was an easier answer than the complicated truth—she was struggling still. She didn't want to bare her soul to everyone before she was ready to make a decision about her job. She wanted to maintain some privacy.

"I thought you might want an update on that case with the runaway—"

"Oh, I'm…actually not on active duty right now," Paige replied.

"Right. Of course. I'm sorry, I'd heard you were coming back to work pretty soon. I'd just assumed you were back since you're here."

What Paige needed was a break from all of this, but she couldn't erase her professional life, either.

"Actually, I do want to know," Paige admitted. "Is this about Quinn Browne?"

"Yes. She ran away again."

"But last I heard everything was going well!" Paige said. "Nadia and her daughter were in family counseling. I set it up myself. Nadia told me it was really helping."

"Well…you know how these cases can be."

Paige did—all too well.

"It gets worse," Layla went on. "Denver PD found her this morning in a hospital. She had no ID and was unconscious. She'd been admitted as a Jane Doe."

Paige felt that old heaviness sink into her chest once more, and her heart sped up, the worst-case scenarios flooding her mind. She pulled a hand through her hair. "What happened to her?"

"A drug overdose. Mrs. Browne thinks her daughter was in contact with the ex-con boyfriend again."

Paige sucked in a deep breath. "But she's alive?"

"She's alive. Nadia is with her at the hospital."

"How bad is it? Is she stable?"

"It was touch and go for a while, they say, but she's recovering," Layla said.

Quinn was a troubled kid. Her mother had been working three jobs to provide for her, and she'd been through a lot in her childhood. She was one of those kids who had slipped through the cracks at school, been dubbed "bad" since about the fifth grade and who was a whole lot more sensitive than anyone realized. And she'd slid into Paige's heart despite her best attempts to keep her professional reserve.

"How is Nadia holding up?" Paige asked.

"Not well." Layla winced. "She's blaming herself for not being enough, and she's a wreck."

"Of course she is," Paige breathed.

"Anyway, when you come back, I thought you'd want to be on top of that one. No one cares about Quinn and her mom as much as you do."

"Thanks, Layla. I appreciate it."

Paige could hear her own professional voice—calm and in control. She knew how to smile, how to act the part, but her heart had a hard time catching up to the image she put out there for everyone else.

"Well, you take care. When you start back at work, give me a call and I'll make sure you've got all the information," Layla said, giving Paige's arm a squeeze.

"Right. Thanks."

Paige's stomach lurched, and she swallowed back the rising bile. Her head was spinning as panic swelled inside of her chest. How much of this was her fault? Did she miss something? If Quinn died, would she only have herself to blame?

She might find herself fired, anyway, if she'd missed something obvious—something she hadn't been able to see because she was too emotionally involved in this one.

Layla moved on to chat with someone else, and Paige took a deep breath, trying some of the calming techniques she'd learned in counseling. She focused on her hands, her fingertips, her breath, her feet on the floor... Centering, they called it. And it did help. The panicky feeling faded away, but the sadness remained.

There. She'd done it. She'd avoided a stress-induced panic attack.

I'm not responsible for fixing everything. My best is enough. I'm making things better a little at a time, and that is helpful.

All the lines her counselor had taught her to repeat to herself. They were true. She understood it all on an intellectual level. The problem lay with her emotions. She got too attached to her to clients, and instead of doing her best for them and then moving on, she empathized with them too well. And right now, Nadia's heart would be in shreds.

In Quinn's case, Paige had done her best, and it hadn't been enough.

Mike came toward her, Benjie in his arms. He nodded at a couple of cops as he passed.

"Hey," he said, coming up beside her. "I'm ready to head out. Are you?"

"Sure," she said, and she forced one of her professional smiles again.

"Are you okay?" he asked, frowning slightly.

"Fine." Her smile faltered.

"You look—" He adjusted Benjie in his arms. "I don't know…upset, I guess. You're pretty pale."

"I'm fine." Or rather, she'd have to be. "We've got to get those gifts into the trunk. Do you want me to carry the baby, or the presents?"

"Would you take Benjie?" he asked. "I've been ribbed all afternoon about my ability to bench-press, so if I let you carry anything more than this baby, I'll never live it down."

"Fair enough."

Mike eased the sleeping baby into her arms, and Benjie wriggled and made a grunting noise. She smelled a dirty diaper. She looked up at Mike.

"Yes, I smell it," he said. "Can it wait?"

Mike looked from Benjie, then over his shoulder toward the room of chatting colleagues. He wanted out—he'd told her from the beginning that he'd been dreading this, and he'd cooperated with all the games, revealed personal information about himself and even made a little speech thanking everyone for their kindness. He'd done everything expected of him.

"You load up the car, and I'll change him," Paige said. There would be other opportunities to let him fend for himself.

Speaking of allowing her emotions to lead her with her clients, she could see how Mike was another example. He was overwhelmed, tired, shier than people realized when they first met him. And for the first time in his life, he was responsible for a newborn. And she could empathize.

If only she was the kind of person who could turn her heart off when she needed to. But she wasn't. And when people told her she was "the best," they never realized the price she was paying for the compliment.

MIKE PULLED INTO his driveway and heaved a sigh. He was back—the weird new dad social obligations were complete, and he was glad. That had been stressing him out more than he liked to admit.

He looked over at Paige—she looked tired, a little pale still.

"That wasn't so bad," Mike admitted as he undid his seat belt.

"I'm glad." She smiled faintly. "And you need those gifts—all of them. Your colleagues were really generous."

"Yeah, they were."

"Did Ellen give you the list of who gave you what?"

Mike grimaced. "Yeah, but I'm not doing flowered notes. I'm doing emails—personal ones, mind you. But emails."

"Fair enough." She undid her seat belt, and glanced over her shoulder into the backseat. "I think he's sleeping."

"You okay, Paige?" he asked.

She lifted her shoulders. "Yeah, I'm okay."

"Because you looked upset earlier, and…" He paused, unsure if he should push this. She didn't look exactly pulled together right now, either, in his humble opinion. "Did something happen in there?"

"Before we left, I got an update on a case I was working on before."

"Oh, yeah?" He paused, watching her expression change. She was trying to hide her deeper feelings from him. "It's bad news. I can tell."

"You know how the job is," she said. "Why don't I bring Benjie in and you can unload the car."

She didn't want to get into it apparently. He wished she would. It might make things easier for her. It would make him feel a bit better to know the worst of it, too.

"Sure. That'll work," he replied.

Paige opened her door and got out, and Mike sat in the driver's seat for a moment, watching her. Whatever that update had been, it had gotten to her. She opened the back door and leaned in to undo the car seat.

"Paige—"

She put a hand on his seat to brace herself and met his gaze. "Yeah?"

He wanted to know what had happened, what had freaked her out so much. He wanted to make it better, if he could, but that was probably overstepping all sorts of boundaries. She was here as a nanny and a teacher, but her career, her professional contacts, her emotional world…none of that was his business. So instead he said, "Thanks for being there with me. You made it all a whole lot easier."

"My pleasure." Paige smiled, and this time it made it to her blue eyes. "You've got this, Mike. You're better at it than you think."

He hadn't been looking for her to reassure him, though. He'd been trying to knock down that wall she'd put up since whatever had happened at the party. But she obviously didn't want to talk about it. Mike passed her the house key, which she plucked from his hand, her smooth skin slipping over his before she picked up the car seat. Mike popped the trunk and got out, watching her thoughtfully as she headed for the front door. She was beautiful—petite with those blond, tangled waves. But there was a lot more going on under the surface, and he felt her refusal to let him see it.

The back of the SUV was packed full of gifts—most of them baby clothes. A few larger gift bags were stuffed full of various sleepers and outfits, most of which looked the same to Mike. But there had been other gifts, too—a gift pack of bottles, several packages of diapers, the stroller Paige had predicted. He could see how much he'd need all of this, and Paige was right—he was grateful.

Mike pulled the first few bags out of the trunk. Then he pulled the new, collapsible stroller out with one heave. He shook it open, then piled the other gifts into the seat. Two trips felt like weakness. He'd do this in one.

Mike pushed the loaded stroller up the front walk, pulled it backward up the two stairs and let himself in the front door.

All was quiet. He pulled the stroller inside and kicked the door shut behind him. He left the gifts by the door and wandered through the living room toward the kitchen. When he got there, he stopped short.

Paige stood by the kitchen window—the baby lying in the bassinet next to her—and her shoulders shook with silent sobs. She looked thinner, smaller. It was like she'd closed in on herself, and he felt a mixture of anger and worry. Anger at whoever had done this to her, even though he had nowhere to vent it. She must have heard him come in, but she didn't turn around, either, and he stood there frozen.

"Paige?" he said softly.

She sucked in a deep breath, and seemed like she was trying to get some control, but he wasn't going to stand around and wait for that. He crossed the room, put a hand on her shoulder and turned her to face him. Her eyes swam with tears, her cheeks were splotchy, and she pressed her lips together in a trembling line. Hell…he only knew how to do one thing when a woman fell apart, and he wrapped his arms around her and pulled her in against his chest. She hesitated for a moment, then sank against him, and he smoothed one hand over her hair, then rested his cheek against the top of her head. This was how he'd wanted to hold her this morning when it would have been all kinds of wrong. But now, it was different.

He could feel her hot tears soaking into his shirt, and he wished the thing that was breaking her heart were an easier target— then he could go kick it down for her. He longed to stomp off and beat on something. That was just a whole lot easier than standing here with a crying woman in his arms.

"You said you were fine," he murmured against her hair.

"I am." Her words were muffled against his shirt, and he laughed softly.

"You're a terrible liar," he said.

She pulled back and he released her, not that he was ready to exactly. She wiped her cheeks with the palms of her hands.

"I'm okay," she repeated.

"Paige, just stop—" He reached out and caught her hand. "You're not okay. All right? You're crying in my kitchen. Just tell me what's going on."

Paige looked up at him, the delicate skin under her eyes puffy, then her gaze turned toward the bassinet where Benjie was sleeping peacefully. Paige hadn't pulled her hand from his yet—her fingers warm and soft in his grasp.

"Just tell me," he said. "You said you got updated on a case, right? Maybe I can help."

"I doubt it."

"Well, maybe just telling me about it will help," he said with a faint shrug. "Try it."

"The news I got was about my client," she said, sucking in a shaky breath. "A teen girl I'd been working with, Quinn Browne, ran away again. She was gone for four days this time, and the cops just located her this morning in a Denver hospital. She overdosed. I know this happens more often than not, with runaways. Quinn's run off before, so it isn't like I shouldn't have expected her to try it again, but…" She shrugged weakly. "I get too personally attached, I guess."

"You thought it would be different this time," he clarified.

"I really did!" Her eyes brightened and she turned toward him. "I got them into family counseling and I kept tabs on both the girl and her mother. The mother, Nadia, is working three jobs to try and keep her daughter in a safe neighborhood. She's done everything she knows how to do. And she's not abusive or anything, either. She was married to a man who'd abused Quinn, and she left him and pressed charges. He's in prison now because of her bravery. She made her daughter her top priority, but it wasn't enough. I know the statistics, but I also know people. And this time…"

Paige rubbed her hands over her face, then fell silent. A runaway—yeah, he could identify with that one pretty personally, too.

"You feel responsible?" he asked quietly.

"It's hard not to." She straightened. "I should have seen the warning signs. I was too optimistic—I believed Quinn when she told me things were getting better. That's on me—I was downright naive."

"It can happen to the best of us," Mike said quietly.

"I just…know how much this is breaking Nadia's heart. She adores her daughter. I know how much Quinn has already been through, and I don't know who she trusted this time, but… Can you imagine having your little girl out there on her own, thinking she can handle it all and knowing exactly the kind of creeps that are waiting for vulnerable girls like her?" Color tinged her cheeks and she looked away. "Sorry, you do know. At least, you know what it's like to have your sister out there."

"Yeah," he agreed quietly.

"You see?" she said. "This is my problem! I care too much! I can't handle the heartbreak—I used to be able to put up a nice little divider between work and my personal life, and I don't know how to do it anymore."

He could see that much. He hadn't realized what she'd meant by needing the break, but he'd just gotten a glimpse into what she was going through.

"What's her condition?" he asked.

"Stable, but Layla said she was in trouble for a while." Paige looked over at him. "The thing is, even after a scary event like this, she'll run away again. Mike, not every problem has a solution—at least, not that I can provide. That's the part that breaks my heart. Sometimes there are just these ongoing tragedies that never seem to improve, no matter how hard you try."

"Yeah, I know..." He leaned forward, resting his elbows on his knees.

"And I hate it," she breathed.

He looked over at her, and found those blue eyes fixed on him.

"I know exactly what that's like," he said quietly. "I found my sister a few times, but by the time I did, she was an adult, legally. Even now, I know she needs help. She's just given birth and given her baby up—she's going to be a physical and emotional wreck.

She needs medical care, at the very least, and I can't do anything about it. All I can do is wait for her to contact me—if she ever does."

"How is that not killing you?" she whispered.

"Who said it isn't?" He met her gaze. "Sorry, that isn't helping, is it? I don't think you should blame yourself for what happened with your client. You did your best and you were working with the information you had. But what happened with my sister—that's on me."

Mike pushed himself to his feet. His recriminations of himself weren't going to help Paige with hers. The last thing she needed was for him to pile his problems onto hers. She was already struggling with clients—he wasn't about to become another one.

"Why?" Paige asked.

He met her gaze. She looked so sympathetic, so filled with concern, and he had no doubt that it was completely sincere. But he wasn't another problem for her to worry over.

"It doesn't matter," he said quietly. "I'm

the one who has to carry that around, and I manage it."

"You said that sometimes it helps to talk," she said.

"And sometimes it only puts a load on the one listening," he countered. "Paige, I'm not your job."

"Right." She nodded quickly, then wiped her fingertips under her eyes.

And now he'd probably offended her. That wasn't his intention, but he couldn't let her shoulder his issues, either. He could handle his own stuff.

"Paige..." He wasn't even sure what he wanted to say. He just wanted to make sure that they were okay. She looked up at him, and he realized in a rush exactly what the problem was. He wanted to be the one taking care of her, not the other way around.

"Yes?" she said.

Mike cleared his throat and dropped his gaze. He couldn't be the one to support her, either, though. He wasn't here long term, and she had her own choices to make.

"Why don't you head home?" he said. "Take that break. You deserve it."

"What about Benjie?" she asked.

"I'll be okay for the rest of the day. Bottles, diapers…if I get in over my head, I'll give you a call. Fair?"

Paige nodded, then rose to her feet. "Fair. But do call me if you need me."

The thing was, Mike was trying really hard not to need her. He wanted to protect both of them, there. She didn't need his personal issues, and he couldn't get used to her gentle presence, either. Besides, having her here—so warm and soft, her emotions so close to the surface—he couldn't guarantee that he wouldn't open up. She was beautiful and so tempting. He had to get used to doing this on his own sooner or later. This wasn't long term. Wasn't that the agreement?

CHAPTER SIX

THAT AFTERNOON, PAIGE walked down the street, holding her coat shut at her throat as a brisk wind whipped her hair around her face, making her shiver despite the warm autumn sunlight. Main Street was lined by businesses and restaurants—a ski rental shop currently closed, a candy shop, a dry cleaner. A few cars were parked along the street, blocking the tumbling flight of crisp leaves that were sent sailing in the cold wind.

The fresh air was helping to clear her head, but she still had a knot of sadness in her chest. This was her problem lately— her inability to separate her own emotions from her clients' situations. And then there was the fact that Mike had asked her to leave. Well, maybe not exactly that, but it amounted to the same. She should have been able to hold things together a little longer.

Mike was her job, too, and she wasn't at her post. Paige was supposed to be a professional, and she'd never felt less like one than when she'd buried her face in Mike's shirt and cried. She hadn't been able to hold it back any longer, and she could only imagine what he thought of her right now. She wasn't handling any of this very well, was she?

Paige's cell phone vibrated in her pocket, and she pulled it out, checking the number.

"Hi, Nathan," she said, hunching her shoulders against the wind. "How's my favorite brother?"

"Not bad. I just wanted to say hi. How're you doing?"

It felt good to hear Nathan's voice again, and she slowed her steps, relaxing a little bit. "Well, I'm still on stress leave, so I'm not up to much. I'm actually standing in as a nanny for one of the officers here for a few weeks. But you probably know about that already."

"So you know I've been checking up on you," her brother said with a chuckle. "I'm not even going to apologize for that. You're my sister. It's my job to care."

"I know, I know. Honestly, there are worse things than having people who want to help."

"Glad to hear that," her brother said. "So how do you like the nanny gig?"

"It's nice. He's such a tiny little guy, and I'm smitten."

"The cop?" Nathan asked with a short laugh.

"Har, har. The cop could bench-press you and a friend," she retorted. "He's new here—Mike McMann."

"At least you're in good hands," her brother replied. "Have you talked to Dad and Irene lately?"

"Not in the last couple of weeks," she said. "What's going on?"

"Dad's been diagnosed as diabetic."

"Oh, no. Is it serious?"

"Serious enough that he needs insulin. He's not telling people, though. I only know because I went down there to see him last weekend and Irene slapped a donut out of his hands."

Paige laughed. "So she's taking good care of him."

"Always." Nathan chuckled. "He's fine, though. You don't need to worry. Irene has his diet under control, and Dad doesn't seem to have slowed down any."

"Good."

"I'd better get going," Nathan said. "I've got a date."

"Yeah?" she asked, her interest piqued.

"Yeah, and that's all the information you get right now," he shot back. "I'll talk to you later. Just wanted to make sure you were okay."

"I'll give Dad a call tonight. Talk to you later."

Paige hung up and slipped the phone back into her pocket. She was lucky to have such a close-knit family, and she could understand why Mike had worried about his sister all these years. If you couldn't count on family, then who could you count on?

For too many people, the answer to that was social services. Guilt wormed up inside of her, and she tried to push it back. She didn't know where she was headed right now as she paused at a curb, waited for a minivan to pass and then headed across the street.

Hylton Books, Liv's store, was coming up on her side of the street, and she decided that a quiet bookstore would be perfect place to warm up for a few minutes. She paused at the window, looking over a murder-mystery-themed display complete with a puddle of fake blood and a large magnifying glass. Liv always had fun with her displays.

Paige pushed open the door and stepped into the welcome warmth, a bell tinkling softly overhead. Liv was behind the counter, perched on a stool. Her belly curved out in front of her, and she held a coffee shop cup to her lips. She looked up and shot Paige a smile.

"Hi," Paige said, undoing the first couple of buttons of her coat. The store smelled faintly of vanilla and that delicious scent of paper and binding that Paige had always liked.

"This is nice," Liv said. She put down her cup and got off the stool carefully. "Where's the baby? I thought you were on nanny duty."

"I've got the afternoon off," she replied. Sort of. "Speaking of which, I thought you had the day off, too."

"My part-timer is sick," Liv replied. "And when you're the owner…"

Paige nodded. "I guess there isn't much choice, is there?"

"Oh, I'm not exactly suffering," Liv said.

"I love being in here. This is my happy place."

"Do I smell coffee?" Paige asked. "I thought you were strictly a tea drinker."

"Call it a pregnancy craving." Liv chuckled. "So how did Mike like the baby shower?"

"I think...he survived it." Paige smiled, feeling her nerves already start to relax. There was something about her friend's bookstore that was just calming.

"He looks like he's settling in with the baby," Liv said. "Jack says he eats every hour?"

"Benjie has a lot of catching up to do," Paige replied, then she fell silent. They could chitchat about the baby for an hour if they wanted to, but Paige's heart wasn't in it. She looked over a shelf of cookbooks, perusing the covers that showed smiling cooks and delectable dishes. Maybe she needed to cook herself some comfort food, because her other coping strategies obviously weren't working.

"How are things with Mike?" Liv asked after a beat of silence.

Paige looked up. "He's taking over with Benjie this afternoon to give me a break."

She felt her eyes mist again. "I, um, kind of broke down and cried."

"Seriously?" Liv came around the counter and reached for Paige's hand. "What's going on? What happened?"

"It's just…more of the same, I guess," she replied, and she blinked back the tears in her eyes. "I got a bad update about a family I was supporting within Social Services. It just hit that nerve again."

"I'm sorry." Liv nodded toward a couple of overstuffed easy chairs she had arranged in the back of the store. "You want to come sit down?"

Paige shrugged. "Yeah. That would be nice."

Liv snagged her coffee cup before leading the way to the seating. Paige sank into the chair opposite her friend, and then glanced around at the fully stocked shelves of books. Across from her was a shelf labeled *Eagles*—bestsellers here in Eagle's Rest during the tourist season, Liv had once told her.

"So what happened?" Liv prodded.

"It was when the baby shower was wrapping up," Paige said. "You and Jack were already gone. That's when Layla Sanders gave me the update. I held it together until I got back to Mike's place, and I really thought I was doing better. I mean, I had a panic attack, but I was able to use the techniques the therapist taught me to get it under control pretty quickly. And then…"

"You broke down," Liv said quietly.

"I've got to stop doing this." Paige sighed.

"It's an improvement from before, though," Liv pointed out.

"Yeah. But I want better than that." Paige forced a smile. "Anyway, I started to cry, and Mike hugged me, which probably made things worse. I don't know. Anyway, he told me to take the rest of the day off. And I figured it was a good idea."

"He hugged you?" Liv smiled hopefully.

"I think it was an instinctive response to having a woman sobbing in his living room. It was either hug me or just look at me."

"In my experience, a man doesn't hug a crying woman on instinct," Liv said with a teasing smile. "They tend to just stand there looking mildly confused, hoping it will stop."

"Does Jack do that?" Paige asked.

"No, the first time I cried he kissed me. And we ended up married."

"That isn't what's happening here."

Liv took another sip. "Jack knows Mike from the Denver PD. They worked together."

"I heard," Paige replied.

"He's a good guy."

"As much as I love your hinting, our relationship is strictly professional," Paige replied with a shake of her head. "Or it will be again tomorrow." She shut her eyes and grimaced. "I'm really embarrassed."

"You were upset. You can't beat yourself up for having feelings."

No, she couldn't. But something was going to have to change around here, because she couldn't go on this way. Her heart just couldn't take it.

"I'm not ready to go back to work, Liv."

"Then don't. This is your life, and you have to live it your way."

"I don't think it's quite so simple as that. I have to do something! I can't just be a lapsed social worker forever. I have bills."

"Want a part-time job here?" Liv asked. "I'm looking for another part-timer…"

"Don't tempt me," Paige said with a laugh.

"I do need something that's easier on my emotions. I can't just keep going through the wringer."

Liv was silent for a moment. "Mike told Jack that he doesn't know what he'd do without you. Maybe he'd consider keeping you on as a nanny for a while longer."

"He can't afford that on a police officer's wage," Paige said. "I'll need more than that. Besides, I know I might be reading too much into this, but I think it's getting…personal between us."

"Oh?" Liv asked, rubbing a hand over her belly.

"He's cute—really cute," she said with a wince. "And I don't know… Maybe it's just been that long for me between boyfriends, but a muscle-bound cop who needs me—it's a tempting combination."

"I could see that." Her friend chuckled.

"There was this moment between us— we kind of ran into each other, and…" She felt heat hit her cheeks. "Look, I don't know how he'd describe it, but on my end it almost sizzled. We went from colleagues to…a man and a woman, if you know what I mean. I've had enough romantic experience to know that if it were anyone else, that hug might have turned into a kiss. So maybe this isn't one-sided."

"Yeah?" Liv's eyes widened.

"And obviously that's a really bad idea."

"I might have to disagree there," Liv said.

"I'm sure you would." Paige smiled faintly. "But I'm vulnerable right now. And I have to tell you, I want to get away from it all—law enforcement, social services, all of it. It's more than I can handle. I can't date a cop. Do you remember what it was like for you before Jack? Just a normal person seeing flashing lights and standing back, wondering what was going on and not worrying too much?"

"That was a very long time ago," Liv said softly, then she rubbed her hand over her belly again and pressed her lips together. "Oh…"

"You okay?" Paige asked, leaning forward.

Liv rubbed her hand in a slow circle over the top of her belly. "Yeah. It must be indigestion or something."

Or something.

"I shouldn't be stressing you out with

my stuff," Paige said. "I'm sorry. Let's talk about you."

"I'm not stressed," Liv replied. "I'm just really pregnant. There's a difference."

"I'd still rather talk about you," Paige said. "How are things going with Jack? You two seem really happy."

Liv's expression relaxed at the mention of her husband. "He's really excited about the baby."

"He would be," Paige said with a grin. "He wanted kids, didn't he?"

"As many as I'm willing to give birth to," Liv replied ruefully. "But I'm not complaining. I want kids, too—" Liv sucked in a breath and rubbed her hand over her belly again. "I shouldn't have had the coffee."

"Liv, are you sure this isn't something more?" Paige asked, leaning forward. "You look like you're in pain."

"I'm eight months pregnant. Something always hurts," Liv retorted. "And I'm not ready to have this baby yet."

"Do you want to stand, walk around a bit?" Paige wasn't sure what to offer.

"Yeah, maybe that will help." Liv tried to get up, then grimaced and leaned forward. Her auburn hair fell over her face. This wasn't ordinary pregnancy discomfort, and Paige stood up and fished in her pocket for her phone.

"Okay, I don't care if it is just indigestion, I'm calling your husband," Paige said.

"I'll be fine," Liv said through gritted teeth.

"Give me his phone number, or I'm calling 911. You pick," Paige retorted.

Liv recited the number. The phone rang twice and Jack picked up.

"Hello?"

"It's Paige," she said. "Are you close by? I think Liv is in labor."

"I'm not in labor!" Liv said loudly enough for her husband to hear, and she pushed herself to her feet, sucking in another deep breath. She pulled her hair away from her face and exhaled a slow breath. "I'm just kind of twingey."

"She's in labor?" Jack's voice turned terse.

"I think so. She's in quite a bit of pain and—"

"At thirty-six weeks pregnant, this not labor," Liv interjected. "It's false labor. This happens, and I'm not going through all the drama of going down to the hospital, just to be sent home again. My cousin went through this and got sent home three times before it was the real thing. This will pass. I'm sure of it."

"She's insisting it isn't labor," Paige said. "I don't know what to say."

"When did it start?" Jack asked.

"A few minutes ago."

"Okay, I'm just at the grocery store. I'm leaving the cart and I'm on my way. Tell her to sit down—"

"Jack says to sit down," Paige said, and Liv shook her head, blowing out another long breath.

"I'm more comfortable standing. It's just the coffee. I'm sure of it—" And then she shot out a hand, catching herself against a bookshelf and let out a soft moan.

"Whatever it is, she needs a doctor," Paige said. "Get here soon, Jack!"

THE DAY WENT by slower than Mike anticipated. He hung out with Benjie—watched some sports, did some workouts during Benjie's naps and fed that little guy bottle after bottle. The day crept by and the sun set.

Mike fixed himself a quick dinner of a hamburger and oven-baked fries, and he put his energy into finding places to store his new haul of baby stuff. Wipes, diapers, clothes, mysterious bottles and jars of ointments and bubble bath... Next, he flicked on the TV and watched some sports highlights. The evening trickled away, measured out with bottles, diaper changes and *The Big Bang Theory* reruns that reminded him of how Paige had laughed watching the show earlier. But even as he tried to keep himself distracted, everything seemed to remind him of Paige. He was worried about her, and every time he thought he was distracted, he'd remember the feeling of her sobbing in his arms.

And he'd had no idea how to help her. That was the part that he hated the most. He kicked some dirty baby clothes into a pile by the laundry room door.

Once, he dialed her number, but he pressed End and tossed his phone aside. He cared—but he shouldn't intrude. There were boundaries to respect and all that. He wasn't a complete idiot.

Hers hadn't been tears of weakness,

though. She was the strongest woman he'd come across in a long time. It was just that she'd finally found her limit. Everyone had one—even the toughest of cops. Even teenage girls, like Jana had been, who thought she knew so much more about the world than the adults around them.

There seemed to be a whole line of women in his life who he hadn't known how to help, and it had started with his little sister. Why couldn't he have noticed more when Jana was young? Why couldn't he have fixed a few things for her earlier? He went to the same school. He didn't like to admit this to people, but he'd been friends with her loser boyfriend, too. Whatever that said about him—birds of a feather, and all that.

He'd noticed when other girls ignored her, and he'd been proud of her rebellious attitude. She wore black lipstick and dog collar cuffs. He'd figured she was taking care of herself, that it proved she was tough enough to get past it. He'd been the naive one—she hadn't been half as tough as him, and certainly not as tough as she'd looked. He'd missed the signs.

Mike had become a cop because he

wanted to finally make things better. He was aiming for SWAT because his big, beefy body and his bad attitude were the perfect combination to get in there and kick some butt. But they weren't the right combination for whatever his sister had needed.

From the bassinet, Benjie started to cry, and Mike turned off the TV and headed over to him. He'd had a bottle and a diaper change ten minutes ago. Mike reached down and scooped Benjie up the way Paige had taught him—one hand under his diaper, and the other under his head. He propped him up against his chest and patted his back in a comforting rhythm, but this time the baby didn't stop crying like he had earlier.

"Hey, buddy," Mike murmured.

He felt the diaper, but it was still dry. Maybe he was cold. Mike grabbed the blanket and draped it over the baby's tiny form, but it didn't do any good, either.

"Maybe you're hungry already," Mike murmured, and he headed for the kitchen. He had a bottle prepared and ready to go, but when he leaned Benjie back to pop the nipple in his mouth, Benjie spat it out and cried all the harder.

A bottle was supposed to be the quick fix here—so he tried adjusting Benjie a little bit, and tried again, nudging the nipple into the baby's open mouth, but Benjie turned away from the bottle, coughing as a drop of milk went down his throat. Mike put him back up onto his shoulder and patted his back a little more.

"Hey, hey..." Mike wasn't sure what to do, what to say. "Come on, buddy. We've been okay so far, right? Come on, now."

The baby balled up his fists, his little face turning red with the exertion of his wails. He was so small, and so angry—it was a strangely intimidating.

Mike had heard crying babies, and he figured he could wait this one out. He'd just hold him, and eventually Benjie would calm down. Right? The kid wasn't on his own— he had Mike. He'd be okay. That was the theory at least, and for the next hour Mike walked back and forth through the house, alternating between rubbing his back and rocking him back and forth. He walked, and he sang every single song he could think of from the national anthem to "The Wheels on the Bus." He was a little teapot, he was an itsy bitsy spider, and he even did the hokey pokey until his own bedrock of calm began to crumble.

Who was he fooling? He didn't know what he was doing! He could do bottles and diapers, and that's where his baby skill set ended. He needed help.

Mike picked up his phone once more and looked down at it. If he called Paige now, it wouldn't be personal, and he wouldn't be crossing lines. But it was also nearly midnight, and he paused before heaving a sigh and dialing her number.

Maybe there was something wrong, and she'd know what Benjie needed. A baby so small shouldn't cry for this long, could he?

The phone rang three times, and then a breathless Paige picked up.

"Mike? Everything okay?"

She could probably hear Benjie loud and clear, Mike realized.

"Uh—" He adjusted Benjie in his arms again. "This has been going on for an hour. I'm not sure what's wrong."

"Is he hungry?" she asked. "Wet?"

"I've tried bottles, changed his diaper, walked with him, sung to him… I've worked my way over to the Metallica songs in my repertoire. I'm out of ideas!" He didn't mean to sound quite so panicked, and he shut his eyes for a moment, trying to recenter himself.

"I'm still up," she said. "I'll be there in ten minutes."

"You sure?" he asked. "I mean, I should be able to do this, right?"

"I'm your nanny, aren't I?" she said. "I'll be there. Just keep doing what you're doing."

"Okay, thanks."

Dropping the phone on the couch, he pleaded, "Come on, Benjie." He put the infant up onto his shoulder again. Benjie thrust out his thin legs and continued his cry. "I'm trying, buddy."

Paige would be here soon...that was something.

Ten minutes later, Mike saw a sweep of headlights come up his drive, and he felt a flood of relief. He pulled the blanket up around Benjie so that he wouldn't feel the blast of autumn air, then headed for the front door. He opened it, waiting for her.

The night was soft and dark, the stars brilliant on this side of town where there were few streetlights and most of the neighbors' windows were black. A dog barked a few times, and Benjie's cries filtered out into the night air.

"Hi," Paige said as she came up the walk. She wore a pair of jeans and a bulky, wine-colored sweater. She hitched her purse over her shoulder, and met his gaze easily enough—whatever she'd been struggling with before seemed back under control. Benjie wailed from just under Mike's chin, albeit a little softer now. He seemed to be tiring himself out.

"You look rough," she said when she reached him.

"I'll bet." Mike stepped back to let her in.

Paige put her purse on the couch, then reached up and slid Benjie out of his arms. Mike released him, hoping he didn't look quite as relieved as he felt to hand the baby off. She pulled the baby against her chest as she made soft shushing noises against his downy head.

"Is that the trick?" he asked, swinging the front door shut.

"No idea," she said with a smile in return. "Now we take turns."

Except he'd just spent all afternoon wondering what he could do to help her, and here she was smoothing over his own problems with that gentle smile of hers and her confident ways with a baby.

"Go make a cup of tea or something," she said. "I'll take over for a while. You need a break."

He did—and he was ridiculously grateful that she was here.

"Thanks," he said, and instead of going for tea, he sank onto the couch and shut his eyes. He rubbed his hands over his face, sucking in a deep breath as he listened to Paige's soft voice murmuring to the baby under his plaintive cries.

Raising this little boy was going to be a whole lot harder than he'd even imagined, and how he'd deal on his own, he had no idea. But with Paige here, he could get through tonight.

CHAPTER SEVEN

PAIGE ROCKED BENJIE back and forth, listening to his desperate cries. She held him close, tucking him up against her chest as she rested her cheek on the top of his head, wrapping her very heart around him if it were possible.

"Poor boy..." she murmured against his downy hair. "It's a tough night, isn't it? You'll be okay, little one. You'll be fine."

This baby had been through so much— a premature birth, drugs in his system, losing his mother from his life, being brought to a new home... He might be only a few days old, but the trauma was real, and as she rocked him, she slowed her breathing, attempting to give him some of her calm.

Earlier this evening, Paige had gotten a quick text from Jack thanking her for her help and letting her know that labor had progressed and Liv was doing well. That was the last she'd heard. Then she'd called her father, told him that she knew about his diabetes and proceeded to listen to him insist that cheesecake didn't have all that much sugar in it, and that he should be allowed more than one scoop of mashed potatoes. Her dad could be a handful, but she wasn't worried. Irene had him under control.

Now, as she rocked the wailing Benjie, Paige looked over to Mike where he sat on the couch. He rubbed his hands over his face and heaved a deep sigh.

"He's tiring out," Paige said, lifting her voice to be heard over his cries.

"You sure?" Mike asked.

"Yep." She patted Benjie's diaper, and didn't slow her rocking. The baby was tired—a yawn interrupted his cries, then he started up again. It was only a matter of time now before he fell back asleep.

"I thought I had it all figured out," Mike said. "Diapers and bottles. I'm in over my head, Paige."

"You're doing fine," Paige said. "This wasn't exactly planned for you. You didn't have nine months to get used to the idea. You and Benjie are both adjusting."

"Yeah, maybe…"

"Everyone takes some time to get used to being a parent," she added. "Even the biological parents. All these feelings of being completely out of control are normal. I promise you that."

"I'm just glad you're here tonight," he said. "What am I going to do if that happens later on?"

"You'll rock him," she replied.

"Right."

"You're doing better than you think, Mike," she said. "Besides, you're a week more experienced than Jack is right now."

"What…did Liv have the baby? I just saw them this morning—"

"They're at the hospital in Colorado Springs now," she replied. "The hardest part was convincing Liv that she was indeed in labor and needed to get in the car. She was fully convinced she had heartburn from her coffee."

"Wow." Mike sat up. "So Jack is going to be in the trenches here pretty soon, too."

"Yep. He sure is."

Benjie's cries had softened to whimpers,

and Paige reached for a bottle sitting on a windowsill.

"Is this fresh?" she asked.

"What?" Mike squinted. "No, it's old. Let me get you another one."

He pushed himself to his feet and headed for the kitchen. The water ran for about thirty seconds, and then he remerged, tapping the bottle nipple against his wrist. Then he handed it over.

Benjie was interested in the bottle this time, and he latched on and started to drink. The sudden silence was filled with soft sucking.

"There you go," Paige crooned. "Is that better, sweetie?"

"Finally," Mike breathed. "What was wrong?"

"Sometimes babies cry," she said with a shrug. "Upset tummy, maybe? Hard to tell. Did you want to take him now?"

"No." Mike backed up a step. "No, he's finally quiet. I'll let you hold him."

Paige stayed where she was and Mike scrubbed a hand through his short-cropped hair. His gaze was locked on the baby in her arms, a look of tenderness in those dark eyes.

"Am I paying you overtime for this?" he asked seriously.

"No," she chuckled. "Don't worry about it."

"Hauling you out at midnight—I kind of feel like you deserve some compensation for that." Mike lifted his gaze to meet hers with a rueful look.

"I'll survive," she said, but it was sweet of him to offer.

"Are you hungry?"

She was, come to think of it. With all the excitement surrounding Liv going into labor, Page had forgotten to eat. "What did you have in mind?"

"A BLT." His gray eyes were still locked on hers, and a smile turned up one side of his lips. "Thick slice of tomato, fresh lettuce, smear of mayo…with the bacon nice and crispy. And all on toast."

"That sounds really good."

Mike nodded toward the kitchen. "Want to come keep me company while I whip up a couple sandwiches for us?"

"Sure."

Paige followed Mike into the kitchen. When Benjie stopped drinking, she put the bottle on the table. He still needed to be burped, even if he was sleepy, so she grabbed a rag from a laundry basket of clean baby things and tipped Benjie up onto her shoulder. Mike turned the stove on and heated a pan on the front burner. Benjie let out a whimper and Mike looked over his shoulder.

"Hey, buddy," he said softly. "You're okay."

Benjie quietened again, and Paige couldn't help but smile.

"You're more of a dad than you think," she said.

"I didn't say I wasn't trying," he replied, heading to the fridge and grabbing a bag of lettuce.

"Aren't we all…" she breathed. Paige was always trying—giving her clients the benefit of her experience, her education, her heart…

Benjie let out a wet burp, and Paige lowered him from her shoulder and wiped his chin. He was pretty close to being asleep.

"I'm going to put him into his bassinet," she said. "You okay with that?"

"Yeah, that works." Mike's gaze slid from her down to the baby in her arms. "He's okay, though, right?"

"He's just fine. Nothing to worry about," she replied.

Mike nodded, then turned back to the counter. He cared—she could see it every time he looked at the baby—but he was still unsure of himself. She'd do her best to get him more comfortable with caring for Benjie, but she was going to have to let go when their time together was up. Benjie wasn't hers to worry over, and neither was Mike.

Paige went in search of the bassinet. She found it in the living room, and as she lowered Benjie into it, she heard the sizzle of bacon start up from the kitchen. The baby let out a whimper as she laid him down, and she kept a hand on his chest while he settled. She could feel the patter of his tiny heartbeat against her fingers, that frail chest rising and falling as he drifted into a deeper slumber. At last, she slowly removed her hand.

She was getting attached—she could feel it. This was a job, and a very short one at that. She'd hoped she could get a "win" with this arrangement with Mike and the baby. Maybe it would bring everything back into perspective for her so she could get back to work where she had always belonged before. But right now, nothing was any clearer, even when she felt like she was succeeding in helping Mike to bond with Benjie.

She went back to the kitchen, and Mike glanced over his shoulder at her. He scooped the bacon out of the pan with a spatula and onto a plate.

"He's down, then?" Mike said.

"For now," she said with a shrug. "No promises."

Mike smiled tiredly, then turned back toward the counter where he assembled two sandwiches. He moved quickly—he'd obviously made these a lot in the past—and his last step was to slice each sandwich in half diagonally. Then he handed her a plate.

"This looks really good," she said.

He leaned against the counter and picked up half of his own sandwich and took a bite. She followed his lead, the tang of mayo mingling with bacon and tomato in her mouth.

"Mmm," she said, swallowing. "This hits the spot."

"Yeah, it does. I eat these when I get off a late shift."

"I guess this counts as a late shift," she said.

"I *am* just as tired," he agreed, and they

both smiled. "If you won't take overtime, I'll have to make it up with food."

"I'm happy with that," she said.

They ate in silence for a moment, Paige finishing up the first half of the sandwich and moving on to the second.

"Mike, I've been wondering about something," Paige said, licking her finger.

"Yeah?"

"You blame yourself for your sister running away, and I don't understand why."

Mike was silent for a few beats, chewing slowly, then swallowing. He glanced over, gray eyes meeting hers, then flicking away. "The loser boyfriend that my sister ran off with—he was one of my buddies."

Paige stopped chewing. "You knew him?"

"Rather well. He was a funny guy—always making jokes, making me forget about real life. I liked him. He met Jana through me."

"Was he into drugs at the time?" she asked.

"Yeah, and I didn't think it was that big of a deal. I was young, kind of dumb. If it weren't for me, Jana would never have hooked up with him."

That explained it. She reached over and

put a hand on his arm. "You couldn't see the future—"

"No, but I didn't deal with the present, either," he said tersely, then he sighed, putting a hand over hers. "There was a lot I could have done but didn't. It was my fault, Paige. There's no getting around it."

"Have you looked for him?" she asked.

"Yep. I found him, too—in Denver, living with another woman. He hadn't seen my sister in years. He wasn't doing too badly. He had a job, a few kids… Jana was the one to slide downhill, and he'd managed to catch himself. Hardly seems fair."

"Was he sorry at least?" she asked.

"Oh, yeah. He was real apologetic. He said he'd been running away from a bad foster home situation, and he felt really badly for dragging her into it. He told me she ended up hooking up with another guy, and he broke up with her. That was the last he saw of her."

"Can I point something out?" she asked quietly.

"Sure." His agonized gaze met hers.

"Seventeen-year-olds aren't as grown up as they think."

"Are you defending him?" His voice was quiet.

"I'm defending you."

He was silent for a couple of beats. "I think I was more grown up than most at that age."

"No, you weren't," she replied. "That's a trick the mind plays on all of us. We remember our younger years as if we had adult brains in our heads. But we didn't. Your teenage brain was still developing. You weren't any more grown up or responsible than any other seventeen-year-old. You didn't have the life experience to know where things would go. You might have wished you did. You might have learned some painful lessons when your sister left, even. But you were still a kid yourself. This wasn't your fault any more than any other victim. You were a *kid*."

His eyes misted, and for a moment, she saw a crack in that armor he carried around with him—the pain that lay so close to the surface.

"You really believe that?" he asked.

"I know it. You're able to forgive your sister for her youthful mistakes, and you're going to have to forgive yourself for your own."

He closed his hand around her fingers, and he stood so close to her that she could feel the heat from his chest emanating against her.

"Well, I'm a man now," he said quietly, his gaze meeting hers. "And I can do a whole lot now that I couldn't do then."

His gray eyes were filled with tenderness, and he reached out and touched her cheek with the back of a finger. Her breath caught in her throat. Yes, he was definitely a full-grown man now... Those eyes moving over her face seemed to captivate her. She wasn't looking for anything more than a break from the pressures of her career right now, but looking up into that rugged face with the shadow of his scruff along his jawline and those searching eyes made her thoughts drain from her head.

Mike leaned in, his gaze still locked on hers. She hadn't thought she'd moved, but then she found her hands on his chest, and his lips hovered over hers, the tickle of his breath brushing against her face...

From the other room, Benjie's whimper broke the stillness. Heat rose in her cheeks, and she dropped her gaze.

Mike cleared his throat and stepped away. "I'd better—" He gestured toward the living room, and Paige nodded.

"Right. Yes. You should."

Mike moved past her, his hand brushing against hers, and then he was gone, and she stood in the kitchen, her heart hammering in her chest. What had just happened here? He'd been about to kiss her…except it wasn't quite so one-sided as that, either. Because she was about to kiss him back. She licked her lips and put her hands up to her cheeks, wondering how obvious her blush was.

If he'd closed that last whisper of space between them, would she have had the presence of mind to stop him?

That might be a better question. It shouldn't matter. She didn't want to be a part of the life he saw for himself—more than that, she couldn't handle it. She was here to help him adjust to being Benjie's primary caregiver. This was wildly inappropriate, and she'd very likely be kicking herself come morning.

"I should get home," Paige said as she headed into the living room to find Mike holding Benjie, who had fallen back asleep in his arms.

"Yeah…" Those tender eyes met hers again. "If you think that's best."

Putting it on her—did he want her stay? The only thing she was sure about right now was that she was in this too deep. Her emotions were already entangled, and she needed to get that under control.

"I need to go," she said, and she reached for her coat.

"Don't worry, I'll be fine," he said, but that direct look he gave her told her that he knew why she was leaving.

"Call me if you need me again," she said, picking up her purse. "And thanks for the sandwich. It was…" She faltered when his gaze met hers again. "Delicious."

"Do you want to stay?" he asked.

What was he asking? Did he want her to stay the night? Or to just stay a bit longer? Or was that just in her imagination?

"I can't, Mike."

Even if she wished she could.

He met her gaze hopefully for a moment, then nodded. "Okay. It probably isn't a great idea—"

"It's just…" She inwardly grimaced. "I mean, if we—"

"You don't have to explain. I'll see you tomorrow." He smiled.

Off the hook. Paige turned for the door and pulled out her keys. She had to leave right now, get home to where she could think straight. The very last thing she needed was to end up kissing this rugged cop. Because whatever was brewing between them wouldn't take much encouragement to get out of control.

THE NEXT MORNING, Mike was exhausted, but while Benjie now seemed to want to be held all night, he was going an hour and a half between bottles. That meant Mike was able to sleep in his easy chair with Benjie on his chest between feedings. It wasn't a long-term solution, but it had gotten him through the night, and he was rather proud of himself for that. When Paige arrived that morning, Mike was in uniform and ready to walk out the door. He'd planned it that way—not wanting to prolong any awkwardness between them.

"Hi," Paige said. She smiled hesitantly, then shrugged out of her jacket and hung it up.

"Hi…" Mike had wanted to just head to work and hope that last night could evaporate, but seeing her this morning, he wasn't so sure that was possible.

Paige went over to the bassinet and peeked in. Benjie was sleeping.

"He, um, he's going about an hour and a half between bottles now," Mike said.

"Okay." She nodded. "That's good to know."

"And, um…" Mike winced. "Look, Paige, about last night. I'm sorry if I made you uncomfortable."

Paige shrugged and a small smile tugged at her lips. "It was nothing."

It had definitely not been nothing. "I asked you to stay. And I meant it… I mean, I'd wanted you to stay longer. I was caught up in the moment, I guess, but I wasn't asking for…what it probably sounded like."

"To stay the night," she said.

"Yeah. That wasn't exactly my intention. And this morning, I'm realizing how out of line that was of me. You're here because I'm paying you. I'm clear on that. I'm sorry."

"Well, it feels like it's getting a bit more personal," she said.

"Yeah?"

"It can be hard to keep things clearly professional when we're dealing with a baby. I feel it, too. So don't beat yourself up." She smiled slightly. "It's part of my problem with the job—keeping myself professional." Her cheeks pinked. "Not that I've ever flirted with a client or anything. Oh, God, this isn't coming out right."

He chuckled, but it was forced. She was letting him down easy, and he didn't blame her. "I get it."

"It's not your fault, is what I'm saying," she said. "It feels personal because it is. It's your life. There's nothing more personal. We'll just have to work at keeping things… in perspective."

"Thanks." He felt a wave of disappointment. It sure did feel personal to him, but she obviously knew better. "And if I ever seem… I don't know…less professional than I should be, feel free to let me know and I'll correct that."

She squinted at him for a moment. "Mike, relax. I don't need you to be some polite and proper cop. You have no idea how tired I am of all of that. Just be you. I can handle you. Trust me."

He raised his eyebrows. He'd been himself in the kitchen last night, and that hadn't worked out so well. She probably didn't know what she was asking here. Besides, he was used to being careful around women or people smaller than he was in general. But with women especially, he didn't want to give the wrong impression—like he'd already managed to do. "I've been told I can be a bit intimidating sometimes."

"You don't intimidate me. I could take you."

He laughed. "You probably could."

Because he'd be too shocked to stop her.

"Look, all the same, I was out of line."

"I cried in your living room. I think we're even," she said. "Things can get emotional and overwhelming. I'm working on it, too."

Mike met her gaze. "Okay. Well, I'd better get to work. I left a fresh pot of coffee and some muffins. Thought you could use some caffeine after last night."

"I really could," she said, and she smiled, her eyes lighting up this time. "Have a good day, Mike. We'll be fine."

He wasn't sure if the "we" referred to her and Benjie or to him and her. Whatever, he felt better, and as he drove to work, he tried to push thoughts of the beautiful blonde out of his head. What he needed was to get off the waiting list and secure a full-time position at Eagle's Rest Day Care. Chief Simpson had promised to pull a few strings on his behalf, but so far, Mike had plans to visit a couple of in-home babysitters who were open to caring for a newborn during the day.

Right now, Mike wasn't sure how he felt about that. He liked having Benjie at home with Paige. He wasn't worried, because he knew the baby was in good hands with her. Paige hadn't been here long, but she was fast becoming his touchstone when it came to Benjie. She made him feel like he could do this, and maybe that was why he was finding himself attracted to her. Whatever the reason, he had to shut that down. She was right—it was getting personal fast between them, but they wanted different things, and no amount of chemistry was going to change that.

When Mike got to the precinct, he went into the gym and funneled his frustration into lifting weights. After an intense workout, he showered and headed into the bull pen to start his shift. A couple of other cops were arriving at the same time.

"Can I have your attention, everyone!" Chief Simpson called, and the bull pen quietened. "Officer Jack Talbott is taking some vacation time this week. Liv had the baby last night—a girl! So Jack'll be busy, and we're all going to cover for him."

There was a whoop of celebration, and Ellen's voice pierced through with, "We need a few more details, Chief. How big? What did they name her?"

"The baby is just over seven pounds," the chief replied. "They didn't tell me a name yet—I guess they're still deciding. Mother and baby are doing well, and Jack is a very happy wreck."

Mike couldn't help but smile at that. He was happy for his friend—Jack had been looking forward to this for a long time, and he'd make an excellent dad. He had what he wanted—beautiful wife, new baby. And Mike would have to be dead inside not to feel a little twinge of longing for those things, too. Except Mike wanted more than that. He wanted SWAT. And to find a way to protect his sister.

Mike turned on his computer at his desk and took a seat. He had a bit of paperwork to catch up on before he went out on patrol. The chief wove through the desks toward him.

"Mike," Chief Simpson said. "A word."

"Sure thing, Chief," Mike replied.

The chief pulled up a chair and sat down opposite him. "How are you holding up with the baby?"

"Uh…" Mike searched for words. "I'm pretty tired, but I'm managing."

"Is there anything you need help with?" the chief asked. "I know this was a shock, becoming a guardian like this."

Mike looked up at the chief, his thoughts spinning. His last boss hadn't liked him much, and this personal attention was hard to get used to.

"I still need to arrange some child care moving forward," Mike said cautiously. "You mentioned before that you might have a bit of influence at Eagle's Rest Day Care?"

How far did the chief's concern stretch?

"Thanks for reminding me. I already

spoke with them, and they'll squeeze you in for an interview Sunday morning at ten. It's just a formality. The spot is yours."

"Thanks, Chief. I really appreciate that. One less thing to worry about."

"Not a problem. Glad I could help," Chief Simpson replied, then he pressed his lips together. "And Paige…how's she doing?"

"She's…" Mike paused. How much should he say? He'd stick to her professional contributions. "She's a real lifesaver. Benjie loves her, and she's been showing me how to do all the baby stuff. She's pretty amazing."

"We all know it," the chief replied. "She's one of the best. I was always glad when Paige was sent in for some of the tougher cases, because she's got an instinct that other agents just don't have."

"An instinct—yeah, I know what you mean." She seemed to know how to make everyone feel better—including him when he'd seriously overstepped.

"But how is she?" the chief pressed. "I'm worried. She's a good agent, but she's also a friend of my daughter's, and…well, you know how these things are in a town this size. I've known her since she was a teenager."

"Honestly, sir," Mike said slowly. "I'm not sure. I mean, she's great with Benjie and she's taken me in hand pretty successfully, but she got an update about a case during the baby shower, and it really undid her. She was pretty upset."

"Which case?" the chief asked with a frown.

"I don't remember the names—a runaway teen. It just broke her heart."

"Right. I know the one. Quinn Browne." The chief was silent for a moment. "As much as we'd all lose if Paige changes careers, we care about her, and we want to make sure she's okay, first and foremost. She's so good at her job because she's got the instinct for what people need, and she genuinely cares. But that's what makes the best agents burn out, too."

"Is there anything I can do?" Mike asked.

"I think you've got your hands full as it is." The chief stood. "Besides, only Paige knows what she needs right now, and all we can do is stand back and let her make up her own mind about her future."

"Right. Of course."

"There is one thing you can do for us here,

though," the chief added. "There's a community picnic coming up. I sent an email out about it, so you should have seen that. We had pretty big scandal here a couple of years ago when a cop from Denver was defrauding a bunch of locals. So we're in a tight spot—we need the community's trust, and a uniformed officer broke it."

"Yeah, I heard about that," Mike said. "Evan Kornekewsky."

"That's the one. Jack was going to be there this year. I want to have a relaxed police presence. An officer goes in uniform with the family, and it helps the community to see us in a better light, as part of the community. Obviously, Jack has a few days off, and we need another officer there."

"This weekend, right?" Mike said.

"Saturday, more specifically. It wouldn't interfere with the appointment with the day care."

"So I just…make myself seen," he clarified.

"Pretty much. Make nice. This is an exercise in public relations. We want to make up for the past."

"Sounds easy enough," Mike replied. "Sure, I can take Jack's place."

"Thanks. I appreciate the team mindset. Take care," the chief said. "Have a safe shift."

Mike nodded a farewell as the chief headed off to talk to another officer. Maybe Paige wouldn't mind coming along with him, and they could be all family friendly for the day for the precinct's public image.

It would be nice to have her there. And maybe it would be good for her, too—an honest to goodness break from it all, getting out and enjoying some fresh air. Maybe this was a way to relax a bit without the temptation to take it too far in the privacy of his home. He picked up the phone and dialed Paige's cell. She picked up after the first ring.

"Mike?" she said.

"Hey." He lowered his voice. "I had an idea, and I wanted to see what you thought."

"What kind of idea?" He thought he could hear a smile in her voice.

"On Saturday, I'm going to be the neighborly police presence at the community picnic. I was wondering if you might want to come with me... Go together."

"Like a date?"

"No, like…time together in a public setting so it doesn't get weird between us."

"That's not a bad idea."

"Right? What do you say?"

"Sure."

"Good. It'll be fun. You deserve some of that."

She chuckled softly. "I do, don't I? All right. It's a plan."

"That's for this weekend, though," he said. "There was one other thing I wanted to ask of you. Would you help me to buy one of those cloth things that straps on and lets a guy carry a baby around? You know, in the interest of getting me self-sufficient."

"A wrap? A Snugli?" she asked.

"Something like that."

"Sure. How about this evening? It won't take long."

"Yeah. That would be great," he said, and he smiled. "I appreciate this."

"Not a problem. That's why I'm here."

Right. Her job.

"I'd better get back to work," he said. "I'll see you tonight."

"See you, Mike."

He liked the sound of her saying his name.

And he was definitely going to have to stop thinking stuff like that. He hung up and turned back to the computer feeling cheerier already.

They were a surprisingly good team, and he liked being around her. More than he should. After last night, he felt like he'd messed things up, but the conversation just now had felt normal. Maybe they'd fixed it.

When this was all done, and he had other child care lined up, and they parted ways, he wanted her to have some pleasant memories of him. Maybe that was just his ego, but he wanted to be more than a job for her. Her job was burning her out, and he didn't want to make things worse for her. He wanted to be the shoulder she could lean on.

He wanted to be her friend.

CHAPTER EIGHT

THAT EVENING, MIKE stood next to Paige in Eaglet Baby and Kids, Eagle's Rest's one and only baby supply store. He felt awkward. Shopping for baby paraphernalia was outside his comfort zone, and he was glad he'd asked Paige to come along with him. Eventually, he'd be doing this stuff on his own, but for now, he'd accept some help. Besides, it might help to give them a bit of a fresh start.

Darkness had already fallen, and outside the shop windows he could see the headlights of cars passing by in the chilly autumn evening. A couple of women were shopping together on the other side of the store, and Mike glanced around the showroom, mentally mapping it out. He would probably need to come back here one of these days without Paige. There were bound to be doodads he didn't even know he needed yet, and that was intimidating.

"This is a baby wrap," the saleswoman said, pulling out a long piece of cloth. "They are really simple to use once you get the hang of them. If you want to carry the baby on your back, you just—"

And the woman took a stuffed bear, balanced it on her back and started to wrap that long cloth around both the bear and her body, talking as she worked.

Paige stood next to Mike, and she leaned in, her arm pressing softly against his. He looked down at her, inhaling that soft, vanilla scent that he'd come to associate with her.

"Those are popular," she murmured.

Looking down at her soft, blond waves, he swallowed hard. She was distractingly beautiful, and he'd been noticing that more and more lately. What was wrong with him? He wasn't normally this easily diverted by a pretty face.

"So what do you think?" Paige asked, and Mike turned his attention back to the older woman, who had finished securing the teddy bear onto her body.

"No, sorry," Mike said, his voice low.

"No?" Paige said. "Too finicky?"

"Yeah, that's it." He just couldn't see himself balancing Benjie on his back while he wrapped him in place. That was a recipe for disaster.

"You could also wear him across your chest. There are several different wrapping methods," the woman went on. "For example—"

"No, not that one." He scanned the section. He didn't know what he was looking for—something made in the vein of a sturdy backpack, maybe. "You don't have anything bulletproof, do you?"

The older woman eyed him uncertainly and Paige rolled her eyes.

"Har, har," Paige said. "He's a cop. Don't mind him."

"Oh…" The older woman chuckled. "Got it. So you're looking for something…"

"I don't know," Mike said. "Something a little more masculine, I guess."

"They're all considered unisex," the saleswoman said with a shrug. "Dads use them, too."

"Actually, could we just look around for a little bit?" Paige interjected.

The saleswoman shot them a smile. "Sure

thing. You let me know if you have any questions."

She crossed the store to the other customers, and Mike looked around the section of baby carriers dubiously.

"Stop scaring salespeople," Paige said.

"Sorry." He shot her a grin.

"I should remind you that you wanted to come here."

"Yeah, I know. And I do. It's just...this is all a little...feminine." This stuff wasn't made for dads, it was for the mothers, and he was suddenly realizing what he was thrown into. He was a single dad now—at least functionally speaking—and that was a whole new world. He understood weights, hand-to-hand combat and sharpshooting. He understood guns! But he was now in the deep end of baby care, and that was more intimidating than any SWAT test.

"Other men do this stuff," Paige said.

"But they have the moms with them to help them figure it out, for the most part," Mike said.

"There are probably lineups of women who'd gladly step in to give you a hand,"

Paige said with a small smile. "Just look around from time to time."

Yeah, he knew that, too. He was a relatively good-looking guy, and whatever flaws he had were smoothed over by the uniform. He wasn't blind to what he did to women, except he didn't want a different woman besides Paige.

"I'm not the kind of guy who flirts in exchange for shopping assistance," he said.

"I'm not suggesting you flirt," she countered. "You could make a friend."

"I thought I had." He dealt her a meaningful look.

"Not me." That stung, and he eyed her for a moment. "I'm not a long-term solution, am I?"

"That's why I've got you here today," he said, attempting to smile, show that he hadn't taken her last comment to heart.

"There are parenting groups," Paige went on. "Baby classes, library reading circles, all sorts of opportunities to meet other parents. Now that Jack is a dad, I'm sure he's going to be a big help, too."

"Yep," he agreed. "You're right. I'll be fine."

"You will be." She looked up at him, and

those blue eyes glittered with encouraging warmth. "You're doing a lot better than I expected."

"Yeah? What did you expect exactly?"

"The first time I met you, you were afraid to touch him," she said.

"In my defense, he was pretty tiny."

"He still is," she said with a shrug. "You're settling in."

"Yeah, I am." He paused, eyed her for a moment.

"And now...you're shopping for baby carriers. You've come a long way quickly."

She picked up a baby carrier, looked it over, put it back, then picked up another one.

"I'm no baby carrier expert," she said. "But this one seems like it might be easier to use." She held up the tag that included some pictorial instructions. "See? It goes around your waist, Benjie goes in here and this flap goes over his back. You wear it around your shoulders and put Benjie front or back. Plus, it's a nice sensible black."

Mike put the car seat down between them and Paige helped to adjust the straps to his size. Her fingers moved around his waist as she snapped the carrier into place. She stayed there for a moment, a look of concentration on her face as she sorted out the clip that held it around his waist, and he could look down at her golden waves and smell her vanilla scent.

She was so close, her arms against his sides, and his breath came shallower as he tried to pretend that he wasn't feeling this... Dammit, why couldn't she just be older and less attractive? It would make everything easier.

"There." Paige stepped back, and he licked his lips and swallowed. She didn't seem to notice any effect she had on him, and she picked up the teddy bear and plopped it inside the carrier.

Mike turned toward the mirror, and eyeballing their reflection together—slender and petite Paige next to his bulky form—he liked the way they looked.

"I do like that it's black," he said, tugging at the contraption and peering inside of it. "And it seems pretty sturdy."

"They're built to stand up to a lot," she said. "And according to the tag—" She paused, plucked at the tag under his arm so that he raised his arm just an inch over her shoulder as she cocked her head to one side to read it.

"It looks like this adjustment here makes it for Benjie while he's tiny like this..."

She stood straight again, and he couldn't really be blamed for noticing how neatly she'd fit under his arm. Then she went up onto her tiptoes and looked down into the carrier and plucked at an extra flap inside.

Mike nodded, looking it over. This was a carrier he could use alone without needing Paige to dive in and rescue him. That mattered to him.

"Okay," he said. "I'll get this one."

"Have you decided, then?" the saleswoman asked, bustling up next to them. "Excellent. Good choice. Is there anything else you were shopping for today?"

"No, this is it," Mike said. He reached for his wallet, and Paige picked up the car seat.

"This is a great baby carrier," the saleswoman went on. "It fits a smaller frame like Mom's, too." She nodded at Paige. "This carrier will survive in your little family for years. My daughter has one, and it lasted all three of her babies."

The woman chattered on, and Mike glanced down at Paige. There was color in her cheeks, and she shrugged faintly when she felt Mike's gaze on her.

Mom. He had to admit that they did look like a couple, and it wasn't just because they were shopping for a baby carrier.

Paige was what Benjie needed—a woman with a big heart full of wisdom and a reassuring way of making a guy feel like he could do just about anything for that smile. Maybe it was what he needed, too.

If he were sticking around.

PAIGE TRIED TO keep things as professionally distant as possible the rest of the week. Mike seemed to have things under control after she left his house at night, and there were no more panicked, late-night calls for help. He seemed to be settling in, and while she was proud of him, she was also a little melancholy. He didn't need her quite so much anymore—the goal all along, of course.

They were getting more comfortable around each other physically, which wasn't something she normally had to worry about with a client. But Mike was different, obviously. She'd gotten to the point where she could lean into his arm or put a hand on his back when she eased around him in the kitchen and it didn't feel strange or too familiar. Granted, it probably was too familiar, but this was a strange situation, and she'd decided to just make the best of it. It would be over soon enough, anyway, and she could get her balance back.

SATURDAY MORNING, PAIGE looked through the diaper bag, making sure they hadn't forgotten anything for their day out at the community picnic. She'd done the baby bag packing, but she'd pointed everything out as she put it in: bottles, burp cloths, diapers, cream...

"Always remember an extra set of clothes for Benjie," Paige said. "The minute you go out, they have an explosive diaper."

"Oh, yeah?" Mike looked around, then snatched up a freshly washed sleeper from the laundry basket.

"That will do." She folded it and tucked it inside, then put the bag over her shoulder. "We're ready."

Benjie slept in his car seat, his tiny chest rising and falling in those short breaths that newborns took, and Mike caught the car seat by the handle and opened the front door.

Mike was in full uniform today—and Paige was glad. When he was dressed down in jeans, that was when it was easier to forget facts. In uniform, he might be steely and good-looking, but he was still a part of that world she was struggling with.

Mike stood back and gestured Paige through the front door first.

"So this is to build a positive police image in town, is it?" she said as Mike pulled the door shut behind them and turned the key in the lock.

"Pretty much." Mike pocketed the key and they went down the front steps together and headed toward Mike's squad car. "Chief told me the citizens of Eagle's Rest have a bad taste in their mouths since that fraud case with Mayor Nelson and Evan Kornekewsky."

It had been an incredibly tough time for the town when their beloved mayor was shown to be an oily manipulator. A fair number of locals had been victim to that crime ring. But it had been more personal for some of them…and it left everyone badly shaken.

"Unfortunately. A cop was intimidating locals into selling their property under market value. But it wasn't only that. He was

Liv's ex, and he tried to implicate her in his fraud scheme, too. It was really scary. She managed to prove her innocence, but still."

"Yeah, I know what it did to Liv. Jack wanted to skin him alive after that, and I don't blame him."

"We all wanted to make him pay," Paige replied. "But it left everyone a little less trusting of the force, too. It was only natural."

Mike paused at the car and glanced back at her. "Is that part of the problem for you with your job? That loss of faith in the system? I mean, one bad officer doesn't mean—"

"I know, I know," she interrupted. "You forget that my brother's a cop. I know that one dirty cop doesn't soil the rest of the force. I wish it were that simple, but it isn't that, Mike."

He pulled open the passenger side door for her. "You sure?"

"Positive." She met his gaze. "It goes a whole lot deeper."

"Okay, then." He didn't move, and his gray eyes moved over her face for a moment, searching.

"You don't have to fix me, Mike."

He smiled ruefully, then tapped the top of

the car and stepped back. "Sorry. The chief is worried about you, is all."

"You seem more worried right now," she said.

"I don't want to be just another one of your burdens," he replied. "And it's true—the chief *is* concerned."

Before he was Chief Simpson, he was just Officer Simpson, Sarah Anne's dad, who gave them lectures about taking care of themselves and carrying pepper spray.

"I know," she replied. "He's a good man, and he cares, but my issues with my career aren't anyone's fault, least of all the chief's."

"It's the cop in me," Mike said. "Doesn't matter if I didn't break it, I still want to patch it back together again. Besides, he says you're one of the best."

"I am," she said with no trace of bragging. "And it's killing me."

She got into the car and put on her seat belt, and Mike did the same. He glanced over at her as he turned the key and the engine rumbled to life.

"I don't want to be just another job that's killing you," he said quietly.

"You aren't, Mike."

"Would you tell me if I was?"

Paige thought for a moment. "No."

He nodded, then smiled humorlessly as he eased the car forward, pulling out of the driveway and onto the street. She'd offended him, and that hadn't been her intention. She didn't know what he wanted from her exactly, but she was too tired to do this dance.

"Mike, you aren't the problem," she said after a moment of silence.

"I don't want to be," he said. "I want to give something back."

"My clients don't owe me anything, though," she said. "I work to better their lives, not the other way around."

"Hey, I serve the public all day, too," he said curtly. "But I don't want to just be your responsibility, either. I get that I'm paying you, but I'm not just another client looking for your help and reassurance. I'm on your team. It's different."

"We *are* on the same team," she agreed. "It's just easier thinking of you as a client, I guess."

"It shouldn't be," he replied quietly.

The community picnic was being held in Central Park, and it spilled out onto the streets that were barricaded off so that the vendors could set up their tables along the sidewalks. There would be food and crafts, some quilts. The local painters who sold prints of their work mostly painted eagles soaring, catching fish or nesting high in the pines. There would be a few self-published authors selling their books, too. On the grass, there would be food booths, some wandering balloon twisters and a couple of caricature artists for everyone's enjoyment. It was the same every year, but it was worth finding parking and wandering through the closed downtown streets. Paige had to admit that Chief Simpson's idea to have smiling, fun-loving officers in uniform was a good one. The citizens of Eagle's Rest could use a little reassurance.

They parked along a side street, and while Paige got Benjie out of his car seat, Mike pulled the collapsed stroller out of the trunk, then fiddled with it until he got it into working order. Benjie was snuggled up in the blanket, cuddling closer to Paige. She kissed his downy head and rested her cheek against it for a moment. He smelled clean and sweet. This baby, like all babies, was so easy to love…

A brisk wind picked up, and she adjusted the blanket around Benjie a little closer, waiting while Mike finished with the stroller.

"Okay," he said. "I think that's it."

Paige leaned over and settled Benjie into the stroller. He was so tiny compared to the stroller around him, and she pulled an extra blanket from the bag on her shoulder and draped it over the first one.

"He needs to stay warm," she said. "You'll want to buy him a snowsuit soon for when the temperature drops."

Mike eyed her for a moment. "How will I know if he's too cold?"

"He'll cry."

"Right." He smiled ruefully.

"Come on," she said. "It's less complicated than it looks. Let's walk."

Some music surfed the breeze toward them, coming from the direction of the park. It sounded like folk music—a banjo and some singing. A swirl of leaves spun across the sidewalk ahead of them, and Paige sucked in a breath of fresh, mountain air.

A young couple, holding hands, passed them on the sidewalk, and Paige moved closer to Mike to give them room. His well-muscled arm was warm against her sleeve, and when she put her hand on the stroller handle, her fingers brushed his. She was about to move her hand away when he stroked his little finger along her index finger, slow and warm. That was intentional! Her heart sped up, and she looked up at him uncertainly.

"Your hands are cold," Mike said, his voice low. He slid his warm palm over her fingers. It felt comforting, tempting, and she had to hold herself back from turning her hand over and twining her fingers with his.

What was she thinking?

"A little bit," she breathed.

The couple was ahead of them now, giving space again for her to step away. She moved her hand out from under his and felt a smile tug at her lips. She wasn't supposed to be enjoying him—not like this.

"You're flirting," she said.

"A tiny bit. Should I stop?"

He should—it would be the right thing to do, but she didn't want him to.

"Paige Stedler!" An angry voice broke the stillness—the tone icy and clear.

Paige sobered and looked around, her gaze landing on a tall, lanky man marching in her direction. He had a bottle of beer in one hand, and he held the neck more like a weapon than a beverage. It was Craig Bolt—the dad who had sobbed in her office, begging for his kids back.

"Paige, get behind me," Mike said, his hand clamping on her arm.

She jerked free. "It's fine, I know him. Stand down. Let me talk to him."

Mike's steely glare was locked on the man, and he pulled the stroller back so that he stood between Benjie and Craig. His hand moved down to his belt where his cuffs were located.

"I know him," Paige repeated, putting a hand on Mike's arm. "I can handle this."

"Paige Stedler!" Craig bellowed again. "You *liar!*"

CHAPTER NINE

MIKE KNEW THIS GUY—he'd removed him from the local bar twice already when the owner called for assistance. He was belligerent, tough, and it took two cops to safely subdue him when he was riled up. Mike eyed that beer bottle—public drinking being against the law. Paige thought she could handle him on her own? He was only one cop right now with a newborn baby and a woman to protect, and if he had to subdue the guy, it would be a whole lot less gentle than when he had backup.

"Paige, this guy isn't safe," Mike said, putting his hand on her arm again. He wanted to hold her back, get her safely behind him, but she wouldn't budge.

"He's fine."

"He's not fine," Mike growled, his gaze locked on the approaching man. "I'm going to call for some backup."

"Don't do that!" Paige's voice turned hard. "I'm serious, Mike. Do not call in a bunch of cops. This is the guy whose kids I had to have removed. Okay? He's sad, mostly. No cops."

Mike noted the irony that he himself was in uniform, but he didn't have time to argue that. He caught her eye meaningfully. "You don't have to do this."

"Yeah, I do." She pulled her arm out of his grasp once more. "He needs help, not to be arrested. Let me do *my job*."

Was she stepping back into her role for good, or only for now? Even the chief had said that she was the best, and maybe she was rediscovering the passion for her position that had slipped away. He'd just have to trust her instincts.

"Okay… This one's yours."

There was a thank-you in her clear gaze, and she turned back to Craig, who took another swig from his beer bottle.

"Miss Stedler," he sneered. "Fancy finding you here."

"Craig, you've been drinking," Paige said as Craig approached.

"It's the weekend," Craig growled. "I'm having a beer. So what?"

"This is also a public space," Mike said, raising his voice. "You aren't supposed to be drinking here."

He'd let her do her job, but he wanted to remind Craig that she wasn't on her own, either.

"You gonna take it away?" Craig snapped, spreading his arms and glaring at Mike. "Go on! Come and take it!"

"Mike, stop—" Paige snapped, flashing him a look of warning. Then her voice returned to that calm, low tone. "Craig, you always feel terrible the next day for what you've done when you're drunk. I know that. You aren't a bad guy. Don't do something you'll regret today, okay? You don't want to be arrested."

"So full of advice," Craig snarled. "You aren't on my side! You never were! You were just waiting for me to mess up!"

"Not true," she replied. "I didn't want that. Neither did you. But this isn't the end of your story, either. We're here to help you."

"Who's we?"

"Social Services. We—"

"So not you. Not personally. You don't care." He belted out a bitter laugh. "You used to say that if I needed anything I could call you anytime. Directly. Remember that?"

"Craig, you're talking to me right now. It's not in my power to change a judge's mind or stop the process. But I can help—"

"I don't need your help. What I need are my kids!"

"And there are proper avenues to follow to get them back," Paige said. "We've been over this."

Craig took a menacing step forward.

"Watch it," Mike said, putting a hand on the baton on his belt. "Come any closer, and you're dealing with me, buddy."

Craig's glassy gaze moved in Mike's direction, and Mike could see the wheels in his head spin for a second before he stopped his forward momentum.

"You told me that if I cleaned up, you'd leave us alone!" The man turned his attention back to Paige. "You told me that! And where are my kids now?"

"They're in temporary foster care," Paige said. "And I know that's a terrible thing to experience as a parent. I get it. I know you're angry, and desperate to see them—"

"You know how I feel?" he sneered. "Really? I doubt it!"

Paige flinched, and Mike took another step closer to her, his muscles taut and ready. If this guy so much as came near her…

"I can empathize, Craig. You know me, and I know you. We've talked long and hard about what your kids need, haven't we? And I know you love your kids. That's why I know you'll do what it takes to get your life together so you can give them a safe home."

"You want me to jump through hoops!"

"Not at all. I want you to prove to us that you're the dad you want to be," Paige said, her tone firming. "You need to attend Alcoholics Anonymous meetings and get off the booze and you'll take some counseling classes on parenting and personal development. You'll have supervised visits with them until you'll be reassessed to have your children returned to you on a limited basis. That's how this works. We care about your family, Craig. *I care.*"

"So what—" He looked over her shoulder

toward the stroller. "You're out with *your* kid—"

"That's not my child, Craig," she said softly. "Let's stay focused."

"I have *kids*!" Craig's eyes brimmed with tears. "You don't get what that means, do you? You took away *my kids*!"

"I didn't take them," she said.

"Shut up!" he bellowed. "You were part of it! The system. The man. The… The…" Craig looked left and right as he floundered for the words through his booze-fogged mind.

"Your children were alone, Craig," she said. "Do you remember that? You'd left them by themselves. They'd been alone for forty-eight hours while you were out drinking! They weren't safe."

"They need me!" Craig snapped. "Where are they?"

"We can arrange another supervised visit for you—"

"Who do you think you are?" The words came out as a choked sob, and whatever control Craig had been maintaining snapped. He lunged at Paige with lightning speed. His big hand clamped down on Paige's jaw as he hauled her forward and panted down into her face. Tears welled in his eyes and his hand trembled.

The seconds seemed to slow down as Mike saw those thick fingers press into the tender flesh of Paige's cheek, and cold anger billowed up inside of him. Mike pulled out his radio and barked in a request for backup as he crossed the grass. He dropped his handset and pulled out his baton. He gave Craig's wrist a solid whack with the metal rod and the beefy hand dropped, Paige staggering backward, her hands flying up to her face.

Mike pulled Paige farther away from the man just as Benjie's thin wail came to them from the stroller. Paige touched her cheek gingerly where Craig's fingers had pressed into her. She was pale, the red marks that brute's fingers had left behind standing out. She'd bruise—there was no doubt.

"Get on the ground!" Mike barked, grabbing Craig's wrist and twisting it up behind his back. "Now—on the ground!"

Craig stumbled, and Mike used the opportunity to push him forward, at the same time pulling his wrist back. Craig fell heavily, letting out a grunt as he hit the grass. The beer bottle lay on the ground next to him, slowly emptying into the grass.

"You're going to the station," Mike said, breathing hard. He slammed a knee into the other man's back and reached for his cuffs. "I told you you'd be dealing with me…"

"Mike—" Paige began, then she looked back toward the stroller. Benjie's cry was getting more insistent, and underneath that veneer of icy efficiency, Mike's heart tugged toward the little guy.

"Get Benjie," Mike said. "Let me do *my* job now."

"I wasn't doing nothing!" Craig bawled out. "Police brutality!"

The sound of sirens came up the street, and Mike heard the cruiser pull to a stop at the curb. Paige lifted Benjie from the stroller, pulling the baby close against her chest as two officers got out of the vehicle and jogged toward him.

Benjie was safe, and so was Paige—his adrenaline started to ease off, and he snapped the handcuffs in place, then stood up.

"What's going on?" Officer Jackson asked.

"He assaulted Paige Stedler," Mike replied. "Add to that, public intoxication and public consumption of alcohol."

"We'll take him in," Officer Jackson said, putting a strong hand on Craig's shoulder. "I'll read him his rights."

"Mike—" Paige stood to the side, the baby held close in her arms. "He needs counseling."

"You really think he'll go without being forced to?" Mike asked.

Paige fell silent, but her eyes followed Craig as he was led to the cruiser. Did she still pity him, even now?

Mike brushed off his hands and went to her side. He wanted to hold her, pull her close in his arms and not let anyone hurt her again. He hadn't been fast enough with that idiot. He should have stepped in, regardless of what she wanted.

Or did he do the right thing, letting her try to intervene? He didn't know. All he knew is that she looked deflated right now, small and hurt.

Mike slipped an arm around her shoulders, and she stiffened. Okay, not the right move here. He dropped his hand and dipped his head down to try and see her face.

"You okay?" he asked quietly.

Paige didn't answer, but her eyes brimmed with tears and she looked away.

"Look, I know you wanted me to stay out of that, but you can't possibly be mad that I stepped in when he got his hands on you!"

"I'm not mad at *you*!" She turned tear-filled eyes toward him. "Craig is in a tough place right now. I should have been able to get through to him."

"You did everything you could," he insisted.

"I guess. I just hate it." She looked down at Benjie, who blinked at them. Paige adjusted the blanket around the baby, and patted his back.

"Does your face hurt?" he asked after a moment.

Paige touched her cheek, and shrugged weakly. "Yes."

"What can I do?" Mike asked at last. "What do you need right now?"

"I want to go home," she said, and a tear slipped down her cheek. She leaned toward him, her shoulder resting against his chest, and he put his arms around her. *Finally...* It felt right to hold her. It was about all he could do for her now, and she tipped her head against his shoulder and breathed out a sigh.

Mike stroked a hand down her arm. He wanted to do more than this, wanted to pull her against him and drown the pain and fear that were eating away at her in a lingering kiss. But that would be wrong on too many levels. He couldn't give in to that. She was vulnerable, and if he had to be brutally honest, so was he. He wanted to kiss her for his own comfort as much as hers. He'd only regret it later. And have to apologize for it.

"I'll take you home," Mike said, his voice sounding gruffer than he felt.

"Thanks, Mike." Paige straightened, pulling out of his arms and letting a gust of chilly air pass between them. Mike gently touched Benjie's cheek.

"I can go back to the station and do the paperwork later on," he added, softening his tone. "I want to make sure your house is secure. Craig isn't going to be a threat for next twenty-four hours at least, but it'll make me feel better."

"He needs help," Paige repeated with a

shake of her head. "I'm telling you, he's hurting."

Yeah, and this was why Paige was so good in Social Services. She could be literally attacked by one of her clients, and she was still filled with compassion for his situation. She was a better person than Mike was, because Craig wasn't ranking high on his list of people he felt bad for. Paige was Mike's concern. She needed support, protection and a little understanding.

And maybe some tea. He'd get her home and see what he could do to make things a bit easier for her. She'd been the strong one for far too long.

PAIGE LIVED ON a street just south of downtown Eagle's Rest. As Mike navigated the open roads to get to her address, Paige's mind spun. What had just happened? Her jaw still hurt from where Craig had clamped down on her, and her initial feelings of concern for him had melted away. Now, she felt shaken and scared. And a bit angry. If Mike hadn't been there today, would Craig have done more than he already had?

Paige leaned back on the headrest. She

wasn't having a panic attack right now, and frankly, that was surprising. She'd just been through a terrifying confrontation, and now that an emotional meltdown would be fully justified, her body seemed to not require one.

"You're welcome to stay at my place," he added.

"No, I'm fine." Surprisingly fine—she wasn't sure she even understood why. "What's going to happen to Craig?"

"He'll be in holding," Mike replied. "The state of Colorado will press charges against him for assault and public intoxication, and he'll be one step closer to being forced into getting that help he needs."

"I can understand his anger, though," she said. "He's a father—albeit a bad one right now. And we've taken his kids away."

"To protect them," Mike replied.

"Yes, and I'm not excusing his behavior. Those kids were neglected and scared. They need adults they can trust. And I'm certainly not excusing his behavior today. But I understand what he's feeling."

"That isn't your job," Mike countered.

"It is my job!" she shot back. "What use

am I to my clients if I can't at least understand where they're coming from?"

Mike fell silent, and Paige sighed.

"I didn't mean to snap at you," she said. "I do appreciate you stepping in."

He signaled a turn. "How are you feeling? You think you need a doctor?"

"No, I'll be fine," she replied.

But she might have to explain a bruised face to her friends and family over the next week, and that would prove tiring.

They were on her street now, and Mike slowed.

"There—just ahead. The yellow house with the white shutters," she said. "Number 36."

He pulled to a stop, then looked over at her. "I can see why you might want out of Social Services."

"Ironically, it isn't the confrontation that gets to me the most," she said. "I just got manhandled by a furious client, and I didn't get a panic attack. Don't get me wrong—that scared me. But what really gets to me is my inability to *fix* things. I can't make Craig do what he needs to do to reunite his family. I can't protect him from himself. And if I cared less, I'd just file that away as not my responsibility."

"He has to want to change," Mike said.

"And I know that."

"No one is looking to you to fix him."

"I know that, too." Paige shrugged. "When I started this job seven years ago, I was more optimistic. I thought that given enough time, enough support, enough people who truly cared, that a man could change. I no longer believe that."

"You work in public service long enough and you're no longer the naive kid who thinks they can change the world."

"So you're the same?" she asked.

"More or less," he replied. "I'm just more determined to catch the bad guys. Because there are such thing as truly bad people, Paige. They aren't all redeemable."

"But there are some people who just lose their way, Mike," she said. "Like your sister."

Mike sobered and was silent for a beat. "You're right. There are a few I haven't given up on."

"You're not quite so jaded as you let on."

He met her gaze and a small smile turned

up the corners of his lips. "I dare say, neither are you."

And maybe she wasn't. That was the problem, and the part that hurt the most. She knew that the likelihood of Craig Bolt changing his ways was slim to none, but there was still a fragment of hope.

Mike's gaze moved past her toward her house. Paige gathered up the baby bag and pulled on the door handle.

"You might as well come have a look around," she said. "I'll feel better if you tell me I'm locked in tight."

They got out of the cruiser and Mike got Benjie out of the backseat. Paige unlocked her side door and let Mike go ahead of her into her kitchen. He paused, his gaze sweeping the room.

"Can you hold Benjie while I look around?" he asked.

"Sure." Paige took the car seat and watched as Mike flicked the lock behind them, then headed to the kitchen window. He looked outside, then glanced back at her.

"Your garden has gone back to nature, you know."

Paige unbuckled the baby and laughed. "I

mean to garden, but I never quite get around to it. My mother was a big gardener. She canned and froze everything. It was amazing. I've always been too busy."

She picked up Benjie and cuddled him close. He nuzzled toward her, opening his mouth in a little circle. He was getting hungry, it seemed. She reached into the diaper bag and pulled out a bottle.

"Was?" Mike asked.

"She passed away two years ago from a heart attack. My dad is remarried now, lives in Ohio. So I'm the only one left in town."

"That's a bit lonely," he said.

"A bit," she agreed. "Mom was always so proud of my brother and I for going into careers where we could help people. She'd brag to all her friends about us. But Mom was perfectly happy living her life simply. She gardened. She taught Sunday school. She planned a big family Thanksgiving dinner for all the extended family…"

Paige paused, remembering her mother's smile, her voice, the way she wore an apron all day long, whether she was currently cooking or not. "Mom used to worry about late frosts and tent caterpillars. She believed in judging people by their actions and never trusting a man who didn't have his mother's phone number in his cell phone." Paige went to the fridge and pulled down a snapshot she kept there, stuck by a ladybug magnet. "That's her during our last Thanksgiving together. She was happiest surrounded by family."

Mike took the photo from her fingers, and while he looked at it, she ran hot water to heat up the bottle.

"You look like her a bit," Mike said.

"Yeah, that's me in twenty years," she said. "There's no denying it."

She shook up the bottle and tested it on her wrist, then turned off the water. Benjie was squirming, eager for his meal, and she popped the nipple into his searching mouth.

Mike put the picture back onto the fridge with that ladybug magnet. "You want the garden, don't you? And the white picket fence. Like your mom."

"I do," she agreed. "And I want a few certainties back in my life. I feel like I've lost most of them."

Paige swung her weight from one foot to the other while Benjie drank his bottle. She looked down into that tiny face—so innocent, so new. He didn't know any of the hard stuff yet. And hopefully, Mike could keep this boy protected from the worst of it.

"Your mother wouldn't have trusted me, though," Mike said after a moment. "I don't have the mom to keep in contact with. Hell, I didn't do so well by my sister, either."

"Not everything is your fault, Mike," Paige said, looking up.

"You're only saying that because you've got so much experience in Social Services."

"I suppose that's true," Paige admitted.

"And you're better for your experience, Paige," Mike added. "You can see the gray, not just the black and white. The real world can be an ugly place, but you're wiser for having seen the tough stuff."

"I'm also sadder," she said.

Mike nodded. "Aren't we all."

Would she ever be able to go back to being just an ordinary citizen around here? Mom had a simple life, but a happy one. She'd seen right and wrong, and good and bad. She'd been compassionate, but she didn't worry too much about the stuff outside of her control. And that was a nice way to live. But would Paige be able to step back into that life again? Wanting it might not be enough.

Mike nodded toward the living room. "You mind if I take that look around?"

"Sure," she said.

Mike gave her a small smile. "I'm looking forward to this. A little unedited view into your world."

Paige patted Benjie's back and rolled her eyes. "I suppose fair is fair. I've been in the middle of yours."

Mike headed out of the kitchen, and Paige looked down at the baby on her shoulder. He lifted his head, then let it drop, then lifted it again. There was a burp, a dribble, and Paige wiped his little chin.

"Does that feel better?" she whispered.

Benjie would be one of the lucky ones. He'd be loved. He'd be prioritized. And even if Mike was still finding his footing, Benjie would have an excellent dad.

CHAPTER TEN

MIKE MOVED THROUGH the little house, scanning for security weaknesses. Most windows were closed and locked tight, and the one that wasn't, in her bathroom, he clicked the lock shut. Then came back out into the hallway where she was waiting for him.

"You'll want to keep all your windows closed and locked," he said, glancing over at her. She stood by at the top of the hallway, the baby nestled next to her neck. He paused, noticing just how soft she looked just then.

"Okay," she said.

He nodded, and tore his gaze away from her.

"Leave lights on outside," he added. "And you can even leave a lamp on in the living room tonight. The more light there is, the less someone wants to try something."

"Okay."

"And keep your garage locked, too," he added.

"Right."

Paige leaned her cheek tenderly against Benjie's head. She was soft, gentle and vulnerable to idiots like Craig. She wasn't just a woman who'd been threatened—she was the one caring for Benjie. This was more personal than he was used to.

"So what are you learning about me with all this…unedited reality?" she asked.

"That you're remarkably clean," he said, glancing back into the spotless bathroom. There were a couple things of makeup on the counter, but otherwise, it looked company ready to him. "You must think I'm a pig."

"No…" She laughed. "I live alone. I'm the only one here to mess things up. You've got a baby in the mix. It's different."

"Yeah, it's different, all right," he agreed.

"But you don't have pictures, Mike," she said.

"What do you mean?"

"Like on your fridge, in frames, on your wall—no pictures."

"I just moved in," he said.

"So you've got some to put up, then?" she asked.

She wasn't going to let this go, was she?

"I don't really have any frame-worthy," he replied.

"Oh."

Mike didn't have many pictures, period. He had a few pictures of his mother growing up from his grandmother. Jana looked a lot like her. And he had some pictures from when they were kids, but Grandma had gotten more and more tired as the years went by, and she took fewer photos. There was one he'd always liked of him and Jana standing together when he was about fourteen and she was eleven. They'd been in shorts and T-shirts, squinting into the sunlight. They were both gangly and awkward, but it reminded him of good times. But that one was kind of blurry, and printed off as a three and a half inch by five.

"I guess even my happy memories are a bit sad," he admitted. "I've got one I could stick on my fridge like you, but... I don't know. It would be a constant reminder of me failing as a brother. That tends to bum a guy out."

Mike headed toward her, and she stepped aside as he entered the living room again. The space was tidy—a white couch, dark gray walls with white trim and a white faux fireplace, complete with photos on the mantel.

"There they are—the pictures," he said, pointing across the room. "That's very well-adjusted and normal of you."

"I suppose so." She chuckled. "I have to admit, no one has ever described me that way before."

Yeah, it took someone less well-adjusted to appreciate normal.

"It's all in the perspective," he replied with a short laugh.

He glanced around the living room. It just felt feminine in here. It *smelled* feminine. How did that happen? There were flowers in a vase on a side table—maybe those were the source of the soft scent in here? He went to the front door, which didn't look like it got a lot of use, and checked that the dead bolt was in place. Then he turned back and paused at the framed pictures on the mantel—a couple of pictures that looked to be twenty-five years old of a little girl with her parents. The girl had to be Paige—the blond hair, the impish smile. The mother had a baby in her arms—her brother, perhaps? There was a photo of an older couple posing together by a Christmas tree, and a few other people in the background. A picture of a younger but recognizable Paige with her mother—he recognized the mother from the photo in the kitchen. And the last picture was of Paige and a man in police uniform. He was grinning into the camera, and she was looking proudly up at him.

"That's my brother," Paige said, and he glanced down at her. He hadn't noticed her approach.

"Nathan, right?"

"Yeah. He'd just graduated from the police academy." She smiled. "I was so stinking proud of him."

"Who's older?" he asked.

"I am. I always looked out for him when we were kids. Somewhere the tables turned, and now he's got a badge and a gun."

"You were pretty close growing up, then?" he asked.

"I mean, we drove each other nuts for a few years," she conceded. "But yeah, we stayed pretty close. I taught him how to organize his finances, and he taught me some self-defense." Color tinted her cheeks. "I wish I'd thought to use some of it with Craig today."

"You shouldn't have had to," Mike said. "Look, right now you've got me. And I took care of him, so—"

She turned and looked up at him. Those clear, blue eyes seemed to disengage his ability to answer. "If you weren't there, I don't know what would have happened."

Mike looked down at her, the framed picture still in his hands. Her blue eyes were filled with emotion, and Benjie let out a little mew of protest. She adjusted the blanket around him closer, and the baby's eyes drifted shut. She was good at that—comforting people, making things feel better. For a moment he couldn't think of anything to say that encompassed what he felt. His feelings for her were complicated, mixed up with his attachment to this baby in his care, and all the insecurities he couldn't let anyone see. She made him feel stronger, more capable. Then Paige looked down, and Mike put the photo back on the mantel.

"I could say I was just doing my job, but it was more than that," he admitted softly.

Her expression turned quizzical, but she stayed silent.

How could he even explain this? He hardly knew how to put it into words. "I don't know. You're not a job to me, I guess. You're…one of mine, in a way. When he put his hands on you, I had to physically restrain myself from seriously hurting him."

And that had taken all of his self-control, because the belligerent, threatening look in the man's eyes, the way his fingers had dug into Paige's tender flesh—even now his heart hammered at the memory.

"And I appreciate that." A smile turned up the corners of her lips.

Was she liking that he took care of things, or that he held himself back from doing damage? Maybe it was a bit of both. He returned her smile.

"I'm looking out for you, Paige," he said quietly. "I'm here. If you ever need anything, or…" He sighed. "I want to make sure you stay safe. You can count on that."

He wasn't sure if he'd said too much, but then she smiled.

"I know."

Mike cleared his throat. "I'd better get going. I have to drop by the station and do a bit of paperwork. I'll bring Benjie with me. There's always someone happy to hold him. Then I'll head home."

"This was supposed to be a fun day off," she said.

"Yeah, well…" He shrugged. "You need the break more than I do right now. Call me if anything comes up. Call 911 first if you think you're in danger, though. This little guy slows me down a bit. I mean, I'll still come, but it might take me a few beats longer to get here."

"Okay." She laughed softly. "I'm sure it'll be fine. This isn't the first time I've been threatened."

Not the first time? He eyed her for a moment. She was tougher than she looked, but that wasn't comforting.

"If you get any more threats, I want to know about it," he said.

"Of course." But she sounded a little too relaxed. He sighed.

"I've got an appointment with a day care tomorrow morning. They're squeezing me in. The chief pulled some strings, says the spot is mine, if I want it."

"Well, that's good…"

"I don't want to just leave you on your own, though, after this. I mean—"

"I'm fine," she said. "Really. Go and get things set up. I'm not your problem, Mike."

"You aren't a problem," he said.

"I'm a grown woman. And frankly, this run-in today only confirms my choice to make a few changes. I could use the time to myself to think things through. I'll be just fine. I won't be talking to Craig alone again."

"What will you do tonight?" he asked. Because he cared about that. Was she going to sit here scared?

"I'm going to call my dad," she said. "And maybe my brother. I'll be fine."

"Okay," he said. "You can change your mind and come along with me, though, you know. We could press a few charges, fill out a few forms…"

She smiled, then shrugged. "As exciting as you make that sound, I think I'll pass. Thanks for the thought, though."

Right. This was her weekend, and he'd already intruded on it by asking her to go with him to the picnic. And unlike him, she had a family she could call when she needed support. The chief would understand if Mike didn't head back to the community picnic. At least he hoped he would, because Mike was determined to get those charges laid against Craig Bolt.

Besides, being here in her home was dangerous territory. He was getting attached to her, and he had to put a stop to that. There was something about her home—it felt like her here. The tidiness, the soft, feminine scent… It made him relax a little too much. It made him imagine what it would be like to spend more time here with her, and that wasn't in the cards for them. Because despite the comfort of her home, the enticing femininity of the space, it also reminded him that she was one of the functional people— the ones who grew up loved and protected. She wanted a life free of emotional complication, and he was the guardian of his estranged sister's newborn. His life was going to stay complicated for a long time to come.

"Okay, I'll see you," he said, picking up the car seat and turning for the door.

"Bye." Her voice was soft, and it made

him want to turn back. He wouldn't, though. She was wise enough to know what she needed to be happy—and it wasn't the likes of him.

As Mike backed out of her driveway, his phone rang. His first thought was that it would be the chief about Craig Bolt's arrest. He punched the Bluetooth button to pick up the call on speaker.

"Officer McMann," he intoned.

He heard only silence on the other end.

"Hello?" he said. "Mike here."

Soft breathing. He frowned, slowing the car as he came to a stop sign at the end of the street, and looked down at his phone, checking the number. He didn't recognize it, but it wasn't local.

"Hello?" he repeated, then sighed. "I'm hanging up."

"Michael?" The voice was quiet, but he'd recognize her anywhere, and his heart jumped into his throat. For a moment, he couldn't say anything, but he pulled to the side of the road and slammed on his brakes.

"Jana! Where are you? Are you okay?"

"How's the baby?" she asked.

"He's good. I've got him with me right

now." Mike looked into the backseat at the car seat. "He's real good. But where are you? Are you okay?"

"I really miss him," Jana said, tears in her voice. "I can't sleep. I keep thinking about him. I dream of him…"

"He's safe with me," Mike assured her. "I promise you that. He's eating and growing and going through a ton of diapers. He's doing good. I'm more worried about you right now. I didn't even know you were pregnant! I could have done something for you, given you a safe place to stay, gotten you some doctor's appointments. I could have…" His voice trailed off. She wasn't answering. He was going too far, wasn't he? And he was going to scare her off. "Look, no pressure, Jana. I'm just really glad to hear your voice."

"I'm… I'm okay," she said. "I just wanted to see how Benjamin was."

"He's good," he repeated helplessly.

"I should go—"

"No!" Mike couldn't help the way his voice rose. "Jana, let's talk a bit."

"That's probably a bad idea," she said.

"You must have gotten my new number

from the precinct," he said, hoping to keep her talking just a little bit longer.

"I saw a cop, and I asked," she conceded. "It took them a bit, but they gave me your number and said you're in a different town?"

Good, so the precinct in Denver had done as he asked and made sure she could contact him.

"Yeah, it's a little mountain town called Eagle's Rest," he said. "It's really pretty out here. You'd like it."

"Small town, huh?" There was a sound in her voice he recognized—the old Jana smiling ruefully. He'd forgotten how much he missed that.

"It's not so bad," he said. "Okay, it's real boring, but that's a good thing with a baby, right?"

She was silent, and he shut his eyes. Was talking about Benjie only going to push her away? Or was it going to make her want to come and take Benjie back? Was he going to lose both of them?

"Where are you?" he asked at last.

"Denver."

"Right. Can I come see you?"

"Nah, that's not a good idea," she said.

"I mean, you just had a baby. That's not an easy thing to go through. Have you seen a doctor? Are you doing okay? I want to help."

"I'm fine. A friend of mine used to be a midwife, so…"

What did that mean? He felt so helpless and yet he had her on the phone. And that was something.

"Okay, you don't want to see me right now," he said. "But you can call me anytime, okay? I'll pick up. And if you need help, I'm here."

The same thing he'd been promising Paige just a few minutes ago.

"I'd better go," she said softly. "Kiss Benjamin for me."

"Jana—"

There was a click as she hung up, and he slammed his hands against the steering wheel in impotent frustration. He wanted to help her, but she just wouldn't let him.

Still, she'd called. She was alive—and that was more than he'd been positive about before. Maybe she'd call again. He could even run her number through the computer at the station. Maybe she'd eventually let him help her.

He put the car into Drive and started toward the police station two blocks away. Of the two women in his life right now, Paige was the only one who'd let him lend a hand. But his sister was the one who needed him the most right now.

He'd let Jana down so many times. He wouldn't do it again. He'd be the big brother she'd needed for so long. And hopefully, he could help her out of whatever mess she'd dug herself into.

He might not believe in people changing a whole lot, but he had to believe that a select few *could* change if they wanted it badly enough. And he had to believe that his sister was on that list.

"ANYTHING ELSE TODAY, HON?" the waitress asked, shooting Paige a smile. The older woman had a coffeepot in one hand and her other hand resting on her ample hip.

"No, thanks, just the bill," Paige replied.

"Sure thing."

Paige sat in a booth by herself in the far corner of The Eagle's Nest, a little mom-and-pop joint tucked off Main Street. She'd managed to cover the bruising along her jaw with some foundation and concealer, but she still felt conspicuous, waiting for someone to ask what had happened. So far, she'd evaded notice.

Outside, the day was sunny. There were trees planted along the sidewalk, and most were bare of leaves now, except for a few that clung to the last fiery remnants of their summer foliage. It was a peaceful scene—one she'd enjoyed countless times over the years. She liked this place, especially in the quiet season. But neither the rustling tumble of dry leaves nor Sunday brunch soothed her like it normally did.

Paige's mind had been running in overdrive ever since Mike had left her place yesterday afternoon. If he hadn't been there when Craig had come at her, she might have been seriously injured. She had to consider that fact, because she wasn't going to walk around with a police escort for the rest of her career if she stayed in Social Services.

Her father had been pretty upset when he heard about the altercation, but finding out that a cop with a personal interest in keeping her safe was with her had helped.

"Maybe you should move out here," her

father had suggested. "The housing is really affordable, and you'd have me and Irene. Our friends would love to meet you. In fact, I know a single young fella…"

Her father always asked her to move closer; it wouldn't have been a chat with Dad if he hadn't slipped it in.

Her cell phone was on the table next to her, ready to dial the cops if she needed to. She was more shaken by that altercation with Craig than she'd wanted to admit to Mike or her father. The man had scared her deeply. She'd always thought of him as a troubled guy, and now she could see that he could move past troubled to dangerous rather easily when pressed. She'd dealt with other violent men in the system, but somehow, Craig had slipped under her radar. Had he been manipulating her? Did she have a blind spot somehow? She should have seen this earlier. She should have seen that the counseling wasn't enough for Quinn earlier, too. Everyone thought she was a superstar, but she wasn't. Maybe she never had been, if she'd missed this much.

The problem was, even recognizing that Craig was a dangerous man, she still felt empathy for him. And for his kids. There had been no evidence of abuse with kids, just neglect. And those children deserved a little consistency. But nothing was ever so easily filed away—at least not for Paige. There were no easy solutions to any problem.

The waitress came back with her bill and put it upside down on the tabletop.

When she'd finished paying, she headed out the door. The sun was warm and the wind was cool, but not as cold as earlier. Paige loosened her jacket, undoing the zipper partway. She hitched her purse higher on her shoulder and drew in a deep breath.

She would be okay. It was time to take care of herself instead of everyone else. There was no shame in that, was there? They said you had to put your own oxygen mask on before you helped others. But what would it say about her if she put on her own oxygen mask, and then never went back? Would that be forgivable?

"Paige?"

She knew that warm voice, and Paige turned to see Mike approaching. He was dressed in street clothes—khaki pants and a brown bomber jacket. He was pushing the stroller, and Benjie looked snuggly tucked in with several blankets around him. He was sleeping with a pacifier bopping up and down in an even rhythm. She felt a wave of relief. She couldn't let herself get used to this police presence all the time, but it sure felt good to have him around after yesterday's drama.

"Hi," Paige said. "What are you doing here?"

"Just got out of the appointment with the day care," he said.

"So he has a space?"

"Yeah, they'll squeeze him in. They have a couple of other infants, so he'll have some little buddies as he gets older. The owner used to be a nurse, and after she retired, she opened a day care."

"Sounds like a perfect setup." Paige couldn't help but look down at Benjie again. So little. A small part of her wished she could be the one to take care of him, because having a stranger take over felt weird. But he wasn't hers, and she'd need to stop this.

"You want to walk with us?" Mike asked. "It's a nice day out. I think I read somewhere that fresh air is good for babies."

"I should probably..." She looked around, looking for the excuse she should use to stand on her own two feet and face life without this handsome cop to lean on. But she couldn't think of anything, or maybe she didn't want to.

"It's good for grown-ups, too," he added.

"Sure, I'll walk for a bit. I don't have anything pressing right now."

Mike fell into step beside her, and they walked down the sidewalk together. They passed Hylton Books, and Paige glanced in the window. There was an employee working. She looked up at the windows above where Liv and her husband stayed. A window was partially open, and a white curtain fluttered out.

"How's Liv?" Mike asked.

"I talked to her for a few minutes last night," Paige said. "She's exhausted. Like really wiped. But happy."

"Sounds about right." Mike smiled.

"And you would know," Paige pointed out with a chuckle.

"Funny being the parenting expert right now."

Paige smiled. "I wanted to go to see her

tomorrow. Jack will be going back to work, and she'll be on her own."

"You're a good friend," he said.

"You don't mind if I take Benjie there while you're at work, do you?" she asked.

"Not at all. Thanks for asking, though."

They got to an intersection and stopped at the curb. Paige looked down a tree-lined street perpendicular to them, trees nearly empty of leaves stretching forlorn branches over the pavement. Yellow and red leaves littered the gutter and fluttered from the yards onto the sidewalk. Sunlight blazed through the tree branches, lighting up the scene into cheerful glory.

"You want to go that way?" Mike asked. "Looks pretty."

"Sure."

The thing was, this tree-lined street, the leaves, the autumn sunlight, all of it—she preferred this to the tough stuff she'd had to deal with lately. But she felt guilty about abandoning her career and her colleagues. She felt bad about giving up on her clients, too, because wasn't that what it amounted to? On some level at least.

"I'm glad you sorted out your child care," Paige said.

"Me, too," Mike said. "It's a relief. We don't have that much longer together."

"True." But the truth of it stung. She cast him a wan smile. The sidewalk narrowed, and Mike moved over a bit. It wasn't quite enough space for them to walk easily, so he reached down and grabbed her hand, put it on the handle of the stroller and covered her fingers with his broad palm. It tugged her closer, and her arm pressed against his.

"That's better," Mike said.

His hand felt warm and strong, and she was ever so tempted to tip her head over onto his bicep. Not that she'd do such a thing. She felt some heat hit her cheeks at the very thought. But he smelled good—musky and clean—and there was something about walking pressed up against this muscular cop that awoke the woman inside of her.

"I heard from my sister," Mike said, breaking the companionable silence.

"What?" Paige looked up at him in surprise. "When?"

"Just as I was leaving your place yesterday actually," he said. "She called me."

"What did she want?" Paige asked. "Do you know where she is?"

"All she'd say was that she's in Denver." Mike paused. "She, um, she was calling to see if Benjie was okay."

"Oh…" Paige's heart gave a squeeze of sympathy. "Does she miss him?"

"Yeah. A lot." Mike's voice tightened. "She said she thinks about him all the time, and she even dreams about him. Giving him up was just as hard on her as I thought it would be."

"Do you think she'll want him back?" Paige asked softly.

Mike slowed his pace, but he didn't look over at her. His gaze stayed drilled onto the sidewalk ahead of them. "That's what I'm afraid of. She sounded like she was pretty desperate to see him. I suggested we meet up, but she wouldn't. I'm kind of scared that she's staying away because seeing Benjie again would hurt too much."

"She's given him up, Mike," Paige said. "Legally, she had twenty-four hours to change her mind. That's long past. You're Benjie's legal guardian, and after the paper-

work is complete, you'll be his adoptive father."

"I know."

"Is that what you want?" she asked more
hesitantly.

"Yeah." He looked down at her, his intense gaze filled with repressed emotion.
"I knew that getting into contact with my
sister again would complicate things, but
I couldn't just leave her on her own. I've
been looking for her for years. She needs
me, too."

"But you're afraid she's going to want him
back," Paige whispered.

"Yep."

Mike fell silent, but he held her hand a
little tighter over the handle of the stroller.
She adjusted her hand under his grip, and
instead of letting go, he wrapped his fingers around hers and dropped his arm to
his side, holding her hand more naturally.
He was scared—she could tell. And she felt
the distinct honor that he was opening up to
her about this.

"What will you do if she does?" Paige
asked.

"I have no idea," he murmured, and he

stroked his thumb across her knuckles, then slowed to a stop and looked down into her face. "Have you ever had to choose between which person you helped?"

"It happens," she said softly.

"For me, it's Benjie or my sister. Or at least it feels that way."

"Mike, there is no right answer here," Paige said quietly.

"There are several wrong ones," he replied. "I need to make things up to my sister, but obviously I can't just hand Benjie over to her if that's what she's hoping. And that isn't just because I'm attached. I mean, I am. I've been thinking seriously about it, and I want to raise this boy myself, but I'm also convinced that Jana can't take care of him. If she could, she wouldn't have walked away to begin with."

"Benjie is better off with you," she said with a nod. "He really is."

"I'm stuck weighing what's best for Benjie against what's best for my sister. Benjie has to be the priority, right? But what about her?"

Paige was silent for a moment, and she

squeezed his hand. "All I know is that you're a good man."

"I'm not sure that helps." He smiled faintly.

"It's all I've got."

Mike raised his free hand and touched her cheek, his thumb moving tenderly over her bruised skin.

"I feel like I'm not enough. I'm better with guns and bulletproof vests and battering rams. I'd make one hell of a SWAT member. This stuff… I'm not great at."

Not enough? He was more than enough. He was strong and sweet, and his heart was stubbornly set in the right place. Why couldn't he see that?

"You're a good man," she repeated, and Mike's gray gaze moved over her face, then rested on her lips. She sucked in a breath. A whisper of cold wind pushed through her hair, and his strong hand tightened on hers. She stepped closer, the warmth from his body emanating against her.

"Is that your job talking—encouraging me? Or is that you, encouraging me…personally?" he murmured.

"That's me."

"Good." Then he dipped his head down

and he stopped just a whisper away from her lips. He hovered there, and she let out a trembling breath, then his lips came down over hers. His hands both moved up to her face, and he stepped closer still, sliding an arm around her waist, holding her firmly against him. He could feel the solid beat of his heart, and her head swam as his mouth moved over hers. She clutched his jacket as she felt the world around her drift away. And then he pulled back, and her eyes fluttered open. His eyes were closed as he pressed his lips together, resting his forehead against hers.

"Oh…" she whispered, and she released his coat, smoothing it down with her fingers.

"I don't know why I did that," he breathed, then he let go of her, his hands sliding off her waist as he took hold of the stroller handle once more.

The wind suddenly felt colder, and Paige tugged her coat closed at her neck. He was a good man—she stood by that—but they were playing with fire here. Kissing her like that, she was liable to get her heart involved.

CHAPTER ELEVEN

MIKE RAN HIS fingers through his hair, looking down at the petite woman in front of him. Her blue eyes locked on his for a moment, and she smiled. She looked mildly rumpled from that kiss, but her eyes glittered and her cheeks were flushed pink. Yeah, it was taking a whole lot of self-control to keep himself from kissing her all over again.

But she'd kissed him back—rather passionately. He could still feel the spot where her fingers had dug into his coat, pulling him closer. A front door opened a few houses down and an older man came out with a small dog on a leash. Mike and Paige both looked in his direction. Standing on a street, kissing her like that, wasn't exactly private. They were on display for the whole street to watch. He was feeling foolish now.

"That was less private than I'd intended," he said with a wince.

Paige chuckled softly, but didn't answer. Benjie let out a mew of complaint, and Mike rolled the stroller forward and back a couple of times.

"We should keep walking so Benjie keeps sleeping," he said.

"Right," she agreed, and she fell into pace beside him again. Her arm next to his felt warmer, even more tempting than before. Now that he'd kissed her, he couldn't get the thought of kissing her again out of his head. It was stupid, he knew, and he'd beat himself up for it later, but whatever he'd been feeling for her the last few days hadn't just gone away. It was growing, and she seemed to be feeling it, too.

She leaned into his arm ever so subtly, and he couldn't help the smile that came to his lips. This felt good—too good, maybe. But at least he wasn't denying it right now. Still, he knew why it wouldn't work. He was heading in a direction that she couldn't live with. And he couldn't just give it up, either.

"Is there…something between us?" he asked.

"I don't think it matters," she said quickly. And maybe she was right. There was no future for them, so whatever this was between them was inviting heartbreak. He couldn't deny what drove him—his need to face the harshest reality in order to make up for his own inadequacy. And she deserved that clean, simple life she craved. So what was he doing here?

"It matters to me. Look, I know why this won't work—I don't need a lecture on that. But there's something here, regardless." They started walking again. He touched the side of her hand with his pinkie finger, and her finger raised, stretching toward his, then she pulled her hand back.

Paige looked up at him with an agonized look on her face. "Do you want me to say that I feel it, too?"

The wind ruffled her hair, and she pulled it back out of her face with a swipe of her pale fingers.

"Yeah, I really do," he admitted. He wanted it more than anything right now, because he couldn't be alone in this—he couldn't be the only one wrestling with these feelings.

"Then...yes." But she shook her head as she said it. "I do. I feel it—whatever this is. We're obviously attracted to each other.

We're two healthy adults, and we probably have pheromones in common or something."

"Pheromones." Mike eyed her. That was what she was going to blame this on—some chemical excuse for the emotional connection between them?

"Or something." She shrugged weakly.

"I think it's more than pheromones," he said.

"Whatever it is doesn't matter! You want SWAT, and I want—" she glanced around at the street "—that picket fence and the garden."

"I know," he said.

"If anything, that altercation with Craig proved that I can't do this anymore. I need peace, and calm. I'm not emotionally equipped! Whatever thick skin I'd had before is gone. And I can't put my heart through the wringer for the sake of my clients anymore!"

"I'm not just a client, Paige." Whatever became of them, he needed her to acknowledge that.

"I know." She swallowed. "You've become a whole lot more than a client."

Hearing her admit it made him feel better.

"I wish there was some middle ground,"

he said. "I don't think feelings like these come around too often in one lifetime."

"I can't be a part of this public service life anymore, Mike," she said quietly. "I can't. I'm so tired of it all, and if my…guy… were going out there in a bulletproof vest, crashing through windows and rolling cars, shooting back at bad guys… I can't just wait at home and hope for the best. I know your future isn't here in Eagle's Rest. You've been really up front about that. Besides, what use is a picket fence if my…guy…is constantly facing all the mayhem I'm trying to avoid? My heart would be out there with him!"

"Your boyfriend," he said.

"What?" she asked feebly.

"Say it. Your boyfriend."

Color tinged her cheeks. "I don't want to."

He laughed. "Fine. I get it. You can't deal with mayhem anymore, even by proxy."

"I can't."

"Got it." He was trying to stay upbeat here, but the joy of the moment was seeping away. And this was where the regret came in, because she was right. There was no use starting something if it couldn't go anywhere. It didn't matter how beautiful she was, or how she stirred his heart. There was no future here. There was no middle ground.

The older man with the dog sauntered toward them down the sidewalk. He walked with a limp, and he stopped every couple of feet while the dog sniffed the leaves, bushes and grass of the next lawn. The dog raised a leg and peed.

"Hi," Mike said with a nod as they passed him on the sidewalk.

"Nice day, huh?" the older man said with a smile.

"Oh, yeah," Mike agreed. "Great weather."

They waited until they'd gotten past him by another yard before Mike said, "So what do we do?"

"What do you mean?" she asked.

"We both feel this," he said. "What do we do about it?"

"We don't kiss each other," she said simply. "Or hold hands. Or… I don't know… anything that would be romantic."

Mike had a feeling that the most mundane of activities could turn romantic with this woman. But if she wanted to keep things professional, he could respect that.

"You're right, of course," he said. "I'm

not planning on staying in Eagle's Rest, and playing with feelings this strong seems foolish."

"It does, doesn't it?" She looked up at him in relief. "I don't want my heart broken, Mike."

"I don't normally admit to this, but I feel the same way," he said. "I've got a boy to raise now, and I've got to figure out how to help my sister, and I'm aiming at SWAT. I need to keep things on an even keel in my private life."

"And that makes sense, too. Okay," she said, her voice firming. "So we're agreed. We don't do that again—no more kissing. We keep things on a strictly professional level."

"Yeah, sure. We can do that."

They turned down another street, and Paige pointed at the next stop sign. "That's my street there."

"Oh…yeah." He hadn't noticed the direction they'd been walking.

"I'll just head home," she said. "I'm sure you have other things to do."

He didn't, but now didn't seem like the time to admit to that.

"Paige, I think we could call ourselves friends at this point," he said.

"I don't tend to kiss my buddies," she said with a shake of her head. "That's a line for me."

He could hear the mild sarcasm in her voice.

"I'm just saying, we don't have to act like strangers to get this balanced out," he said.

She met his gaze for a moment, then smiled impishly. "It's not just you, Mike. I feel this, too. We've got a really powerful attraction between us. I think it's probably safer to stay as far from that line as possible. For me."

That changed things a bit, and he swallowed. "Okay."

"So about that visit to Liv and the new baby tomorrow. I'll take Benjie with me in the morning, and we'll be back at your place by lunch."

So professional. He could already feel the change in her.

"Yeah…sure. No problem," he said.

"Okay." She met his gaze one last time, and he could see the emotion swimming in those blue eyes. She was holding things together, and he wasn't making it any easier. "I'm going to head home. I'll see you tomorrow."

"See you tomorrow," he said quietly, and she slipped past the stroller and headed down the street. He watched her go, then heaved a sigh.

If only these feelings *were* a simple chemical thing. This wasn't pheromones. This could be blamed on the fact that she was perfect for him in every way except the most important one. She couldn't accept his career, and being a cop was a part of him on a bone-deep level. Plus, he wanted his sister in his life, and that would never be smooth—there would be drama, pain, complication. He was going to be the guy raising his sister's child—and nothing was going to be easy about that.

He knew full well a relationship with Paige wouldn't work.

But he had a feeling that with that kiss, he'd just lost a friendship with the one woman who really understood him.

PAIGE HEADED UP the side stairs to the apartment above Hylton Books the next morning,

Benjie's car seat in one hand. Outside it was chilly and overcast, and the warmth of the hallway was a welcome relief from the biting wind. She'd glanced in the display window on her way in, and the store looked pretty busy—several shoppers were waiting in line at the register, and a few more were browsing. That was good news for Liv.

Benjie's car seat was growing heavier by the second. He might be a tiny baby, but with the car seat added in, her arm was getting sore. At the top of the staircase, she put down the car seat and the gift bag she'd brought. She knocked on Liv's door. She could hear a soft voice inside, and the reedy cry of a newborn.

Benjie was still asleep, and when the door opened, she saw Liv with a baby in her arms and her hair pulled back in a messy bun. Her eyes looked heavy, and her pale skin showed the discoloration beneath her auburn lashes caused by lack of sleep.

"Hey, girl," Liv said, stepping back. "Come on in. Is it ever good to see you!"

Liv cuddled a pink-wrapped baby in her arms, looking down into the little face with an exhausted expression. The baby started to

whimper again. "What do you want, Ava?"
Liv asked helplessly. "Oh, my goodness. I've
never been this tired in my life!"

Paige picked up the car seat and came inside. The apartment had all sorts of baby
accoutrements—a swing, a bassinet, three
boxes of diapers piled up in a pillar in one
corner. Liv closed the door behind her, and
Paige pulled the blankets off Benjie so that
he wouldn't overheat, leaving just one blue
afghan tucked around him.

"Ava is twice as big as Benjie already!"
Paige said with a grin. "She's beautiful, Liv."

"Isn't she?" Liv smiled. "I'm smitten, I
must say. Come on in and sit down. I put
the kettle on."

"Sounds great." Paige followed Liv into
the kitchen.

"I think she's hungry," Liv said. "Again.
She just eats and eats."

"Sit down and feed her," Paige said. "Benjie's sleeping. I can make tea."

"Would you?" Liv shot her a grateful smile
and grabbed a baby blanket from the back
of a chair. She draped the blanket over her
shoulder, adjusted herself and then leaned
back with a sigh as the baby stopped her

fussing. "They tell you that you'll never feel rested again, but I didn't believe them."

"Who told you?" Paige chuckled.

"My entire family." Liv smiled wanly.

"She'll sleep through the night eventually," Paige said. "She won't be eating this often when she's ten."

"She better not." Liv laughed, and her gaze moved to the car seat. "That is one cute little guy you're taking care of. How big is he?"

"Five pounds—a bit more now. He's been growing. I have to remind Mike to make a doctor's appointment to check."

"I had the lactation consultant come by yesterday, and she weighed Ava. She's almost eight pounds now. Imagine if she'd been born at forty weeks."

"Right?" Paige laughed. It felt good to settle in for a chat with her friend at long last. "Oh, I brought you something." Paige held up the bag. "You want me to open it for you?"

"You're a mind reader."

Paige lifted out the tissue paper, and then pulled out a set of newborn pants and tops.

"So cute!" Liv gushed. "Thank you so much, Paige! I'll get a lot of use out of these."

"So how was the delivery?" Paige asked.

"Twelve hours of active labor, and the worst pain I've ever experienced." Liv smoothed a hand over the baby's rump. "Jack was amazing. He sat next to me the entire time and told me I was a titan for doing this. He got me ice chips, helped me walk, helped me sit on the exercise ball... I mean, he was so patient. As for me, I wasn't at my most graceful. I told him he'd never touch me again."

Paige belted out a laugh. "In your defense, you were in agony. How'd he take that?"

"Like the perfect husband he is," Liv replied with a smile. "He was great. When she was born, he was the first one to hold her, and he passed her over to me, and we just stared at her. And...it made every minute of childbirth worth it."

Paige blinked back some tears in her eyes. This was what Paige wanted one day—a husband, a baby of her own, maybe her own business. But not with a cop.

"I'm really happy for you, Liv."

"Thanks." Liv licked her lips. "Now I've

been talking baby stuff every waking minute. What's going on with you? I need a window into the adult world."

Paige sobered. "I think I'm going to quit my job."

"Seriously?" Liv straightened, and when the baby gave an irritated cry, she peeked under the blanket, then leaned back again. "So, you've decided?"

"You thought I just needed a break, too, huh?" Paige said.

"Kind of. You really did love your job. I mean, for a long time you did at least. It was everything to you."

"I can't take it anymore," Paige said. "I get so emotionally involved. I care too much. I'm making the same mistake with Mike!"

"You mean, you're developing feelings for him?" Liv asked, her eyebrows rising.

Paige felt heat in her cheeks and she sighed. "We, um, kissed yesterday."

"Well, now! That's the window I was looking for!" Liv shot her a grin.

"It was a bad idea," Paige replied quickly.

"The best kisses are," her friend replied with a wink. "So how did that happen?"

Paige sighed. "We were walking down a

secluded street. He had Benjie in the stroller, and we were talking, and it was getting really personal, and our eyes met, and... I don't know! He kissed me. And I...kissed him, too."

The memory of his lips coming down, then hovering over hers as he waited for her to smack him or something, flooded her thoughts. He'd been so strong, so confident, but also so in control. If she'd made any indication that she hadn't wanted that kiss, he would have stopped. She knew that for a fact, but she *had* wanted it—maybe even more than he had—because once his warm lips had covered hers, she found herself pulling him closer.

What was wrong with her? She knew all the logical reasons that Mike wasn't the right guy for her, but the memory of that kiss made her heart speed up.

"I had a feeling you two would click. He's a good guy, Paige. He and Jack have been friends for, like, ten years. He's really decent."

"It isn't about how decent he is," Paige replied. "I need to get away from it all. Cops deal with the worst segments of society. And

PATRICIA JOHNS 253

when cops are done their job, they call in Social Services to help clean the mess up. I was a part of that system for seven years, and something inside me has just...snapped. I can't do it!"

"He's a cop in Eagle's Rest, though," Liv said.

"He doesn't want to stay here," Paige said with a shake of her head. "He wants to join the SWAT team in the city. He wants to go chase down the baddest of the bad guys."

"Do you love him?" Liv asked softly.

"Oh, I don't think we're there," Paige said quickly. "But I like him a lot. He's sweet, handsome..."

"He could bench-press a small car," Liv said with deadpan solemnity.

Paige chuckled. "Yeah, yeah. He's strong and all filled with testosterone. He's definitely hard to resist, but I'm going to have to."

"I remember saying that very thing about Jack to my aunt," Liv said with a small smile.

"I'm serious. I mean, you're married to a cop. You've been married to two of them! So you'd know—is it possible to stay insulated from all the ugly stuff, have your white picket fence and just be a regular civilian?"

Liv's expression fell. "No."

Paige didn't know what she'd been hoping for, but her friend's honesty was sobering.

"The thing is, in a marriage you have to be able to share everything," Liv said. "If you don't, a chasm starts to form between you and it's really hard to bridge. You don't want him to stop telling you stuff! My first husband tried to keep me on one side of that gulf while he worked on the other side. It didn't work. Evan ended up cheating on me. He was also a criminal, so there was that…"

Paige nodded. "Yeah, there was that…"

"Anyway, I made Jack promise it would be different with him. I didn't want to be cut out of his life. Cops are a unique breed. Their job is more than a career, it's who they are. Even ex-cops look like cops, you know? I'm convinced they're born that way. It's in their DNA. So Jack tells me everything. If I love him, I have to be the one he can come to when he needs to talk. I have to be his soft place to fall."

"And that all makes perfect sense," Paige replied, but sadness swelled inside her chest.

"Mike is a good guy, though," Liv said. "I can tell you that much."

"I know," Paige replied, trying to swallow the lump that rose in her throat. "He's a great guy. But I can't be the soft place for him. My heart can't take it—all the pain and heartbreak that happens out there. I'm not tough enough anymore."

Liv shot her a sympathetic look. "I'm sorry."

"Don't be," Paige said, forcing a smile. "I'm fine. He needs help with Benjie, and I'm providing that for another few days. That's it. This is a job, and I know my tendency to get emotionally involved. That's all it is."

Which was a lie, because it was more than that. If he were a client, she wouldn't be falling for him. There had never been danger of that with any client before... But Mike wasn't just a client. He was a cop and part of the same team. He might need her help with Benjie, but she'd needed his with Craig. Still, she could guard her heart. They were attracted to each other—a simple fact. She could curb that.

"We need tea," Liv said, and she pulled Ava out from under the blanket and put her up onto her shoulder. "Tea solves every-thing."

And while that wasn't true, it was the kind of comforting thought that she would cling to. Paige took the teapot and poured two cups of tea, sliding one toward her friend. The life she wanted included a garden, pots of tea and all the regular concerns and joys of ordinary people.

Was it so wrong to just want to be or-dinary?

CHAPTER TWELVE

THAT EVENING WHEN Mike got home from work, he unlocked the front door and let himself into the house. He'd been kicking himself all day about that kiss. He'd crossed lines with Paige yesterday in ways he never should have done. Sure, the kiss had been mutual, but what had he been thinking? He wasn't planning on sticking around Eagle's Rest long, so what kind of guy was he to toy with a woman's emotions? It wasn't like him.

Except he hadn't been toying. His kiss had been sincere. There was something about Paige that made him want to open up, and he wasn't normally that kind of guy. He didn't talk about his feelings; he beat up punching bags or went to the gun range like he did this afternoon. That had always worked just as well for him, but with Paige... Whatever. It didn't matter what she did to him or how she messed up his coping mechanisms. He couldn't offer her what she needed, so he had no business putting his ridiculous hopes for something more onto her. She was on stress leave, for crying out loud! What had he been thinking?

Add to that, the chief had asked him to work an overnight shift as a one-time favor. And he hadn't said no, yet. But he should have.

Mike closed the door behind him, and he heard the sound of Paige's voice from the living room. "Is that you, Mike?"

She came around the corner, Benjie in her arms. Her hair hung loose around her shoulders, and she looked sweet, a little rumpled, and for a moment, all thoughts slid back out of his head.

"Hi," she said. "How was your day?"

"Not bad," he replied. "How was yours?"

She lifted her shoulders. "It was nice to see Liv. Their baby is really cute."

"They tend to be…" He could feel the tension between them, and he wished there were a way to break it. But he only had himself to blame. If he'd been thinking yesterday instead of just going with his feelings…

"Are you wanting to get him onto a bottle schedule before day care starts? I think it would be a good idea. I can get him started on a proper feeding schedule tomorrow, if you like. It might make it easier for him to adjust to a day care setting."

"Stop it, Paige. I don't want to be professional," he countered. "Not...like this."

"I don't know how else to do this," she said, shaking her head, and for the first time frustration shone through. That was more real. At least she was showing some honest emotion.

"I don't want to be colleagues with you. I want to be friends," he said.

"Like I said before, I don't have many buddies I've kissed."

"Me, neither," he said. "It was one mistake, Paige. I think we can forgive ourselves that, don't you? Because I can't just talk bottle schedules and diaper sizes with you. We can't pretend that we don't know each other as well as we do. We're more than that now."

"This is my problem!" Tears welled in Paige's eyes. "I always do this! I get emotionally involved with my clients, and—"

"Not like this," he countered.

"Not exactly," she admitted. "Not romantically obviously. This is a novel way for me to mess things up."

He couldn't help but smile. "I think we agreed that I'm a whole lot to blame there. And you didn't mess anything up. I happen to agree with everyone else about you—your heart in your work makes you one of the best."

"I just… I overstep." She winced. "And I obviously overstepped with you."

"Hey." He lowered his voice and met her gaze. "You know I don't just want to be your job."

"Like it or not, you are," she said. That stung—even if it was technically true.

"Then I'm letting you off the hook when it comes to me. You're here for Benjie, that's it. And with me…whatever this is? It *is* personal. Okay?"

"I think we covered that," she said with a shake of her head. "We can't do this!"

"I didn't say we'd cross any lines," he countered. "But we can admit that we're more than professional acquaintances here. You mean something to me. And if that complicates things, so be it."

"What do I mean to you?" she asked softly.

"I don't even know. I just… I care about you. And a whole lot more than I care about the chief, if you know what I mean. And I know we can't be more than friends—I've accepted that. But I'm not going to pretend that we're less than friends, either."

She licked her lips. "Okay."

"Yeah?" He eyed her uncertainly. "What part of that?"

She laughed. "We're friends. Maybe with weird boundaries, but we're definitely past professional. I'm okay with that."

"Okay, then…" He nodded a couple of times. He wasn't sure what else to say now that they'd agreed on that.

"Benjie's diaper is changed," she said. "Did you want me to stay for a few minutes until you've settled in, or…"

"No, I'm fine," he replied. Friend or not, he had to learn how to do this on his own. "I appreciate all of this, Paige. I really do."

"My pleasure." She reached out and gently punched his arm. "Buddy."

He chuckled, and Paige eased the baby into his arms. Holding Benjie again felt good…it felt like coming home. When had that happened? Mike looked down at the little guy with a smile.

"Hey, there," he said softly.

Benjie blinked up at him, suddenly still. Those round eyes struggled to fix on him, so he lifted Benjie a little higher. He'd missed the baby while he was gone today. Like, really missed him. That was a new experience for Mike, and coming home was a relief. But he'd been thinking about Paige all day, too. This new experience of family seemed to be folding Paige into his heart at the same time as the baby.

"I guess I'll see you in the morning, then," Paige said, and she paused, her blue gaze meeting his for a moment before she grabbed her purse and jacket.

"Actually, just as I was leaving this evening, the chief asked if I'd take an overnight shift tomorrow," Mike said. "I said I'd get back to him. I can say no. I'll have to say no when Benjie's in a day care, so—"

"You'd want me to watch Benjie overnight?" Paige asked. She fixed him with an unreadable stare. Was he overstepping again? Maybe. He'd asked her to stay longer before—and it had sounded a whole lot like an invitation to stay the night. Was she questioning his motives here?

"If you wouldn't mind," he said. "You could come here—he's got all his stuff here. You could sleep in my bed if you want—I won't be here, after all. And Benjie's bassinet fits in right next to the bed. I know that's kind of a lot to ask, but…" He paused.

"I suppose I could," she replied.

"You could take the day off tomorrow, then. You know—get some time away from me—us." He smiled hopefully, and she didn't refute that, so maybe some time away from him was more welcome than he thought.

"All right," she said. "I suppose I could do that. So, I'll see you tomorrow evening, then. What time?"

"About six."

"Six. I can do that." She opened the side door, and a finger of cold air swept around her and into the house. "Bye, Mike."

He still liked the sound of his name on her lips. She closed the door firmly behind her, and he ambled into the living room, watching as she drove away.

"Just you and me, Benjie," Mike said, tucking the baby into the crook of his arm. "Did you have a good day? I got to escort a belligerent drunk guy out of a bar. That's as exciting as it got for me. But you got to be snuggled by Paige all day… I'll bet you liked that."

Mike flicked on the TV to a channel with some sitcom reruns, the tinned laugh track filling up the space in the little house. The day had been frustratingly slow, and he'd been looking forward to coming home to Paige this evening, even though he knew his time with her would be brief. But he missed her already.

Heck, she wasn't just someone to pass the time with, and they'd admitted that whatever they felt was probably beyond friendship. For him, it was stronger than anything he'd experienced before. Maybe it was just that Paige was so unlike the women he usually dated. She'd asked him if he ever wished he could be a civilian again. He didn't. But he did wonder what it would be like to be romantically involved with a civilian woman—someone normal and sweet. He wasn't sure he could hold it together, but he'd entertained the thought. And Paige lacked that tough veneer. She didn't have a strong exterior to chip away. She was tender and soft, and it was all on the surface.

"Stop being stupid," Mike muttered to himself. Because that's what he was—really dumb. Why was he torturing himself with this?

Mike glanced toward the kitchen, hungry. Some meat sauce and noodles would hit the spot. Besides, he needed to get his mind off Paige, if he could. As he turned, there was a knock at the front door.

Mike frowned. Was Paige back? Had she forgotten something? He halfway hoped so—seeing her again tonight would be real treat. Maybe he could convince her to stay for dinner.

He grabbed a baby blanket off the back of the couch to wrap around Benjie before he opened it, and he pulled open the door.

For a moment, his mind only registered the sight of a slim woman standing on his doorstep. She had a floppy bag over her shoulder and a jean jacket that didn't look warm enough for the cold night. Her hair was stringy, her skin gaunt and pockmarked; her eyes looked too big for her head. A gust of wind blew her hair against her face, and when she reached up to push it back, he saw the fingernails had all been chewed down to the quick. She stared at him for a couple of beats, holding her hair away from her eyes, then that agonized gaze turned to the baby in his arms.

"Is that Benjamin?" she breathed. "Oh, my God..." Tears welled up in her eyes. "Oh, my God..."

"Jana?" he gasped. He hardly recognized her—she was a shell of the girl he remembered, and she looked so much older than he was, even though she was the younger sister. Her life—the drugs—had worked her over, and his heart swelled, hammering past the overflow of unnameable emotions. She looked so broken, so fragile, and yet so hard. And against all those odds, his little sister had found him.

Jana's gaze hadn't moved from Benjie, and tears welled in her large, brown eyes. "I just need to hold my baby..."

PAIGE WAS ALMOST HOME, and the streets were dark. The houses she drove past were glowing from within, people passing windows, TVs flickering. There was something so lonely about looking in from the outside.

One day, she hoped to have a family of her own. She wanted to come home to a family—kids, homework checks, a husband with a great smile. She wanted all of that so badly she could taste it some days, but until her own life was in order, she wouldn't be able to look around for a nice guy.

Why was it that when she imagined that future family lately, the husband was muscular and sweet, and looked a whole lot like Mike McMann? And when she thought about holding a baby of her own, the little face looking up at her was Benjie's. It was only further proof that she needed to get herself emotionally untangled. She was setting herself up for heartbreak here. She knew that. Mike and Benjie weren't hers, and she wouldn't allow herself to get more attached than she already was.

Friends. She could handle that—with a few boundaries. This wasn't about what Mike needed anymore, but what she needed. If she quit her job, she'd have to make sure she started fresh in everything, for her own good. Her heart was no game, and if she wouldn't allow her career to break it, then she wouldn't be less vigilant when it came to this burly cop.

Paige paused at a stop sign. She was tired, and a quiet evening at home was just what she needed right now. Her phone rang, and she idly wondered if it would be Nathan again. Or maybe Dad. Before she pulled forward again, she hit the speaker button, then stepped on the gas.

"Hello?" she said.

"Paige? It's Mike." His voice was tense, and Paige's anxiety ratcheted up a notch in response.

"Everything okay?" she asked.

"I, uh, could use a hand back here at the house, if you could come back."

"Yeah, sure." She signaled and pulled to the side of the road. "What's happening?"

"My sister's here."

His sister! Paige looked both ways to make sure the street was clear, then pulled a U-turn.

"I'm on my way," she assured him. "Is Jana okay?"

"More or less. I just need your insight. It's…complicated."

Wasn't it always? Human lives were never cut and dry. There were no good or bad people, for the most part, just hurt people trying to cope. And Jana had been through more than most. If she'd come to her brother, was she hoping to get her baby back?

"How did she find your house?" Paige blurted out.

"She asked at the coffee shop across the street from the police station, and some helpful citizen told her," he said, his tone emotionless. "A place this small, and there's no privacy at all. Not that it's bad. I'm glad she came out here. I'd asked her to, it's just—" He stopped.

"I know," she said. "It's complicated."

"Yeah. She misses Benjie something fierce. She's holding him right now."

She could hear the tremor of worry in his voice, and she had to wonder if that was a good idea…for Mike and Benjie at least. But Jana must be heartbroken, too. She'd given up her child. Paige could only imagine what that had done to her.

"Do you want me to contact my office? I can bring someone with me," she offered. She wasn't exactly the best person for this job, given her own emotional involvement.

"No," he said curtly. "This is personal. I don't want anyone else here right now. I haven't seen my sister in years, and… I'm asking you as a friend."

A friend with the right experience, though, she realized.

"I'm on my way, Mike," she said. "I'll see you soon."

Paige hung up and stepped on the gas, her heart accelerating with the speedometer. She didn't know what to expect, but she did know that Mike was torn between the sister he'd never been able to rescue and the vulnerable nephew he wanted to raise.

Ten minutes later, she pulled into Mike's driveway. There was an extra car there—the beaten up little hatchback must be Jana's. The curtains in the house were drawn, so she couldn't see inside, but the lights were on. She got out of the car and sucked in a lungful of night air. She could smell the smoke from someone's fireplace, the moldering of leaves, and she did her best to calm her own nerves with a breathing exercise. The last thing Mike and Jana needed was for her to be rattled.

Paige headed around to the side door, and she paused a moment and listened. She could hear voices from the kitchen. She knocked, and when the door opened, Mike gave her a look of unmitigated relief.

"Paige," he said, and he reached out, grabbed her hand and tugged her inside. There was something so natural about the gesture, but desperate, too. He didn't let go of her hand right away, and when she tugged her fingers free, his gaze flickered back down to her.

The kitchen was warm and smelled of toast. A woman sat at the kitchen table, a plate of untouched toast and a mug in front of her. She had Benjie in her arms, and she held him close, rocking back and forth in a gentle rhythm. She curved her thin body around the baby protectively.

"What's happening?" Paige whispered.

"I let my sister hold her son—she was desperate. And now she won't let him go." Mike scrubbed a hand through his hair. "Maybe she just needs more time. I don't know."

Jana looked up, watching them pointedly, her rocking not changing a bit. She had bags under her eyes and costume jewelry rings on her fingers. She looked like she'd applied a bit of makeup, but it was smudged around her eyes from tears.

"This is Paige," Mike said. "Paige, this is Jana, my little sister."

Jana eyed Paige suspiciously. "What does she want?"

"She's Benjie's nanny, at the moment," Mike said. "And my friend. I asked her to come by to help us talk it all out."

"There's nothing to talk about," Jana said, fresh tears brimming in her eyes. "This is my son. I gave your name at the hospital so I'd know where to find him and get him back. And now I'm here. That's it. There's nothing else to say!"

Paige dropped her bag on the counter and rubbed her hands together. "I could use some tea."

Mike and Jana both blinked at her. Paige shrugged out of her jacket and hung it on a hook by the door.

"It's cold out there," she said. "I feel frost in the air."

Jana didn't say anything, and Paige sat down opposite Jana with the table between them. She didn't want Jana to feel threatened right now, and she looked up at Mike, who stood frozen in the middle of the kitchen.

She needed to normalize the situation, calm everyone down.

"Tea?" she prompted, and Mike nodded, and headed for the kettle.

"You a cop?" Jana asked curtly.

"No," Paige said. "I'm a Social Services agent. On leave. So I'm not sure how much I even count. I've been standing in as Benjie's nanny."

"Benjamin," Jana said tersely. "His name is Benjamin."

"Sorry. Benjamin." Paige met the woman's gaze and gave her a smile. Jana didn't react. She was scared—that they'd forcibly take her son away? Maybe. She was running on maternal instinct right now, it seemed, and what mother could be blamed for wanting her own baby? But if she had drugs in her system, her anxiety might be off the charts for chemical reasons, as well.

"Here you go," Mike said, sliding a mug in front of her, a tea bag floating on top, and Paige smiled her thanks.

"I call him Benjie for short," Mike said, his deep voice reverberating through the kitchen. "It's my nickname for him."

Jana's gaze flickered up to her brother.

"So you're bringing in Social Services to handle me?"

"Jana, I'm just—" Mike pulled up a chair and sat down next to Paige. "You gave him up. I'm his legal guardian. You had twenty-four hours to change your mind, and it's been two weeks."

"I made sure he went to you," Jana retorted. "Because out of everyone, I thought I could trust my brother!"

"I know, and I'm glad you did," Mike said. "It was a solid choice. He should be with family. Jana, you can trust me. I want to help."

"And you have." Jana looked down at Benjie, tears misting her eyes. "So thank you. Now, I want him back."

Mike shot Paige a panicked look, and under the table, Paige put a hand on his.

"You should eat something," Paige said, nudging the plate of toast toward Jana.

"I'm not hungry."

"I know," Paige said. "But you're a mother, and you have to take care of yourself, too. You're still healing from childbirth."

Jana softened at that, and she reached for a piece of toast, nibbling the crust. A couple of crumbs fell onto Benjie's head, and she flicked them off, then took a proper bite. She chewed quickly, then shoved half the slice into her mouth.

"Did you see a doctor after you left the hospital?" Paige asked.

Jana shook her head and answered past the toast in her mouth. "Who can afford that?"

"I could get you in to see a doctor—no charge." Paige shrugged. "I know people who'd help."

Jana shook her head. "No."

She'd be scared of doctors, no doubt. And that was understandable.

"Are you in any pain from the delivery?" Paige asked. "Because if you are—"

"I'm fine, I said."

Paige didn't believe that. Childbirth was traumatic, at best. Her body would still be recuperating.

"What do you need?" Paige asked.

"My son." Jana's eyes flashed.

"I know, but in order to take care of him, you'll need some support, right?" Paige said. "Do you have an apartment? Do you have baby things—a crib, a car seat, formula?"

"He's mine!" Jana snapped. "You can't just take someone's baby away from them because they're broke! That doesn't make me any less his mother! I gave birth to him! I made sure he was safe. I dreamed of him, and thought of him, and tried to find a way to get out here to your dumpy town so I could get him back. I'm his mom. I'll figure it out. You can't just take away someone's baby!"

That wasn't exactly what had happened here. Jana had voluntarily given him up, and now she wanted him back. But pointing that out wasn't going to de-escalate this situation. Jana's hand trembled and Benjie started to cry. She shushed him and started to jiggle him—the movement not soothing to Benjie at all, because he started to cry louder, and Jana started to jiggle harder.

"Jana, slow down," Mike said. "You're going to hurt him."

"I'm not hurting him!" Jana's voice started to rise. "He's fine! He needs *me*!"

Benjie's cry intensified. Paige's heart hammered in her chest. All she wanted to do right now was to pry Benjie from his mother's arms, get him still, soothe those cries, but Jana was getting more and more agitated. She pushed her chair back and stood up, swinging back and forth as the baby wailed.

"Jana—" Paige rose to her feet at the same time as Mike. "Stop shaking him—"

"Shut up!" Jana shouted, and Paige wasn't sure if she was talking to her, or hollering at the baby.

"He's scared," Paige said, trying to keep her voice even. "I can take him for a few minutes, give you a break—"

"Shut up!" Jana repeated, stepping away from the table. "You think I believe you?"

Mike moved subtly toward the door.

"Jana," Paige began, but all she could see right now was Benjie's red, tear-streaked face, his little mouth open in a cry that was starting to get hoarse. He was terrified, his head lolling from side to side as she jerked him up and down in an effort to silence his cries. Jana was equally terrified, but Benjie was the one who'd get hurt.

"Stop acting like you know me!" Jana shouted. "You don't! What do you even know about me? I'm Benjamin's mother! I am! You can't have him! You can't take him away from me!"

And with that, Jana lunged for the door.

CHAPTER THIRTEEN

MIKE BOLTED INTO ACTION, sliding between the side door and his sister. He caught her by the shoulders, scared that she'd drop Benjie, or that he'd accidentally hurt her. The baby wailed, stretching out his arms and legs, his whole body rigid with anguish. Mike held Jana tight, and she struggled against him, twisting this way and that for a moment or two before she seemed to realize that she wouldn't get past him. Jana stopped, breathing hard.

"Jana, you can't just run off with him," Mike said. "And if you shake him, you'll give him brain damage. He's tiny—his brain can't handle that."

Tears rose in Jana's eyes and she looked down at Benjie in her arms. "I'm not hurting him—"

"Not on purpose," Mike said, and he loosened his hold on her shoulders. "But what felt like just a little jiggle to you is a whole lot more to him. He's too small for that. Let me hold him. I'm not running off. We'll sit down together and talk this out."

Jana looked toward the door once more, and for a moment he thought she might try to make another break for it, but then her face crumpled into tears. And she was just the same old Jana, again…the little sister who'd cried when she got frustrated, who'd yelled when she got mad and who seemed to have a storm of energy in her heart.

Even as kids, he'd been surprised when she'd suddenly cry. She'd go from Amazon woman to sobbing, and it had always thrown him off how thin that line was for her—what she could face and what she couldn't.

Paige came up next to Jana and slipped Benjie out of her arms. Paige cuddled him close against her chest, and the baby started to calm down, his sobs turning into hic-cuppy shudders. Mike's shoulders relaxed and he sucked in a stabilizing breath. He'd been a fool to just hand Benjie over to Jana, but what was he supposed to do?

Benjie was his sister's child. And she was heartbroken at having given up her baby. All this time, he'd been so scared that she needed more care than she was getting. She just wanted to hold her baby, to be near him, and what mother wouldn't want to take her baby back again?

Except Benjie needed more than Jana could give him.

"Jana," Mike said quietly. "Come talk to me."

"I have nothing to say to you!" she hissed.

"We've got a whole lot to say to each other!" he snapped. "Fifteen years you've stayed away from me! What did I do to you? How did I deserve that?"

Jana blinked up at him, then wrapped her arms around herself. "Like you even cared!"

"Me?" Mike shook his head. "I looked for you! Every weekend, every evening, I went to the city and I combed the streets hoping to catch sight of you somewhere. I became a cop *for you*!"

"For me?" Jana shook her head. "That was dumb. I hate cops."

The irony was thick, and he knew it. But it hadn't only been for his ability to track her down.

"If someone was going to hurt you, I

wanted a gun and a badge so I could do something about it."

Plus, he never wanted to be sideswiped like that again. He wanted to know the worst, not hide from it. If he was going to be emotionally gutted, he at least wanted to see it coming.

Jana's gaze softened, and Mike nudged her back toward the chair.

"Eat some toast," he murmured, and she sank back down again. She'd always liked toast back when they were kids. She'd butter it so meticulously, making sure every square millimeter was covered, and now toast seemed like the best thing a brother could offer.

Jana reached for the slice she'd started, and she took another bite. She looked skinny—the hungry kind of skinny.

"Why did you run away to begin with?" he asked quietly. "I've asked myself that a million times. Because you had a family! Grandma might have been tired, but she loved you. And I was always on your side."

"No, you weren't," she said, shaking her head. "You were on your own side."

"If I'd known—"

"And you never liked my boyfriend."

Not when he'd seen what the relationship was doing to her, at least.

"You aren't with him anymore, so maybe my instincts weren't so off," he retorted.

"And when I did call you, you wouldn't give me money!" she added.

Yeah, not quite how it all went down. He'd given her money several times until he realized he was just helping her get more drugs. So he'd stopped—begged her to get help. But this was the addict talking, the woman who would say anything to get her next fix.

"Jana, you love your son," he said seriously. "I know that. But you can't go on like this. You won't survive, and you're no good to him in this state."

"I'm no good?" she demanded. "And you ask why I ran away to begin with."

Her words stung, and he sucked in a shaky breath.

"I didn't mean it like that," he said with a sigh. "You need help. You need to get off the drugs, get your life cleaned up. Like this, you won't be able to be much of a mom. I'm sorry. And you could be better than this."

"Or what?" she demanded. "What will you do? Keep my son away from me?"

"No," he said with a shake of his head. "I'm not threatening you, Jana. I'm your brother—I care. Look, you gave Benjamin up, gave him to me. And I'm going to take good care of him. And he'll always know who his mom is. I'm not going to keep you from him. I want him to know you! You need to be in his life. But you have to think—what is Benjamin going to think of a mom who's strung out? What's that going to do to him?"

Jana's lips trembled, and she looked away.

"But if you got clean," he went on, "if you kicked the drugs and got a job and an apartment, then he'd be proud of you."

Jana's hands trembled and she looked toward Paige, who stood at the door into the living room, rocking Benjie back and forth. Benjie had settled against her neck, snuggling in as close as he could, and Paige met Mike's gaze.

"Here—" Paige came over to the table and slid into the seat next to Jana. She adjusted Benjie in her arms, then reached out and took Jana's hand, laying it gently over Benjie's leg. Tears spilled down Jana's cheeks again as she touched her baby's soft skin, her fingers running over his leg and foot.

"I can't do it," Jana whispered. "I tried quitting before. I can't stop."

"There is a detox program close by here," Paige said quietly. "I could get you in, if you wanted it. Once you were checked in, though, it would be fifteen weeks before you were allowed back out again."

"What would they do there?" Jana asked.

"They give you counseling, help to get the drugs out of your system, help you get a plan for the future. There are other narcotics programs that could help you after that. I'm not saying it would be easy, Jana, but you could do it if you decided it was worth it."

"And if I fail?" Jana whispered.

"You try again," Mike replied. "Jana, Benjie needs to know his mom, and he needs a mother he can look up to. Don't be like our mom—"

"I'm not like her!" Jana retorted. "She just left us. She never came back. Where am I right now? I came back!"

Had their mother ever wrestled with her choice to leave them? Did she lie in bed in night like Jana had, dreaming of the kids she'd walked away from?

"You're right," he admitted. "But you

know as well as I do, if you don't get off the drugs, they'll get stronger than you are, and you won't be able to fight them anymore. It won't be you, it'll be the drugs. And Benjie will grow up like we did, wondering why his mom disappeared on him."

"I love my baby!" Jana said, her voice trembling. "I'd do anything for him."

"Then get clean for him!" Mike pleaded. "Do it for me, too, while you're at it. I need my sister back."

Because every day that she'd been gone, he'd missed her. And he'd blamed himself. She'd wanted freedom with a druggie boyfriend who was too old for her. She'd wanted her family to stand back and let do whatever felt good. So maybe he couldn't fix everything for her.

What felt good to his sister right now could be lethal to her newborn.

"I don't know," Jana breathed. "I have to think about it."

"Okay, that's fair," he said.

"But I need a place to stay tonight."

She couldn't stay here. Mike knew the chances of her taking off with Benjie were just too high.

"There is a women's shelter here in town. There are some private rooms available," Paige said, glancing over at Mike. It was like she'd read his mind, and he smiled gratefully. "I can get you set up in one of those."

"And I need some money," Jana added.

"No," Mike said quietly. "I'm sorry, Jana. No more cash."

Jana didn't respond. Her hand slipped off Benjie's leg and she reached for the last of her toast.

"I'm going to call the night line," Paige said, standing up. "I'll arrange a place for you to stay, Jana."

She slipped Benjie into Mike's arms and went to her purse to get her phone. Benjie snuggled in close to Mike, and he looked down at the baby and wondered what life would throw at this kid.

But this much Mike could swear—he'd protect Benjie better than he'd managed to protect his sister.

PAIGE STOOD ON Main Street with her umbrella in one hand and a hot coffee in the other, the rain pattering down in a soothing rhythm. Last night had been intense. She'd driven Jana to the women's shelter and seen her comfortably settled. Mike had sent a pair of Benjie's tiny socks so that she could have a small reminder of why she was doing all of this.

It was after midnight before Paige got to bed, and the next morning, her boss had called her in to get all the information about Jana's situation to pass along to the agent who would be taking her case.

"Would you like to take the lead on Jana's case?" her boss, Genevieve Martin, asked earnestly.

"No, this one is personal for me," she said. "I can't stay objective."

And it was far too personal, because she was falling for this cop, whether it was smart or not. And when she'd seen Jana desperate for her baby, Paige had been wondering just how heartbreaking it would be to be the stepmom in that family dynamic—the one who wasn't Benjie's biological mother, but who would do all the emotional heavy lifting. Except she couldn't be that stepmom—what was she even thinking?

"You're good at this job," Genevieve had said. "Really good. You're one of the best I've ever worked with. You de-escalated that situation, provided a solution and even managed to convince the client to take this next step in her sobriety. You make a difference, Paige. You really do."

And those were the words running through Paige's mind as she crossed the rainy street. She didn't know where she was going—just walking. It felt good to be out in the fresh air, on these familiar streets.

Home was more than a place, it was a feeling, a collection of memories and hopes for the future. And Eagle's Rest was all of those things for Paige, including an image in her mind of the future she longed for. Was it selfish to want some peace and beauty for herself?

Paige glanced over at the hardware store display—this time of year, it was showing a selection of metal fire pits. She continued on, passing another few shops, crossing another street, before she came to Hylton Books. Paige glanced inside the wide window, taking in the shelves of books, the stuffed chairs by the colorful children's books. She loved Liv's store, and as her gaze swept through her view of the store, she spotted her friend, baby Ava strapped across her chest with a brightly patterned wrap. Liv saw her at the same time and a smile broke over her face. She waved, then beckoned for Paige to come in.

Paige wasn't in the mood to talk, but being alone wasn't helping much, either. She headed for the side door and shook out her umbrella as she came inside, the bell overhead tinkling cheerfully.

"Hey, girl!" Liv said. "Where's Benjie?"

"I have the day off," Paige said. "I'll take care of him overnight tonight."

"Oh, okay." Ava squirmed, and Liv smoothed a hand over her baby's back. Liv smiled tenderly down at her daughter, then shot Paige a grin. "It's nice to see you."

"What are you doing here?" Paige asked. "Aren't you supposed to be taking a few weeks off?"

"My part-timer called in sick again." Liv leaned over to give Paige a one-armed hug. "Is it terrible that I was relieved? It's an excuse to get back down here, smell some new books."

Paige cocked her head to one side to get a peek at Ava's little face. "It's your store. You have every right, I figure."

Liv moved the wrap so that Paige could

get a better look. Ava was fast asleep, nestled against her mother's chest. So small. So sweet.

"Are you getting any more sleep?" Paige asked.

"My aunt came over yesterday morning and held Ava for four hours while I slept like the dead," Liv said. "She's a saint."

"Sounds like it."

This was how a new mother was supposed to be supported—family and friends who checked in on her, helped her rest. Jana didn't have any of it, and Paige could empathize with how hard it was for her.

"I feel so much better," Liv said. "You have no idea."

"I'll get a small taste of what you're going through tonight," Paige said.

"Yes, you will." Liv laughed softly.

"I'm not sure I like how much you're enjoying that." Paige chuckled, and the two women exchanged a grin.

"You'll survive," Liv said. "It's good for character, or something."

It was a taste of being a mom. Paige hadn't thought of it that way until now. She was trying to keep herself from getting too emotionally involved with Benjie, though it didn't seem to be working. This time with him and Mike was a bittersweet taste of the life she longed for—kids of her own, a husband. A family.

"Did you hear about that vacant lot on Belleview Avenue?" Liv asked.

"No," Paige said. "What about it?"

"Well, the town council is voting to turn it into a community garden," Liv replied. "Old Lisa Ellison died last month, right? Turns out that she left it to the town, and they've been considering what to do with it. Jack heard about it this morning. I thought of you right away. I mean, I know you have your own garden you never quite get to, but I figured it might interest you, anyway."

"A community garden?" The idea did spark a certain excitement inside her. "How would they run it? Would it be rented out in plots, or would everyone work together on one large garden?"

"No idea," Liv said. "They'll probably need someone to run it, too, for that matter."

"My mom would have loved that."

"Your mom could make anything grow," Liv replied. "Remember when she won the biggest pumpkin contest?"

Paige smiled. Yes, her mother had had a

green thumb, and Paige had inherited that penchant for plants. Except she'd been too busy the last years to do much about it. Her own garden plot was horribly grown over, but there was still potential there.

"So what are you going to do with yourself today?" Liv asked, changing the subject.

"I think I'm doing it," Paige replied. "I already had a quick meeting with Genevieve."

"Oh?" Liv perked up. "Going back to work?"

"No, Mike's sister showed up at his place last night," Paige replied. "Benjie's mom. She was a wreck, and I helped get her set up at the women's shelter. We're trying to help her get into a rehab center, and…" She winced, remembering the agony in the distraught woman's eyes when Paige had taken her baby back out of her arms. "She misses her baby."

"Do you think she'll get him back eventually?" Liv asked, her hand fluttering protectively to her own baby's rump.

"She gave him up," Paige said. "But Mike loves his sister, and he wants what's best for her. From what I can tell, he wants Jana in Benjie's life, but he wants to be the one raising him."

"And is there room for a stepmom in that equation?" Liv asked.

A stepmom… The question echoed Paige's earlier thoughts. Would Jana be able to stay clean? And if she could, would she try to get her son back? There would be constant complication there—nothing would be easy. Paige knew that from experience—life got messy. Paige was trying to get away from this heartbreak, not court more of it.

Paige shook her head. "That isn't my business, is it?"

Liv smiled faintly. "It sounds tough."

"Yeah." Paige sighed. "But she's in no shape to care for her son, love him though she does."

"It would be really hard to give up a baby," Liv said, and tears sparkled in her eyes. "I don't know how she did it."

"She wanted him to be safe," Paige said. "And she knew he wouldn't be safe with her. She missed him just as much as you'd imagine she would." A lump rose in her throat. "She just wanted to be with him. It was hard to watch."

"What did you do?" Liv asked, a catch in her voice.

"Once she was at the woman's shelter, I handed her care over to one of my associates, and then I went home and cried," Paige said, and she blinked back a veil of tears. "And after a good long cry, I knew I couldn't keep doing this—any of this. I can't take it."

Outside, a crack of lightning lit up the street, and then a couple of seconds later, a roll of thunder peeled. Paige looked out the window, watching the downpour. It was getting heavier, and the wind gusted blasts of rain against the window. Inside, the warm book-and-coffee-scented air wrapped around her like a favorite sweater.

"I get it," Liv said softly.

"Is it selfish?" Paige asked, turning back to her friend. "I want *this*." She glanced around herself, wondering how to put that aroma into words. "I've been thinking about opening a day care—just a small one. I think about taking the kids on walks, you know, where the kids are holding a rope. I think of coffee at the corner coffee shop on a Sunday morning, gardening in my backyard… I want to get married, have kids of my own.

I want to stop in your bookstore on a slow morning, and just browse the titles. I want to plan a nice dinner for my family…learn how to make strudel. I just thought of that now—but I do! It wouldn't be an extravagant life, but it would be happy, and I'd finally have an evening where I wasn't plagued by my most recent client's heartbreaking situation. I want all the sweet things, without the steady dose of heartbreak. But that means I'm giving up on all the people who need me!"

"Paige," Liv interrupted. "That life sounds beautiful. And you deserve it."

"But what about my clients?" Paige asked, lifting her shoulders helplessly. "While I build that life for myself, fenced off from the things that break my heart, what about them?"

"Not everyone wants that fenced-off life," Liv asked. "For some people, a calm life of gardening and day care management in Eagle's Rest sounds painfully boring. So does running a bookshop, for that matter. Not everybody wants what you want. You shouldn't feel guilty for following through on building the life you long for. Isn't that the very skill you're trying to teach your clients?"

It was true—even Mike wanted out of

here, off to some exciting city where he could be a SWAT cop in the middle of the action.

"And for the clients that do want the kinds of things I want?" Paige asked.

"There are people who can pick up the torch where you laid it down," Liv replied, "people who are put together a little differently. You don't have to burn yourself to cinders to keep other people warm."

And yet, the guilt was real. But that thought of the community garden was still tickling at the back of her mind. A garden where people could push their fingers into the soil, clean up weeds, see plants grow and thrive. Kids could learn how to grow their own food. Neighbors could harvest and share the produce. There could be meaningful work for people who wanted to find the serenity of slow growth.

Maybe for the people who wanted the same life she longed for, there could be a little garden waiting for them as they worked their way through their own tough stuff. Was it okay to be a guidepost farther down the path?

CHAPTER FOURTEEN

MIKE PUT THE tabs down on the tiny diaper, then slid Benjie into his warm sleeper. It was almost second nature now, and it took only a couple of minutes to get Benjie dressed. There was one regular newborn sleeper that Benjie finally fit into. Only one. The others were all too big. But it still felt like an accomplishment.

"How're you doing, buddy?" Mike said, snapping the clasps shut as the baby stretched his arms and legs, making a disgruntled face. "I know, I'm almost done. You want your bottle, don't you?"

A week ago, he'd been looking around for Paige to tell him what to do, and now he knew Benjie's cues as well as she did.

That morning, he'd taken Benjie to the doctor for a checkup. He just wanted to be sure, and he needed to take him anyway. The doctor had squeezed them in and reassured Mike that all was well—the drama from the night before hadn't hurt the baby. He'd been so relieved he'd teared up.

All the same, Mike had to wonder what it was like for Benjie to have seen Jana again. Did Benjie know that Jana was his mother? Had his little infant heart felt a connection to her? Benjie seemed happy enough to stay snuggled in Mike's arms, but Mike couldn't help but wonder what the future would hold. Would Benjie resent Mike for having kept him from being raised by his mom? How would Jana tell this story? Was Mike the bad guy in her version?

He picked up the baby, using his fingers to support the back of his head, and he looked down into that little face. His sister was thinking about this baby right now, he had no doubt. Her heart was aching for him. The image of his sister's desperate longing as she looked at Benjie in his arms had seared itself into his brain, and he wasn't sure that he'd ever forgive himself for the pain he'd caused her. But what choice did he have? If he left her alone with Benjie, she'd run, and Benjie might not survive it. This baby needed more.

But was Mike enough? Was the fact that

he'd bonded with the baby, fallen for the kid in spite of it all, enough to make this moral claim to raise him? Legally, he was Benjie's guardian, and when he sorted out the paperwork, he would be his adoptive father.

And yet, when he thought of his sister, he was still just as protective of her as when she was that lanky eleven-year-old from his favorite photo. Just a kid. Hopeful, kind of ticked off with the world already, and so vulnerable to all the bad guys out there. He hadn't been strong or insightful enough to protect her back then, either. He still felt out of his depth.

Mike was already in uniform and had some futile hopes of getting out the house without milk or spit-up on his dark blue uniform shirt. At the very least, he knew that Jack would be in the same situation. Mike cradled Benjie in the crook of his arm and reached for the bottle. He'd already warmed it—the kid was primed for food. He popped the nipple into Benjie's searching mouth, and the baby settled into slurping back the formula.

Mike looked at the clock on the cable box. He didn't have much time until his shift started, and he was looking forward to see-ing Paige again. In the midst of this confu-sion, she was his one light. She made him feel calmer, more in control. She made all of this feel just a little less crazy. And hav-ing her here tonight—watching over Benjie, keeping the peace, would make him feel a whole lot better.

As if on cue, he heard the rumble of an engine in his drive. He went to the window. The sun was sinking low behind the moun-tains, the shadows from the trees in his front yard stretching out long. Paige got out of her car carrying a slightly larger bag over her shoulder. He watched her for a moment, her movements as she hitched the bag up onto her shoulder and fiddled with her key fob. A beep announced the car was locked. She looked up and saw him in the window, and he waved.

The relief he felt in having her here wasn't just for Benjie. It was for him, too. It hadn't been the plan to start relying on her for him-self. He'd been so sure he could keep those lines clear. But this had become more about his jumbled feelings for her…and he didn't want to take the lid off that.

Paige waved back, and she angled her steps around the side of the house. Mike met her there and opened the door.

A blast of cold air hit Benjie and he set up a wail. Mike mentally chastised himself for not thinking of that, and he stepped away from the door and grabbed a folded blanket from the kitchen table. He shook it out and draped it over the baby. He nuzzled the nipple back between Benjie's angry lips to get him drinking again.

"Hi," he said as Paige came inside and shut the door behind her. She dropped her bag on the counter.

"It's cold out there," she said, then she reached out and touched Benjie's blanketed foot, giving it a tender squeeze. "Hi, Benjie."

"Just finishing up this bottle," Mike said. "Thanks for doing this tonight."

"It's no problem." She paused. "So how are you?"

"I'm—" He was going to say he was fine, which was the socially acceptable answer, but then he stopped. There was something about the way she was looking at him, so open and patient, that he changed his mind. "I'm worried about Jana," he admitted.

Paige headed to the counter and looked into the electric kettle. Then she brought it to the sink to fill it. She was comfortable in his home, and he liked that. She fit into his space—something he hadn't been able to say about women in his life before.

"I don't know how I'm going to balance all of this," he said, looking down at the baby as he drained the last of the bottle. "I mean…how do I explain this to Benjie?"

"A little at a time, as he gets old enough to understand," she replied, putting the kettle back and flicking the switch to turn it on. "This is an adoption, really. And when you adopt a child, it's important that they understand the truth early on, so there aren't any shocking revelations later."

"Right." He met her gaze, then shrugged. "Except this is a little more complicated. What about Jana? What do I do if she wants him back?"

"You mean, if she gets clean," Paige clarified.

He sighed. "Yeah. This is so hard."

"It is," she agreed. "But life often is. That's both the beauty and the frustration of it."

Hard. Messy. Heartbreaking. Nothing

about this was going to be easy, and he doubted that it was going to get any easier as he went along. Jana had relinquished Benjie, but she was still Mike's sister.

"I don't want to give him up," Mike said, and his heart sped up as he realized that was what he was most afraid of right now. "I'm already attached, and I know how awful that is for me to say, because does me having bonded with this little guy mean more than his own mother's love? I hear how selfish it is."

"You aren't selfish," Paige said. "You're stuck in a complicated situation, and you know that Jana isn't a fit mother right now."

"And if she pulls it together later, then what?" he asked. "Am I supposed to just hand Benjie over?"

"Kids need to know that they belong somewhere no matter what," Paige said. "They need to feel that belonging, and to know that the adult who loves and cares for them wouldn't be happy or complete without them. Every child needs an adult who thinks the sun rises and sets with them. Mike, that's you. You aren't selfish for wanting to protect Benjie and keep him close—you're loving him the way he needs to be loved so he'll grow up secure and happy. You're loving him like a dad."

"But I'm not his dad," he murmured. "I'm his uncle. Technically."

"Adoption counts, Mike."

Mike met her gaze. Once more, she'd taken a complicated mess and made it feel a little more manageable.

"And my sister?" he asked hopefully. "What do I do with her?"

"You love and support her as much as you can. You draw some boundaries about what you'll accept and what you won't, and you stand by them."

"I want Benjie to know that Jana's his mom," he said.

"And Benjie should. That's a solid decision. But that won't change who you are to Benjie—his parent, his number one supporter, his biggest fan."

She made it seem possible, even functional. This balance wouldn't be an easy one, and if he ever got married, it wouldn't be an easy situation for a woman to take on, either.

"I wish I could have you with me for all this," he said softly.

"I can't." She shook her head, tears in her eyes.

"I didn't mean—" He stopped. He wasn't sure what he was trying to say. He didn't mean to pressure her, he just wanted her around. But that was hard to communicate. "I'm not asking anything of you. I want you to know that."

"I know…" She smiled. "And this is my fault, too. I think that I was hoping that by helping you out with Benjie, I could get an easy win. I could help someone settle in, feel like I'd contributed and see a happy ending for you and Benjie. I was hoping that would give me the fuel I needed to get back into my career. But that's not fair to you, either."

"Hey, if I can help." He shot her a smile.

She shook her head. "You have to take care of Benjie and Jana. You've got your own balance to keep. You shouldn't be trying to hold me up, too."

"Am I burning you out?" Mike asked.

"No…it isn't you, Mike. But I can't be your Social Services contact for your sister. It's too much for me. I do hope that she finds the help she needs, but I can't help in that way. Not anymore."

"I shouldn't have called you back that night," he said, the realization sinking in. "I'm so sorry, Paige. That really was selfish of me. I was calling because I wanted you there for me, and I should have thought of what that would do to you."

"It's okay. You called me as your friend," she said. "And I did what I could. But now I have to step back."

"With Benjie, too?" he asked. Was she quitting as nanny, as well?

"We have a few more days until our time is up, and I'll honor that," she said. "But after that, even though I'd love to be a part of his life, I have to step back. For me."

He and Benjie had become a burden on her. That had never been his intention. He looked at the clock on the kitchen wall. He had to get going, or he'd be late.

"I'm sorry if I made things harder for you, Paige," he said.

"I'm the one who's changing," she said with a weak shrug. "I don't blame you."

Right. He shifted Benjie in his arms, and felt a wave of love as he looked down at the little guy. Benjie's arrival was incredibly complicated, but that wasn't the baby's fault. Mike would sort it out.

"I'll be late if I don't get going," he said, and he tossed the burp cloth on the floor next to the laundry room door. "And like before, please don't clean up. I'll take care of that when I get back."

No more burdens or obligations. He'd just have to be grateful for her willingness to be Benjie's nanny for a few more days. He didn't know exactly what he'd been hoping for with Paige...just more time with her, he supposed.

But she'd been clear about where she stood. He needed to respect that. Mike pressed a kiss on the top of the baby's head. "See you in the morning, buddy."

He eased Benjie into Paige's arms, and as he leaned close, he could smell the soft scent of her shampoo. He took an appropriate step back and gave her a nod. She was beautiful and feminine and reassuring. But those qualities were meant for Benjie, not for him.

"So... I'll see you later, then, Paige."

"See you, Mike."

He headed out in the chilly evening. The sun was slipping behind the mountains now, glowing red and spilling rosy light down the opposite mountain sides. Night was falling and his shift was just beginning.

PAIGE'S DREAM WAS unsettling and foggy. She had a basket of puppies that kept crawling out and scampering off, and it was her responsibility to keep all the puppies in the basket. At the same time, she was looking for Mike. Somehow, she was worried about him, and if she could just hear his voice, she would feel better, but as the phone rang, the puppies kept crawling from the basket.

She awoke feeling confused. She was at home in bed, wasn't she? She was wearing her comfy, flannel pajamas, but why was the light coming from the wrong side of the bed? As she slowly opened her eyes, she looked at the pillow, the comforter she'd slept on top of, the throw blanket from the couch she'd wrapped herself in, and it all came back to her.

Paige was at Mike's house, and it was morning. Benjie had been up to eat four times since she'd lain down to sleep, the last time being at about four in the morning. When she fell asleep the last time, she'd slept hard—too hard. She blinked her eyes open and pushed herself up to peer into the bassinet next to the bed, and her heart thudded to a stop.

Benjie was gone!

Her first thought was of Jana, but how on earth would she have gotten into the house without waking Paige up? All sorts of horrible possibilities flooded through her head, and she swung her legs over the side of the bed and dashed out of the bedroom and into the living room. The TV was on, the volume turned low, and a breakfast television show was on the screen. From the kitchen, she could hear some sounds of cooking.

Paige looked into the kitchen to see Mike at the stove, Benjie on his shoulder as he angled his body away from the heat to keep Benjie safe. He was stirring something in a cast iron skillet, the sizzle sending up an amazing aroma.

Mike's attention was on the stove, and he absently patted Benjie's little diaper with one hand. He was in full uniform, and she watched him for a few beats. The crisp shirt, the muscular physique, the tender way he held Benjie with one protective hand. He was a handsome man, but it was more than good looks. It was how he held himself—confident, relaxed, and he had an air of happiness around him, too.

"And a little bit of pepper, Benjie," Mike was saying. He reached for a shaker and shimmied it over the pan. "Pepper is absolutely necessary, little guy. You have to remember that, okay?"

Paige couldn't help but smile, watching him with Benjie. Mike had certainly relaxed over the last couple of weeks. He'd gone from panicked cop afraid to touch the baby to this guy—chatting with Benjie as he cooked one-handed. Mike picked up the spatula again.

"Smells good, right?" Mike said, his voice quiet. "A man has to know how to cook, kiddo. This is one of those cardinal rules. You can't be all helpless. Well, *you* can. You're small enough that I'll let that slide, but in five or six years, you're going to start helping in the kitchen, and I'll show you my tricks."

He stirred the spatula around in the pan again.

"Good morning," Paige said, and Mike turned, surprised.

"Hey," he said with a smile. "Good morning. I didn't want to wake you up. You were drooling into my pillow and looked so exhausted—"

"I wasn't drooling!" She wiped at her face. Maybe she had been, and she felt the heat come to her cheeks. "Sorry. He was up a lot last night. I tried not to rumple your bed too much."

There was something so familiar in the way he'd grinned at her, and she felt her heart flutter. No—she had to keep herself firmly in control here. Last night, it hadn't felt right to crawl into his bed, honestly. His bedroom was masculine, and she'd done a quick perusal of the room after he'd left for his shift—mostly out of curiosity. He had a few books on his bedside table, as well as a few baby bottles that needed washing. He had a digital clock on the top of his dresser, and all the furniture was dark wood. His bedding was charcoal gray, and the room was just so intimately Mike's that she hadn't been able to let herself fully relax. Letting herself go would have felt like overstepping more than she already had. She wasn't supposed to be getting comfortable in this most private space. It even smelled like him—musky, clean, warm. It certainly wouldn't have helped her to curb her feelings for him.

"I was fine," she said with a shrug. "So you were able to come right in there and I didn't stir, huh?"

"You were out cold." He imitated a sleeping face, mouth open, soft snores.

Paige rolled her eyes. "I was tired!"

"Hey, I didn't say you weren't cute all flaked out like that." He nodded to a chair. "Take a seat. I made breakfast."

"What is it?" Her stomach rumbled.

"Just a hash of everything," he said. "My grandmother used to make this a lot."

It did smell amazing, whatever it was, and when she sat, Mike ambled over and handed Benjie to her. The baby squirmed until he was settled in her arms, and he blinked up at her.

"I thought I'd lost you, Benjie," she said softly.

"Sorry, did you freak out when you didn't see him there?" Mike asked.

"I just about had a heart attack," she admitted.

"I figured it would be nice to wake up

to breakfast." Mike opened a cupboard and pulled down a couple of plates. "I hadn't figured in the heart episode."

He dished up two heaping platefuls and carried them back to the table. It did look good—browned potatoes, fragrant sausage, some sautéed onions and clumps of scrambled eggs mixed through. There was a sprinkling of black pepper on top.

"So how did you sleep, when you could?" Mike asked, passing her a fork.

"I dreamed of puppies," she said with a shake of her head, and she related the frustrating dream to him.

"That's got to mean something," he said with a small smile. "I have a feeling I'm one of the puppies."

"No, you were in the dream, but you weren't a puppy." She stabbed a piece of potato with her fork.

"So I was in your dream, was I?" He raised an eyebrow and shot her a teasing smile.

"Don't flatter yourself," she quipped. "You were stressing me out. I don't know how, but I had to call you, or something, and I couldn't reach you, and it was annoying."

"So I'm in your dreams, but I'm annoying." He chuckled.

"Apparently." She swallowed her bite, meeting his gaze. "I don't know how, but in my dream you were capable of solving the puppy crisis. But you wouldn't pick up your phone."

Mike grinned. "That doesn't sound like me. I'd pick up if you called."

"My subconscious doesn't seem to think so," she teased back.

Mike leaned his elbows on the table. "Try me."

"Just…calling you?" she asked.

"Yeah. Call me up. See if I answer. I'll have some guy in cuffs, and I'll still pick up."

"You're flirting," she teased.

"Me? Never. I'm completely serious." But his glittering gray gaze was locked on hers playfully.

"Why the good mood?" she asked.

"I don't know. I'm liking having you around, I guess. It was nice to come home to the two of you. I'm used to coming home to an empty house. It's…better than I thought it would be. Maybe I'm turning into a family man, after all."

"Benjie's bringing out your softer side," she said.

"So are you." His tone dropped, the playful banter gone.

Paige averted her gaze. She'd been enjoying this time with him, too, but it wasn't safe to dwell on that. They didn't have much more time together, before she'd be going back to normal, coming home to her own empty house.

"Here, pass Benjie over so you can eat," Mike said.

"It's okay—" she started.

"You deserve a full meal, Paige. I'm not going to be the guy who just takes and takes. So let me cook for you, and…eat it."

It hadn't come out very smoothly, but she knew what he meant, and she shot him a smile. He was acting like a dad here, taking responsibility for his son and his home. And he was good in the role—strong, sweet, confident. She passed the baby over to him, and he tucked Benjie into the crook of his muscular arm.

"What do you think?" he asked.

"Delicious," she said past a bite of food.

"My grandmother used to make hash with the last night's leftovers. It was never the same twice. Once I got my own place, I started making it with my favorites."

"Sounds good to me," she said. "This is amazing."

He smiled. "I'm no helpless puppy, as it turns out."

"I never said you were." She cast him a grin. "But this is nice."

"Yeah, it is." He took another bite and looked at her thoughtfully.

"I heard a rumor that the town has been left a plot of land, and they were considering turning it into a community garden."

"Oh, yeah?"

"Liv was telling me about it, and it got me to thinking… If I do walk away from my job in Social Services, I might be interested in working for the city, if they could budget me in. If it turned out to be a volunteer situation, I'd still be very interested."

"Running the garden," he clarified.

"It could be a great way to integrate people into the community," she said. "Working together toward a goal. We could use the food to service the food bank, and if I could raise the money for some good greenhouses, we could be producing some veggies all year long, like tomatoes, cucumbers, green beans…"

"You've put some thought into this."

"It would be the garden that I've been longing for, but it would still use my experience in social work. I still want to help people," she said. "I'm just not sure that I belong on the front lines."

"I have to admit, I'm impressed," he said. "It's creative, has a great social benefit and it sounds like it would use all of your talents. You should pitch it at city council."

Paige shrugged. "I'm still ironing it out in my head."

"I'm serious," he said. "You should pitch it before someone else does. This should be your project."

And maybe it should be… The garden in her backyard had grown over, but that was because she hadn't had the time and didn't want to work it alone. She'd wanted kids to help pull weeds, a husband to walk with her down the rows, seeing just how ripe the produce was getting. For her, the garden came with people to love.

But maybe a community garden could give her a different way to have people in her life and let her use her talents without burning out.

A garden to feed the needy...it did sound perfect. And Mike was right—this project should be hers.

CHAPTER FIFTEEN

MIKE SAT WITH his sister in the coffee shop across the street from the police station the next morning. Outside the window, Mike could see the redbrick police department in the cold, watery light of the overcast autumn day.

"I don't like the women's shelter," Jana said, hunching over her cup of coffee.

"Why not?" Mike asked. "The food bad or something?"

He'd picked his sister up for breakfast out, but she hadn't wanted to go back, and so breakfast had turned into an extended coffee, as well. He glanced at his watch—his shift was starting soon.

"It's like a prison," she said, taking another sip from the mug. "You can't just come and go as you please. You have to sign in and out, and they have a curfew like I'm some kid. You can't even have guests."

"It's for safety," Mike said. "For the women staying there who are running away from abuse. Wait—" Her last comment finally landed. "What guests? You don't know anyone here, I thought."

"I meet people." She shot him an annoyed look.

"Okay." He was tired. "Who did you meet?"

"Just a guy. We hung out a bit, but he doesn't have a place right now, and…" Her voice trailed off.

"Jana, you need to build your own life right now," he said.

She had serious problems to deal with, and she was already getting involved with some guy she didn't know? But then, she'd always lived her life by her own rules.

"What's life without people in it?" she replied, and for once the attitude seemed to be gone, and she just looked at him with pain-filled eyes. "Back home in Denver, I have friends and stuff. Here, I just sit alone."

"Yeah, I get that," he murmured. "I work a lot. But I'll try and come by and see you more often."

"Thanks." She hunkered back over her coffee.

"I talked to your Social Services agent—" he began.

"That woman from your place?" Jana asked.

"No, she's a friend. The other one. She says they have an opening in the rehab facility starting Friday." He leaned forward hopefully. "It's a good place, Jana. They're nice there. They really care. I looked into it myself at work, and I think it has real promise."

"But I'd be locked in," Jana said.

"Yeah. That's what makes it effective. When you're really wanting another hit, you can't get it. It helps you detox."

"Right." She nodded slowly. "How's Benjamin?"

"He's good," Mike said. "I got this baby carrier thing so I can carry him around."

"Cute." She smiled wanly.

"And he's just doing the baby thing," Mike said, casting about for something she could hold on to. "He's downing a lot of bottles, dirtying a lot of diapers. He's growing, too. Finally got into a regular newborn sleeper."

"Yeah?" She brightened a little. "I got the pictures of him you emailed me." She picked up her phone and waggled it at him.

"Thanks. I showed this other woman at the shelter. She's got a kid, too, but hers is a teenager."

"Do you want to see him again before you go to rehab?" he asked. "You could hold him for a while—remind yourself why this is worth it."

"Would you do that?" she asked warily. "After last time? I'm sorry if I got weird. I wouldn't really have run away with him."

"Yeah, you would have," Mike said quietly. "Let's not lie to each other."

Jana shrugged. "Maybe I would have. But I had nowhere to go."

That wasn't a lot of comfort. His sister needed so much more help than he could provide.

"I'll make sure I can see you before you go," he said. "And I'll bring Benjie so you can hold him awhile."

In the precinct. Under his supervision. He wasn't taking another chance that she'd run with the baby.

"You think you could tell the women's shelter people that I'm allowed to have visitors?" she asked.

Mike shook his head. "Nope."

"Fine." She sighed.

Mike's phone blipped and he looked down at the screen to see an incoming text from Chief Simpson.

Mike, could I see you in my office before you leave on patrol today? Thanks.

It didn't say much, and Mike shot his sister an apologetic smile.

"Jana, I've got to start work," he said. Do you want me to drop you back off at the shelter?"

"No." She shook her head. "I'll go back when I get hungry."

"Okay." He watched his sister take another sip of coffee, not raising her eyes to meet his. They were so far from what he'd hoped when he'd discovered her on his doorstep. But fifteen years apart didn't evaporate, even if they wanted it to. "Jana, I'm glad you're here."

She raised her gaze then. "Go to work, Michael. I'm fine. I'm going to rehab—you don't have to worry about that."

And while Mike knew she wasn't fine, he couldn't actually fix it, either. So he pushed himself to his feet and adjusted his radio on his shoulder. He'd become a cop to find her, to protect her, to finally face it all head-on so he didn't miss the warning signs again. And even now, with all of his experience and training, he couldn't figure out what he could do for his sister to help start healing that hole in her heart.

"Call me if you need me, okay?"

"Yep." She sipped her coffee again.

"I'm going to pay for your lunch here. Come back to eat, okay? It'll be covered already."

It didn't feel like half enough, but it would have to do.

Mike stopped at the counter and put down a twenty, telling the woman working to let Jana order whatever she wanted. He didn't dare give her cash right now—there were drugs to be had out here in Eagle's Rest, just the same as in the city. It was better not to tempt her.

He'd rather go to the gun range or the gym this morning to deal with his unresolved emotions, but there wasn't time. The chief was waiting.

Mike looked back at his sister as he

opened the door to the outside. She sat staring into her cup, slowly turning it in a circle in front of her. She didn't look up to see him leave.

He jogged across the street and headed inside the station. Ellen looked up with a smile as he came in.

"Hi, Ellen," he said, heading past her desk.

"How's Benjie?" Ellen asked.

"Good. Growing!"

Ellen grinned. "Bring him by one of these days. I'd love to hold him again."

And he *would* bring Benjie by, but not for Ellen to hold. It would be Jana's chance to hold her son a little while. This would never be an ordinary arrangement. His life would be unique from here on out. He'd wanted to find his sister so badly, but somehow he hadn't considered the long-term ramifications of having her in his life while he raised her son. But what choice did he have?

He crossed the bull pen to the chief's office and knocked.

"Come in," the chief called, and Mike opened the door and went inside. "Have a seat."

Was he in trouble? Mike squeezed into one of those narrow visitor chairs, his mind ticking through everything that had happened the last few days. He waited for his boss to begin.

"How are things going?" the chief asked, clicking his mouse so that his computer screen went dark.

"Uh—okay, I guess," Mike replied. "I just had breakfast with my sister, and she's agreed to rehab. So that's good, I guess. It's a start."

"That's good to hear," Chief Simpson replied. "I know you were looking for her for a long time."

"Yeah…" Mike nodded. "A long time."

"It must be hard with her being an addict," the chief said. "There's nothing easy there."

"True, but it's better to know than wonder," he replied. That had been his motto ever since she'd run away—better to look the worst in the face and know what was going on than to stick his head in the sand.

"You know you can't make her get clean, right?"

"I know, sir. I wouldn't pressure her in any way—"

"No, I mean, you've accepted on a heart level that you can't fix her, right?" The chief eyed Mike pointedly. "An addict has to want to get better. You can't want it for her."

"I guess so," Mike replied. "Doesn't mean I won't do my best by her, though."

"And as a new dad," the chief went on, "I know it's a complicated situation. What are you hoping for there?"

"To raise Benjie as my own," Mike said, shaking his head. "With all due respect, what is this about, sir?" Mike was professional, and he did his job well. Things might have gotten a bit messy since Benjie appeared, but he was doing his best, and he hadn't missed any work, either.

"I'm not meaning to overstep," the chief said. "What I'm trying to see is, do you still want SWAT? Have any of your hopes for the future changed with the baby, and your sister, and…all that? Or are you needing more time to think that over?"

"No, sir, no change," Mike said, his voice firming. "That's one thing I'm sure about. I might not be able to fight my sister's demons for her, but I can sure as hell go out there and break the kinds of guys who did it to her. That much has stayed the same."

The chief smiled, then shrugged. "You can't say that kind of thing to me, Mike. Rephrase."

"Uh—" Mike cast about for more appropriate wording. "I want to join SWAT to use my particular skill set to catch the bad guys, bring them to justice and see them charged for the crimes they have committed, sir."

"Better. That's the kind of thing I can use in your recommendation letter for SWAT training."

Mike blinked. "Wait… Did you get my test results back?"

"Sure did," the chief replied. "You passed with flying colors, and while I'll hate having to replace you around here, I'm willing to recommend you to SWAT training. You're good, and I think you'll be a real asset wherever you're posted."

"Thank you, sir." Mike heaved a sigh of relief. "I appreciate that. I really do."

And yet, the chief had a point about things being different now. He didn't feel the elation that he'd imagined he would when he dreamed about this day. He'd done a lot to get here, including transferring to Eagle's Rest. SWAT had been the goal all along.

"You have a good shift, Mike. And congratulations," Chief Simpson said. "You earned this."

Mike rose to his feet and shook the chief's hand. He'd done it—and that certainty did give him a certain flood of satisfaction, but he'd settled into Eagle's Rest in a way he hadn't settled anywhere else. And it was all because of Paige.

She was here. Her life, her touch, her smile, her influence—all here in Eagle's Rest where there was no need for a SWAT officer. And even though he was now about to achieve his most coveted ambition, he couldn't help but feel a stream of sadness working its way through his heart.

This was really it—and it would be goodbye.

PAIGE SAT AT the kitchen table, the bassinet next to her. She took a sip of tea and looked down at Benjie, who was fast asleep, and she smiled mistily. He'd be in Eagle's Rest Day Care in a couple of days. She was sure that the day care employees would treat him well, but she wouldn't be the one caring for him anymore. She wouldn't give him bottles or cuddle him when he fussed. She wouldn't be the answer to his cries, and that stabbed deeply.

This was supposed to be a short-term nanny position where she showed Mike everything he'd need to know about baby care. She'd done what she came to do, and she should be feeling a sense of accomplishment here. Instead, she was just sad to have to say goodbye.

The side door opened, and she startled. Mike came inside the kitchen, his uniform shoes clunking against the linoleum floor.

"Hi," Paige said. "He's sleeping."

She'd brought the bassinet into the kitchen next to the table.

"Right." He smiled sheepishly. "How was your day?"

"Nothing to report," she said, returning his smile. "Bottles, diaper, snuggles." She paused. "Tomorrow is my last day with him."

"I know." He paused, his gaze meeting hers. "You gonna miss us?"

"You have no idea." She blinked back the tears in her eyes.

"Do you have a few minutes?"

She should be leaving, but she could tell that there was something bothering Mike. Her position with him would be over soon enough, and she'd go about the business of piecing her heart back together again. Wasn't this what she always did? What she needed was a job that didn't do this to her—pluck at her heart until it was in shreds.

"Sure," she said.

"Because I've got news."

"Yeah?" Paige leaned against the kitchen counter. "What's going on?"

"I got into SWAT training." He smiled hesitantly.

"Really?" Paige pushed herself away from the counter and looked up at him. Her heart felt like it was tumbling inside of her. "Mike, that's…great. That's what you were aiming for, right?"

"Right." He nodded, but his smile slipped. "It starts in two weeks in Denver, and it'll be four weeks of intensive training."

"Okay… So you'll have to arrange some child care in Denver, then. But you have the day care spot here in Eagle's Rest already.

I'm sure they could hold it for you for a few weeks—"

Her mind was spinning ahead. This wasn't her problem, but she cared.

Mike met her gaze. "And then I'll be assigned to a new precinct where they need a SWAT-trained officer."

His words sunk in, and she swallowed. "So you'll be leaving Eagle's Rest for sure."

"Yeah, it looks that way." He licked his lips. "This was the plan all along."

Paige looked up at him, and his somber gaze met hers.

"You should be happy about this," she said. Even if she couldn't summon up the joy on his behalf, he of all people should be happy.

"I was thinking…" He caught her fingers in his and ran his thumb tenderly over the top her hand. "What if you came with me to Denver? I'd pay you, of course. Like you said, I'll need someone to watch Benjie for me while I'm training, and there's no one I trust like I trust you."

Go with him…they could put off that goodbye for a few more weeks. It was tempting, and she longed to say yes…

"Mike, I can't," she said, shaking her head. She pulled her hand from his grip.

"Why not?" he pressed. "Unless you're going to be working with the community garden..."

"I don't know about that yet," she said, and she licked her lips, trying to find some solid ground inside of her. "Mike, I can't do this. It's putting off the inevitable, and I can't keep breaking my heart in two. We've crossed lines here... There's no denying it. I have feelings for you, and going with you to Denver isn't going to help that."

"You have feelings for me?"

That was what he was latching on to?

"We're playing with fire, here, Mike," she said. "Don't you see that? There's no way for us to walk away unsinged!"

"It might be too late for that, anyway," he said, shrugging helplessly. "When the chief told me I was in, my first thought was that I'd have to leave here, and that would mean leaving you behind, but if you came along—"

"For how long?" she asked, annoyance surging up inside of her. "For a few weeks during your training? And then what?"

"Maybe we just keep it going," he said.

"Not just the nanny thing… Our relationship, too," she clarified.

"Is that part so awful?" He smiled faintly and brushed her hair away from her face.

Did he really think this would be easy? What about her? She'd be leaving her home, caring for his child, falling in love with the man, and all for what—to put off an inevitable goodbye?

"We can't do this!" She batted his hand away from her face, and he let it drop. Benjie whimpered, and they both looked instinctively toward the bassinet.

"Let's go into the other room," Mike said, and she followed him into the living room, but she still kept her voice lower so as not to wake the baby.

"Why would we go through all of that?" she asked. "Do you know how much it would uproot my life? We want different things! What you're suggesting is…is…" She cast about for the word. "Selfish!"

Mike's eyes flashed. "Selfish? Damn it, Paige, I'm not selfish. I'm in love with you!"

Paige stared at him, stunned. His words

hung heavy in the air, and she blinked at him. "You…love me?"

"I…" He looked as surprised as she felt, and then he stepped closer and slipped a hand behind her neck. He bent his head and covered her lips with his. She sank against him as his lips moved tenderly over hers, and when he pulled back, she blinked up at him. His steely eyes searched hers.

"Yeah, I love you," he breathed. "You're amazing. You're insightful and wise, sweet and compassionate. And you're gorgeous… Do you have any idea what you do to me? I'm not the kind of guy who even tries to connect with sweet, gentle women, you know. I normally know better—I only mess it up. But what we have…that's special. To me at least. I don't know what it means to you."

He released her, and the air that flooded between them felt cold and hostile. She wanted to be back in his arms again, enfolded against that strong chest, feeling his heart beat against her. He loved her…and as surprised as she was to hear that, she realized the ache inside of her, the longing she felt to be near him, the way she recklessly let him kiss her, all pointed to the very thing she'd been fighting against. She didn't want to fall for this man, but it had already happened.

"I love you, too," she admitted, her throat tight with emotion.

"Yeah?" A smile tickled his lips. "That's the best news I've had all day."

He moved toward her again, and she took a step back.

"Mike, stop," she breathed. "This can't work—"

"Hey, as of this morning, I was depressed at the thought of achieving my life's dream, and now I've got you in love with me. I think things are moving in the right direction."

"It doesn't change anything!" she said, shaking her head. "You have this life in mind, and you want to take me along with you, but I'm not the woman you need. I can't be. I've talked to Liv about what it takes to make a marriage work with a cop, and I'm not that woman."

Mike was silent for a moment, and then he said, "You could have talked to me instead."

"I needed her insight," she said softly. "And she likes you a lot. But I have to make some changes in my life. I know what I can handle and what I can't."

Mike heaved out a sigh. "Even if it's my job, and not yours?"

"A cop's wife has to sit at home late at night and wonder if her husband is coming home. She has to see news stories, and wonder if her husband is one of the first responders. She has to worry about traffic stops that go wrong… And when her husband gets home, she has to be able to sit down and open herself up to all the stuff that he needs to talk over, because if she can't do that, he'll be talking it over with someone else. And you can't be married, compartmentalizing your wife away from your job. It doesn't work! Marriages like that don't last!" She paused, taking a breath. She felt the tears rising up inside of her.

"I wouldn't hold it away from you."

"And I couldn't handle it," she whispered. "I can't just open myself up to all the difficult things you face during your days. I'm not quitting my job because I'm lazy or just don't feel like doing it anymore. I'm quitting because it's crushing me and I can't go on like this! My job or yours, I can't do it."

They were silent for a few beats, and Paige tried to swallow back her tears. It was no use—one escaped and trickled down her cheek, and Mike reached out and brushed it away.

"What if I stayed?" he asked at last.

"And gave up SWAT?" Paige shook her head.

She saw the competing emotions battling across his face, and he shook his head irritably.

"For you," he said. "I could do that. I could just make my peace with…with…"

He didn't finish the thought, but she could hear what he was saying. He'd try to give up the dream that had fueled him, healed him, directed him ever since his sister ran away. He would try to turn off a part of his own heart…for her.

"No," she whispered.

"Why not?"

"Because you can't!" she said. "You've said it before—you're right for that job. You're tough, you're strong, you shoot, and you want to use your strengths to make this state a safer place for all the families, not just your own. It's noble, Mike. I can't ask you to give that up."

He didn't answer, and she knew what that meant—she was right. It was too much to carve a piece of a man's heart out of his chest, just for the sake of romance.

"Does it matter at all that I love you?" he asked softly.

She nodded, tears slipping down her cheeks. "Of course it does. I love you, too. But that doesn't mean it'll work between us, does it?"

"No." He pressed his lips together and swallowed hard. When he looked down at her again, she saw tears shining in his eyes.

"I should go," she said, her voice shaking. She had to leave before she broke down and cried. She had to get back to her own home, her own space, and grieve this heartbreak alone.

Paige gathered up her coat and bag. Her fingers fumbled as she pulled her jacket on, and Mike stood there watching her with agony in his eyes.

"Paige, I don't want to leave it like this."

There was no solution here, and if she stayed any longer, she'd do something she'd regret. If not right now, then eventually, when she had to leave him because she couldn't take it anymore. It was better not to start.

"Goodbye, Mike," she said, and she pulled open the door. The cold air hit her as she plunged out into the twilight. Her heart was so heavy in her chest that she felt like it could make her double over with the very weight of it.

Loving Mike had never been part of the plan, but it hadn't been avoidable, either. It was just as well that her time with the both of them was over. This was exactly why she'd been doing her best to keep her heart walled off.

Paige needed to heal.

CHAPTER SIXTEEN

MIKE DIDN'T SLEEP that night—at least not much. Whatever had developed between him and Paige hadn't been planned, and it hadn't been wise. But there they were, regardless. He'd fallen in love with her, and having said the words out loud seemed to have cemented them into his heart. Had he kept his mouth shut, he might have been able to delude himself a while longer… But he loved her, and he wasn't a man who fell in love easily. Neither did he get over it very easily. But she was right, their feelings for each other didn't change who they were and what they wanted.

As he came into the precinct the next morning, carrying Benjie in his car seat, his heart was heavy. He nodded to Ellen at the front desk, and she looked like she was about to banter with him, then her smile slipped, and she didn't even ask to take a closer look at the baby.

Mike wasn't hiding his feelings too well, it seemed. He turned back to the well-meaning receptionist.

"Ellen, Genevieve from Social Services was going to meet me here this morning—"

"She's in meeting room A," Ellen replied. "She has someone with her, though—a client?"

His sister. Yes, that was the plan.

"Great. Thanks," he said.

"Did you want me to watch Benjie for you while…" she began, then her smile faltered.

"No, thanks," he said, forcing his own smile. "But I appreciate the offer."

Mike carried on, bypassing his desk and heading toward meeting room A. He'd at least get to see his sister again before she headed off for rehab. And here was hoping against all hope that rehab could help start her out on the right foot.

He tapped on the door, then opened it, poking his head into the room that was dominated by a large table. On the side closest to the door, Jana sat with her hands pressed between her knees, Genevieve standing behind her.

"Hi," he said.

"There he is…" Jana sighed, her gaze pinned to the car seat.

Mike shut the door behind him and brought Benjie over to the table. The baby was still asleep, and as Mike unbuckled the straps and pulled Benjie out, he wriggled a little, moaning in a complaint at being moved.

Jana looked calmer than the last time he'd seen her, less jittery. She held out her arms, and Mike carefully handed her the sleeping baby. She sighed, looking down into his tiny face, and tears filled her eyes.

"Thank you for this, Michael," she said quietly.

Mike glanced over at Genevieve. "You think we could get a few minutes alone, me and my sister?"

"Sure. Of course." The woman smiled and went over to the door. "We have twenty minutes until our transport leaves."

"Thanks," he said, and after the door was shut, he pulled out a chair opposite his sister and sat down.

Jana touched the downy hair on Benjie's head with one cautious finger, then sighed. "You were right, you know."

"About what?" he asked.

"About me needing to make some changes so that Benjie could be proud of me." Her gaze flickered up toward Mike, then back down to the baby. "I don't know how I got this bad, but I want help. I want to get better."

He was relieved to hear that, but he wasn't sure what to say. "You'll get better. I know it."

"Not fast enough to be a mom now," she said quietly.

"Jana, you'll always be Benjie's mom," Mike said. "You getting help doesn't change that."

"But I can't be a good mom," she said, tears welling in her eyes. "I can't take care of him."

"Hey, you're being a good mom by taking care of yourself," he countered. "You need to do this for you. I've worried about you for years, but I can't make things better. I'm not going to disappear on you. When you get out of rehab, I'll be finishing up my SWAT training, and we'll figure out how we'll do things from there. But I can promise you that I'm not going to cut you off from your son. You're going to be in his life. And mine. Jana, you're my baby sister. Nothing changes that."

They were quiet for a few beats, both of them looking down at Benjie as he slept. Jana put a finger underneath Benjie's tiny hand, and he closed his grasp around it.

"I was talking to this therapist at the women's shelter about when we were kids," Jana said.

"Yeah? You were talking to a therapist?"

"She was there," Jana said with a half smile. "I figured I might as well. Anyway, nothing was normal for us, Michael. Grandma was doing her best. But she let us raise ourselves. I remember asking her about puberty and stuff, and she told me the bare minimum. I was confused for years, and I ended up getting all my information from friends. I'm still not sure what's true and what isn't."

"Yeah, try being a boy in that situation," he said with a rueful smile.

"I can only imagine," she said with a roll of her eyes. "But it wasn't just that. Mom dumped us. I remember the other girls talking about their mothers, and I used to think to myself, *Mine didn't want me.* I mean, those other girls were all angry because their mothers grounded them for smoking, or whatever, and mine didn't care if I was okay or not, let alone if I was smoking or going out with boys who were too old for me."

"I should have cared," Mike said.

"You weren't my mother," she said with a sigh. "Was I supposed to take over for Mom with you, too? It's complicated."

"But you're right," Mike said. "It wasn't normal. Not by any stretch."

"You turned out normal, though," Jana said, looking up. "I mean, you went to school, got a good job—you got a badge, Michael! You did okay. Me...not so much."

Mike was silent, and for a moment, neither of them said anything. Then Jana said, "I realized something else. Benjamin will have some normal with you. More than he'd have with me, even if I get clean. I mean, look at this town—it's so normal it hurts." She laughed softly. "Boring as all get-out, but I can see how nice it would be for a kid to grow up here."

"I'm not staying here," he said. "Once I finish SWAT training, I'll be assigned somewhere else. I mean, I'll bring you with me, of course, but—"

"Whether it's here or some other city, you're giving my son something I can't," she said earnestly. "You're giving him a safe, happy, ordinary life. You'll be there for him, listen to him, help him make better choices than we did when we were getting away with murder under Grandma's nose. I remember this one time I snuck out and my friends all got caught. I was the only one who didn't have someone yelling at me, and what I wouldn't have given for a mom or dad to holler at me…to stop me. I just kept on messing up, while my friends stopped. Benjamin needs that. You'll make sure he doesn't get away with anything."

"Yeah, of course." He nodded. He'd raise Benjie right. The boy wouldn't be wandering the streets. He'd be one of the kids getting heck when he tried to push the boundaries too much.

"And this—all of this—is what I didn't have," she said, looking down at Benjie again. "Normal. And it might not seem as important as all the other stuff you do around here as a cop, but…it's more than you think."

"Yeah?" Mike asked uncertainly.

"What would it have meant to you to grow up normal, Michael?" she asked with a shake of her head.

What would he have given to have a mom or a dad to make sure he was doing his homework, or to insist he brushed his teeth? Heaven knew, Grandma tried, but Mike had been more stubborn than her, and that hadn't been good for either of them.

What would *he* have given for some normal?

He'd become a cop to set a few wrongs right, and he'd been aiming at SWAT in order to make sure he saw the dangers coming. He never wanted to close his eyes again, but what if the danger that threatened this little guy wasn't "out there"? What if it was a whole lot closer to home?

"I'll do right by him, Jana," Mike promised. "And I'll do right by you, too."

"I know. This is better for Benjamin if you raise him. I know that. I just—"

"Hey, this doesn't have to be forever," he said. "When you're better, we can talk about shared custody. I'm not stealing him from you, okay? I want to make that really clear."

"Do you mean that?" she eyed him warily.

"It'll be hard at first," he said with a quick nod. "I already love him, too. But we'll figure it out."

He couldn't push his sister off on her own and use the excuse that it was better for Benjie. It wouldn't be—it would just be simpler for Mike. He couldn't do that to her, though. What was best for Benjie was what was hardest for the adults to provide—a fair balance.

The door opened behind Mike, and he turned to see Genevieve looking in.

"We need to get going if we're going to make that shuttle," Genevieve said.

Mike turned back to his sister. "You ready, Jana?"

"No," she admitted softly, tears welling in her eyes. "But this is worth it. I don't want Benjamin making up stories about me to make himself feel better. I want to be a mom he can be proud of."

"Jana, *I'm* proud of you," he said gruffly.

She kissed Benjie's head, and Mike eased the baby from her arms.

"Thank you, Michael," she said, and her voice caught. "I mean that. Thank you."

Mike followed his sister out of the room. Genevieve smiled encouragingly and put a hand on Jana's shoulder.

"All right. Let's get going, Jana," Genevieve said.

Jana waved as she got into the minivan that would drive her out to the rehab center, and Mike waved back. It was a brand-new start, and he really hoped that this first attempt at sobriety stuck. Was that naive of him? Maybe—it was also the brother in him.

Normal—that was what Jana said she'd been missing. All he'd wanted was to fight the bad guys to make things better for her and others like her. But now there was a little boy in the picture, and Benjie needed something different…something slower-paced. Benjie was going to need some "normal," as Jana put it, and that was going to start out with diapers and bottles and turn into play dates and bike rides. Benjie wasn't going to need Mike to throw himself at the bad guys; he was going to need a dad who came to school plays and made him eat a good breakfast. Benjie needed *him*.

Mike suddenly realized that Paige had been wrong. She'd said he couldn't set aside his career aspirations—not without resenting her in the long run. He had a certain skill set, but that selection of skills had been growing lately. He'd been softening, nurturing, falling in love…

When Jana ran away, Mike's life had never been the same. He'd stopped caring about his own silly wish lists. All he'd wanted was to make sure his little sister was safe. And if Mike missed some warning sign with Benjie and history repeated itself with Jana's son, none of his career aspirations would soothe away the self-recriminations for having missed out on the most important part of life—family.

Paige thought he couldn't change course, but he could. His deepest desire to keep his loved ones safe remained the same. But maybe he needed to do that differently than he'd been planning all along.

It wouldn't change that Paige wanted something different than he could give her, but it would change his plans to leave Eagle's Rest. Chief Simpson had been more supportive than Chief Vernon ever had been.

This precinct had acted more like a family—thrown him a baby shower, checked up on him. They'd cared. If Mike wanted to give Benjie some "normal," then he'd need support, too. And Eagle's Rest was the place for that.

And he needed Paige to know that he wasn't going anywhere.

She probably still wouldn't want more than friendship with him, but he'd be around, and if she ever changed her mind, he'd be here. It wasn't about getting her to go with him for SWAT training, he realized. It was about being where he was needed most, and now he knew where that was.

It was time to drop Benjie off at day care. But first, he had to talk to the chief—because something significant *had* changed in his personal plans, after all.

PAIGE HADN'T SLEPT well last night. Going home to her own kitchen, her own mug of tea, and listening to the tickling branches of her front yard tree rattle against her window hadn't done as much to soothe her heart as she'd hoped. But she'd had privacy at least, when the tears overflowed, and she cried herself to sleep.

This morning, she felt dehydrated and tired, her heart aching in her chest. Because she'd fallen in love with the man, against all her better instincts, and proven once again that she was not cut out for this kind of work. Her skin was too thin, her heart too near the surface.

Paige got dressed, printed off the resignation letter she'd typed out the night before and tucked it into a fresh envelope. Her decision was made—it was time for her life to move in a different direction. But as she stepped outside into the crisp fall air, she felt a pang of sadness. Clouds were tumbling in over the mountain peaks, carrying with them the smell of more rain. It matched her mood.

She could change her professional life, but she wouldn't change how she felt about Mike quite so easily. She hadn't realized how hard she'd fallen until he'd told her how he felt, and she'd never been more tempted in her life to follow after a man.

But she couldn't. She knew what she needed. Roots, and a home, and some peace. Mike was the dangerous opposite of all those things. No matter how much she loved a man, her basic needs weren't going to change.

As she drove down to the Social Services office on the east end of downtown, she tried not to think of Benjie and the way he snuggled against her neck when she held him, or about Mike's strong arms and his warm lips as they covered hers during one of their stolen kisses. She wasn't very successful, though, and she blinked back a fresh veil of tears.

No, she wouldn't cry again. She had her own life to arrange, and she had to move forward with that.

She parked in her regular spot behind the building, the first few drops of rain splattering against her windshield. She pulled an umbrella out from the backseat and took a deep breath.

It was time to make a change.

When she went inside the building, shaking out her umbrella, she looked around at the familiar office where she'd spent the last seven years of her life. She'd started her career here as an eager young recruit, and she'd grown both in her position and in her boss's esteem. Paige had been good at her job—there was no denying it, and that success had meant a lot to her. So this goodbye wouldn't be easy.

A small group of young people dressed in business casual walked across the reception area, focused on what one of the trainers was saying. These were newbies, and she smiled wistfully at the sight of them.

"You'll succeed here if you always think of yourself as part of the team…"

Paige glanced around and spotted Genevieve by the water cooler. Her boss smiled and waved, but her smile faltered when she saw Paige's face.

"Paige," Genevieve said, coming up to her. "We've got some new recruits coming through for training today. I think we've got some good ones…but are you all right?"

"Could we talk in your office?" Paige asked.

"Yes, of course," Genevieve said. "I'm glad to see you. The woman you brought to the shelter has left for rehab this morning. I hope it goes well for her, and your quick thinking will have helped. You made a difference there."

"I'm glad," Paige said. "She's had a tough go of it."

They walked together toward the office, and Genevieve stood back and let Paige go inside first, then she shut the door behind them.

"So what's up, Paige?" her boss asked, circling around the desk to her seat. Paige sank into the chair in front of the desk, the envelope clutched in her hands.

"I'm giving my notice," Paige said. "Effective today."

Genevieve sighed, then nodded. "I'd hoped you wouldn't."

"I know," Paige replied. "And believe me, this decision wasn't made lightly. But I have to do what's right for me."

"Is there any other support I could offer to help you through this?" Genevieve asked. "We might be able to manage a longer stress leave, if you need it, or perhaps a staggered reentry into the position to make it easier on you?"

"I appreciate it," Paige replied. "I really do, but no. You've been really great, Genevieve. I've loved working with you. This isn't an issue with you, your leadership or the team here. This is about me and what I can handle going into the future. I need a new line of work."

Genevieve nodded. "I'm sorry to see you go. And I know I'm not alone in that. If you want a reference, I'll provide you with a glowing one, although anyone who knows you in this town won't need it."

"Thank you." Paige put the envelope on the desk, then rose to her feet.

Genevieve came around and held out her hand. They shook, then Genevieve pulled her in and gave her a hug.

"Sorry, that wasn't professional, but you're going to be hard to replace," Genevieve said. "I'll let everyone know after you've left, if you like."

"That would be nice," Paige said. "Thank you for everything, Gen."

It felt like a weight had been lifted off her shoulders as she walked out of Genevieve's office, and she knew she'd made the right choice. She had enough savings to keep herself for a few months while she sorted out her next steps, but she felt, for the first time in a long time, like she had unlimited options. Life would go on…and eventually, her heart would heal from Mike, too.

As Paige moved through the office, she was caught behind the little group of trainees, and she couldn't slip past them without calling attention to herself, so she slowed her pace, waiting for her chance to get by.

"Our clients are just as human as we are," the trainer was saying. "They have come upon hard times, or they're struggling with very real problems. If you were in an identical situation, you might react exactly like they are doing. If you can empathize with your clients on a human level, you'll do well in this career."

Paige remembered this advice from her own training. What they hadn't told her was that by empathizing and opening her heart, she'd empty herself out. Or maybe that was just her, because her colleagues seemed to be doing better than she had about balancing it all.

"Life isn't a continual path of roses for any of us," the trainer went on. "It has ups and downs, sun and rain. Even the most challenged life has beauty in it. And there is meaning and value in the struggle. That's human existence! And that's also where we come in. We're here to help those rough patches to be easier to bear for the most vulnerable in our community. We are strong when they need us to be their champions. We are thoughtful when they're too overwhelmed to think things through. We are the shoulder they lean on."

Paige stopped her forward momentum, and the group of trainees moved away from her down the hallway. The words had struck her a little more deeply than they ever had before, and something had suddenly occurred to her.

Life *was* unpredictable, and while she wanted to run from the pain, she couldn't. She'd done her best to stay emotionally in control, but she'd still fallen in love with Mike. And no matter how carefully she guarded herself, she wouldn't be able to avoid pain. It was part of the human condition, and sometimes the wading through that pain was meaningful in itself.

She'd taken an oath to support the most vulnerable in the community because she cared. And unless she barred herself off from all human contact, she'd continue to care about people who were hurting.

Paige had fallen in love with a man who

was hurting… Pushing him away would mean more pain, experienced separately. Being with him would mean facing that pain together.

She loved him—it wasn't going to go away. It wasn't like a sunburn, something to fade and disappear in a matter of days.

Mike's life would be complicated with the sister he loved, with the nephew he would raise as his own son… But would she love Benjie any less because of his troubled start in life? Or would she love Mike any less because he was courageous enough to chase down the people who caused all that pain in others? Life would surely be painful, and while she knew that she'd made the right choice in her job, Mike *wasn't* a job.

Did she really want to face life, the beautiful, difficult, sometimes painful pathway, by herself without the man she loved? Or was she brave enough to be the shoulder Mike could lean on? Because heaven knew he was doing his best to be the shoulder she could lean on in her tough times.

Her heart welled with emotion, and she suddenly knew what she had to do.

She'd made a horrible mistake. He'd offered to stay in Eagle's Rest, and she'd been afraid that he would resent her later on for his sacrifice. And he well might, especially after having the night to consider his brash offer. Was he really willing to give up his chosen career path to be with her? Had that been the honest truth?

The group of trainees moved off into another room, clearing the hallway, and Paige hurried out. Her head was spinning.

The police station was only a few blocks away, and maybe she could sort out a few of these jumbled emotions before she got there. She didn't know what she was going to say to Mike, or if it would even matter. But she had to see him just once more.

Then her heart could have some closure and she'd stop torturing herself with "what ifs."

CHAPTER SEVENTEEN

THUNDER ROLLED OVERHEAD, and rain pattered down on the pavement. Mike stood in front of Eagle's Rest Day Care, his umbrella up. He'd come to drop Benjie off for his first day of day care, and he hadn't made it inside yet.

This was harder than he'd thought it would be. It wasn't that he thought Benjie would be in danger exactly; he just couldn't quite bring himself to hand the little guy over to a bunch of strangers. Which left him standing here in front of the day care, the rain pummeling his umbrella while Benjie snoozed comfortably against his chest.

His plan was to drop off Benjie, and then go find Paige. They needed to talk—or maybe he needed to talk.

Mike pulled out his phone and dialed the number with his thumb, then held it to his ear while it rang.

"Mike?" Paige picked up.

"Where are you?" he asked, and just then a gust of wind blasted some rain at him, and he had to angle the umbrella down to keep them dry.

"I'm walking," she said, sounding breathless. "I was actually heading toward the station. I was hoping to catch you. I quit my job today."

"Good for you," he said. And he meant it. She was doing what she needed to do to take care of herself, and he was glad.

"I hope so." Thunder rumbled overhead again. "I'm just passing Hylton Books now."

About two blocks away from the station. His heart hammered in his chest. "I'm on my way. I'll meet you in the middle."

"Where are you?" she asked.

"I'm in front of the day care, and I'm on foot, too."

"Okay… See you soon?" she said.

"Real soon."

He hung up and tucked his phone away. He put a hand over Benjie and tugged his blanket a little farther up on his downy head to protect him from the drafts and started down the road. It felt good to walk away from that day care, and even better to be walking toward Paige, even if it was only to see her one more time.

Cars crept down the road, wipers whipping back and forth. A pickup truck went through a puddle, the spray narrowly missing Mike. He walked faster, waited for a car to pass at an intersection, then crossed the street and started to jog. The station came up, and he glanced inside as he carried on past. She wouldn't have arrived yet—not on foot.

It was then he spotted her—her umbrella bobbing as she walked toward him. He couldn't help the smile that came to his face, and he picked up his pace yet again. How could one woman flood him with so much emotion?

"Mike?" she called.

They met each other in the middle of the sidewalk, and Paige collapsed her umbrella and stepped under the shelter of his. She hunched her shoulders up and shivered.

"I had to see you," Paige breathed.

"Me, too."

She looked up at him, then grinned. "You look good with a baby carrier, Mike."

"I brought Benjie to the day care and I couldn't do it. I know other parents drop off their new babies all the time. It's hard, but it's life. I just couldn't do it."

"You're a dad now," she said. "You've graduated."

He chuckled. "I'll try again to drop him off tomorrow. Maybe I'll be more successful."

Another gust of wind came at them, and Mike fumbled with the umbrella as he tried to shelter Benjie from the blast.

"Here," Paige said, and she took the umbrella from his hand so he could adjust Benjie's blanket again. He met her gaze, and smiled.

"I miss you already," he said.

"Me, too."

"And I wanted to tell you that I'm not leaving town."

"What?" Those blue eyes widened in surprise. "What do you mean? I thought you got into SWAT training—"

"I talked to my sister this morning, and she opened my eyes to a few things, namely that I know what my priority is. I need to give Benjie a stable childhood, and a single dad doing SWAT assignments isn't going to be anywhere near that. He's my priority now, and I'm staying here. I'm raising him right."

"In Eagle's Rest?" A smile toyed at her lips.

"Yeah…but it's not going to be easy. I'm not taking Benjie away from Jana. When she's clean again, I want her to be in his life. It's going to be a balance…a constant one. And it's going to be hard." He swallowed.

"It sounds like you're doing what's best," she said softly.

"I also want you to know that I still want something with you, Paige," he said. "I'm going to be here. And I want to see you, if you'll let me. I want to take you out to dinner, cook you hash for breakfast, walk with you in the rain." He reached out and touched her cheek, her skin cold from the wind, and she leaned into his palm.

"So you're really staying," she breathed.

"Yeah." He dropped his hand.

"Because I had a bit of a realization this morning, too." Pink bloomed in her cheeks, and she looked down again. "You aren't a job, Mike."

"That's what I've been telling you," he said with a low laugh.

"No, I mean that in a deeper way. I overheard some training in the office this morning when I was tendering my resignation, and I realized that…it's the right choice to quit my job—that was a necessary change. But I'm also running away from life. I can't protect myself from every bit of pain to come my way. Being without you would hurt more than just standing up straight and supporting you in your career."

"And Benjie?" he asked softly.

"And supporting you with raising him, too…complications and all."

"Do you mean that?" His voice sounded strange in his own ears. "Do you really mean it?"

She nodded, raising her gaze to meet his. "I love you," she breathed. "And I love Benjie, too. I know it'll be complicated, but it's not like I'll just stop loving you and go find some appropriately dull man to take your place."

An image rose in his mind of some guy in a blazer with a toothy smile and hair with a side part. He wanted to punch the schmuck.

"I sure hope not," he retorted, and she laughed.

"So, if your offer still stands of being a nanny for Benjie, I'll like to take you up on it."

Right. That was what he'd offered last night. It felt paltry now. What had he been thinking? He'd asked her to work for him and keep dating him. No wonder she'd run.

"I don't want a nanny," he said, and her smile fell, her clear eyes clouding in confusion.

"You changed your mind, then…"

"I want *you*, Paige," he said, stepping closer and putting his hand over hers on the umbrella. "I want you by my side for better or for worse, raising Benjie together, loving each other through it all. I want a wife. I want a mom for Benjie. If you want to open your day care or run the community garden, I'm fine with that. If you want to stay home with Benjie, I'm fine with that, too. And maybe with a newborn right here, you aren't thinking about more kids—but I'd like a baby of our own one day. You made a difference in a lot of lives, Paige, but you make a world of difference to me and Benjie. I want… I want to marry you."

"Are you proposing?" she breathed. "On a sidewalk in the rain?"

"Yeah, I am." He moved his fingers over hers. "What do you say? Let's do this. Forget halfway. I was an idiot last night. I want the whole thing. I want us to belong to each other, Paige, and to Benjie. I don't want you as a nanny in my house—I want a home with you!"

Paige nodded, and he bent down, just as far as he could with Benjie strapped across his chest, and Paige rose up on her tiptoes to meet him. His lips covered hers, and when another gust of wind blew rain in their direction, they tilted the umbrella down to protect their little family. Finally, he pulled back.

"I love you," he breathed. "You have no idea."

"I love you, too." She moved the blanket so she could look at Benjie's sleeping face. "We'll be okay, Mike."

"We'll be more than okay," he said, catching her hand as they fell into pace side by side under the umbrella. "We'll be together."

The rain hammered down around them, and he shot her a grin. Who cared what the weather did? She'd just agreed to marry him.

"Where are we going?" she asked.

"I don't know." He glanced around at the rainy street, the creeping traffic, the glow of the shop windows, and he felt a rush of joy. "How about shopping for a ring?"

It felt right. He wanted to marry her, and he wanted everyone to know it. Most of all, he never wanted her to doubt it.

"Aren't you supposed to be at work?" she asked with a laugh.

"It'll be an early lunch," he said. "I want to make this official. What do you say? Do you want a ring today?"

Paige grinned up at him, her blue eyes sparkling. "I think I do."

Mike would marry her, and he'd love her with everything he had. He wanted to make a little oasis for Benjie, but also for Paige. She deserved that much—the picket fence and the little garden. Maybe a few more kids to round things out in their home and make sure they were seriously outnumbered. There would be birthday parties, bedtime stories, family vacations and all the good stuff life could offer. They'd be normal—ordinary, completely in love and utterly devoted.

That was about as perfect as he could imagine.

EPILOGUE

PAIGE SAT IN a quiet room in the Eagle's Rest Christian Church, a fan blowing a cooling breeze in the warm June morning. She wore her white wedding dress—a strapless gown that hugged her curves, then fell into a frothy pile of lace and tulle around her feet. She looked down at her hands—the diamond solitaire now on her right ring finger in preparation for the wedding band to come on her left hand.

The manicurist had had a real time getting her hands wedding-ready. She'd been gardening all spring for the Eagle's Rest Community Garden, and the wear and tear had shown in her fingernails. She'd been hired as coordinator in February, and she'd begun getting ready for the first spring plant immediately. There was nothing quite so satisfying as getting her fingers back into the dark, rich soil. And while Paige had been busy with the garden, Mike had used his spare time to put together her wedding gift—a picket fence surrounding the yard of their new house…and he'd even painted it a gleaming white.

Outside, she could hear the murmur of voices as people milled around, and Paige sucked in a stabilizing breath. This was it… She'd be Mrs. Paige McMann after today, and she was oh-so-ready.

There was a knock at the door, and Liv poked her head inside. Liv and Jack were taking care of Benjie during the service, and the little guy was already whimpering.

Paige's heart melted. When they'd started planning the wedding, Mike had started to refer to her as Mom for Benjie's benefit. And truth be told, she felt like a mom.

"He wants you," Liv said, coming inside and closing the door behind her. Benjie held out his hands and cried until he was in her arms, and then he sniffled, stopped his fussing and snuggled up against her, his tearstained face pushed into her dress.

"Hi, sweetie," Paige crooned. "Did you miss me?"

Benjie was a big, bouncing baby now—all

chub and smiles with those first four pearly teeth. Paige had been taking him to the garden with her most days. They still used the day care a couple of days a week, but Paige liked to bring him with her.

"Where are his shoes?" Paige asked, looking down at his pink little toes. He'd had shoes this morning.

"Right here. They keep coming off." Liv lifted up the pair of blue satin shoes.

"These are important," Paige said. "Not only are they my something blue, but they're a gift from Jana."

Jana had been able to get a pass from the rehab facility she was currently in. The first fifteen-week program had been a good start, but she'd needed more support. Jana had been working hard on her sobriety, and she'd graciously agreed to be a bridesmaid in their wedding. She was family, after all— and she had a place with them.

Liv handed the shoes over, and Paige started wrestling with Benjie to get them back on, but he kicked his legs, keeping his toes bare.

"So she's okay with you being Mom?" Liv asked softly.

"As long as he knows she's the Tummy Mummy." Paige planted a kiss on Benjie's forehead, then wiped off the lipstick mark. "He's one loved little boy. There will be no confusion."

Outside, the murmur of voices stopped, the door opened again and her father popped his head inside.

"It's time, Paige."

Paige's heartbeat sped up, and she looked up at Liv. "Do you think Benjie will go with you?"

Liv pulled out a bag of teething cookies and Benjie immediately perked up. "I think I can bribe him. And I'll get these shoes on in time for pictures—I promise."

Paige shot her friend a grateful smile. "Thank you."

Liv picked up Benjie and rewarded him with a cookie, and Paige rose to her feet and took one last look at herself in the mirror. She smoothed her hands down her hips and pressed her lips together to even out her lipstick.

"You look beautiful," her father said gruffly. "Really beautiful."

"Thanks, Dad."

Her father pulled her veil down over her face, adjusting it carefully. Then he picked up the bouquet of red and peach roses and handed it to Paige.

"He's one lucky man, you know that?" her father asked with a teary smile. "I don't care how big he is, if he hurts you—"

"I don't think we have to worry about that," Paige said with a low laugh.

Mike was out there, waiting for her, and while Paige felt like a bundle of nerves right now, seeing him would make it better. She'd never imagined that she'd marry a cop, but here she was, becoming the wife of one of Eagle's Rest's finest. It just so happened he was also the only man she'd loved so much that letting him go wasn't even an option.

Her father and Liv stepped back to let Paige pass out the door and into the nearly empty foyer of the church. The pastor's wife stood guard at the swinging doors to the sanctuary, and when she saw Paige, her face erupted into a smile. Then she looked through a crack in the door, and the organ music swelled.

"That's our cue," she said. "You ready?"

It wouldn't have mattered what she said,

because the doors swung open and there was the sound of all the guests rising to their feet at once. Paige slipped her hand into the crook of her father's arm and he put a strong hand over her fingers.

"Let's go make this legal," he murmured, and Paige couldn't help but smile back.

These were their friends, extended family, the police family, the cousins who'd traveled for the occasion and the people who would dance the night away, celebrating with them. She could see Nathan with his date—a woman who seemed very nice, but Nathan was staying very close-lipped about. Nathan was sitting next to Irene on the other side; she was already dabbing away tears with a tissue, and when she caught Paige's eye, she pressed one hand against her chest in a gesture of love. Past the sea of happy faces in the pews, at the front of the church, there was Jana standing proudly next to Mike, whose dark gaze locked on Paige.

Mike wore his formal blues, his hat exactly straight and his white gloved hands clasped in front of him.

Wow, Mike mouthed, and Paige blinked back a mist of emotion.

Then the organ began the processional, and with a deep breath, Paige stepped forward, her father at her side, into the rest of her life.

With one vow, this complicated collection of people would become her family. She'd truly be Benjie's mom—at least one of his moms—and she'd be the strength that both Mike and Benjie needed, the gentleness this man longed for, the partner at his side through anything that came their way.

And she couldn't wait for the rest of her life to start.

* * * * *

*Don't miss Patricia Johns's
next book for Harlequin Heartwarming,
coming December 2019.*

*And check out the previous books
in the Home to Eagle's Rest miniseries:*
Her Lawman Protector
Falling for the Cowboy Dad

Get 4 FREE REWARDS!

We'll send you 2 FREE Books plus 2 FREE Mystery Gifts.

Love Inspired® books feature contemporary inspirational romances with Christian characters facing the challenges of life and love.

FREE
Value Over
$20

Get 4 FREE REWARDS!

We'll send you 2 FREE Books plus 2 FREE Mystery Gifts.

Love Inspired® Suspense books feature Christian characters facing challenges to their faith... and lives.

FREE
Value Over
$20

BETTY NEELS COLLECTION!

Buy 3 and get **1 FREE!**

Experience one of the most celebrated and beloved authors in romance! Betty Neels will delight you with her signature brand of storytelling: happy romances, memorable couples and timeless tales of lasting love. These classics have been combined in 2-in-1 books for your reading pleasure!

Get 4 FREE REWARDS!

We'll send you 2 FREE Books plus 2 FREE Mystery Gifts.

~~~ FREE ~~~
Value Over
$20

Both the **Romance** and **Suspense** collections feature compelling novels
written by many of today's best-selling authors.

READERSERVICE.COM

Manage your account online!

- Review your order history
- Manage your payments
- Update your address

*We've designed the
Reader Service website
just for you.*

Enjoy all the features!

- Discover new series available to you, and read excerpts from any series.
- Respond to mailings and special monthly offers.
- Browse the Bonus Bucks catalog and online-only exculsives.
- Share your feedback.

Visit us at:
ReaderService.com